Novels by Kelly Cheek

All We Hold Dear
Trial by Fire
The Lost Colony
JackSimile and the Phantom Fury
Spirit Breather
The Piper
Worst Enemies

The SpiritSense Series
In Restless Dreams
First Light
When We Were Gone Astray
Gazing Into the Abyss
Undying Love
Snow Angels
A Life Worth Living
Black Heart

The Facebook Trilogy
Profile
Private Messages
Poked

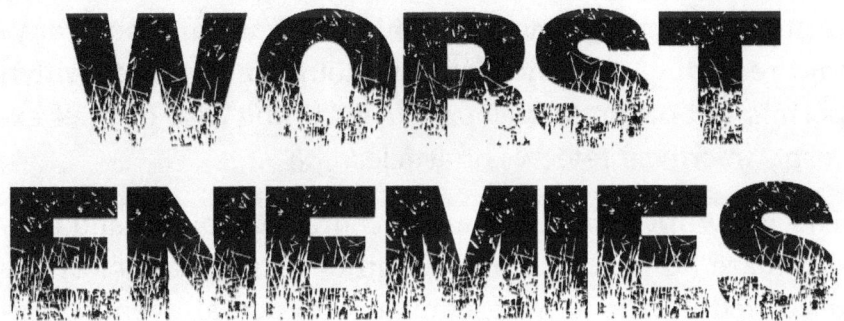

WORST ENEMIES

Kelly Cheek

The world doesn't end just because one thing goes wrong.

Shelley Duvall

This is the way the world ends, not with a bang,
but a whimper.

T. S. Eliot

THE END

have observed that, when the impending death of a world finally becomes obvious to all, when the changing coastlines and deadly weather patterns, the famines and diseases can no longer be denied, the population breaks down, roughly, into four categories.

The largest category is what I call the Passives. It consists of those who feel powerless to do anything. They've lived with hopelessness for so long that any attempt to improve the situation is, in their mind, a useless venture. The fact that the tipping point is long past only proves the validity of their viewpoint. Theirs is an apathy born of futility.

The second category is the Defenders. This group consists of those who refuse to give up, and who heroically fight, against all odds, to try to save some vestige of their world, despite the unavoidable evidence that the end is imminent. These are the ones who, in the past, never missed an opportunity to march in protest of some injustice, some political or environmental issue, whether it directly affected them or not.

Or their fight may have been in verbal or written form, their battle waged in the newspapers, or what was known at the time as social media, a virtual world in which people interacted, often without actually knowing each other in person. Their righteous indignation, in better times, eventually effected change.

The third category is the Raiders. These are aggressors, those who want to take whatever's left for themselves, for however long they have left. These people are an offshoot from the earlier "Deniers" group, thinking that the world will at least go on long enough for them to enjoy their spoils, and to hell with any possible future generations. Armed with weapons and the classic philosophy, "Might makes right," these are the ones who feel that they are entirely justified in taking from those less "prepared" than they are.

Finally, there are the Spectators, those who just jockey for the best seat. One might be excused for lumping them in with the Passives, but the ugly truth is that Spectators are often guilty of fomenting conflict rather than just withdrawing. They want to have something worth watching as they go.

Or at least that's been the case with the impending death of *our* world.

Popular books and movies of the twentieth and twenty-first centuries often cited nuclear holocaust as the catalyst for the end of humanity, and there has certainly been good reason for that. During the entire span of recorded human history, it's been estimated that fewer than three hundred years have been peaceful ones. Having the capability to destroy all life on earth many times over made for nightmarish prospects. And war, certainly, played a part in the end of our world.

Especially when one considers that it's not only soldiers who lost their lives during—and after—wars. War never stopped at the edge of the battlefield, nor at the signing of the armistice. The effects of war were far-reaching, from disease and famine, to collapsed economies and governments, to destruction of infrastructure, to depletion of the labor force.

I imagine all of those things can lead to a certain dissatisfaction with one's government. Therefore, it was not at all uncommon to hear of civil unrest and anarchy breaking out in one place after another. Some countries managed to quell it by force, while others, already greatly weakened by the aforementioned issues, were overtaken by the masses.

By this time, the world economy had pretty much collapsed, as well, causing even further hardships on already weakened governments and cultures. With no financial assets at their disposal, relief was simply out of reach.

When people with illnesses could no longer get their prescriptions or their dialysis or any number of other medical necessities, they died off pretty quickly. Others, weakened by old age or injuries, in hospitals and nursing homes, were quick to follow, as were those who were unfamiliar with life outside of their cities and who found adaptation difficult.

Scientists in the past came up with a theory called the Snowball Effect, in which different systems break down in different parts of the world, one adding its destructiveness to the last, finally culminating in a global catastrophic breakdown.

Perhaps not as dramatic as hurling nuclear fireballs at each other, but rather effective nonetheless.

§

My name is Press. My father, Bookman, was a lover of books, and he claimed that my name was the offspring of that love, being a word that was used to describe the creation of books in the past.

Long ago, in the distant past, people commonly possessed first, middle and last names. By the time I was born, though, that practice had somewhat lapsed, due in large part, I think, to the fragmentation of society that had taken place. Human settlements were small and far apart, based mainly on how many people could be comfortably supported by a particular area. Multiple designations were no longer necessary.

Although I suspect that a certain amount of apathy, and a disconnect from the past, may have played a part in it, as well.

In the more recent past, names often became somewhat descriptive, rather than just labels. My father, as I said, was a lover of books, and was instrumental in developing the scholarly bent that I took on. Eventually, I developed a very great love of learning myself, so I've kept my name.

Others, though, have taken, or been given names later in life that better describe a love of theirs, or a physical feature, or some other defining characteristic. So, one's name in adulthood may not be the name one was given at birth.

My wife is an example of that. Though she learned skills that were considered "useful" in our world, she also possessed an abiding love of art. When she was still very young, she took the name Frida, after an early twentieth-century artist. Her parents, being supportive of her, blessed her desire to become who she was to be.

At different times in her life, she has received criticism for her love of what some consider dead or unnecessary pursuits. It turned out, though, that she was a perfect match for me, a lover of books.

In time, I became what might, in days past, have been called a historian. I took up a study of the past, and how it has affected the present. In doing so, I've become convinced of what I've suspected for a long time.

Humans, in general, are major fuck-ups.

HISTORY OF THE WORLD, PART 1

Humanity *is nothing but a tiny speck of dust in universal history. Even during just the life of the planet Earth, which was formed less than five billion years ago, man has barely been a blip on the geological timeline.*

Throughout those billions of years, the earth had been fine. Yes, catastrophes occurred – certainly, the "Chicxulub impactor" that crashed into the Yucatan Peninsula at the end of the Cretaceous Period was a catastrophe, especially for the dinosaurs and other species that became extinct as a result. But the earth healed. Scars formed, but often those scars gradually became hidden beneath new life.

When humans appeared on the scene, they existed in harmony with the earth. They allowed nature to teach them how best to live. They created gods and goddesses of earth and sky, and they paid homage to them in various ways that reflected their respect for the natural world around them.

As man became more "advanced," though, they tended to concentrate into cities, states and, eventually, great civilizations. They built mighty fortresses around themselves. They seemed to outgrow their earlier belief systems. Humans still worshipped gods and goddesses, but frequently, that worship had less to do with respecting the earth, and more to do with condoning their own hatreds and indulging their passions.

Neighbors became enemies, not to be trusted. They attempted to conquer them, to acquire more land and property for themselves, and to eliminate competition for the abundant resources that they craved. They endeavored to make great names for themselves, spreading their dominion over greater portions of the land, while sometimes taking the women (and men) for themselves, thus satisfying consuming passions and cultivating long-lasting hatreds at once.

They erected great monuments to themselves, some of which have survived for thousands of years, though in many cases, the meaning and object of the commemoration were lost to the passage of time.

Earth endured much at the hands of man, but she always survived. The things that man did to her were little more than tattoos, cosmetic marks of a small and localized nature.

Throughout the millennia of man's existence, he marked the earth with multiple proofs of his intelligence and demonstrations of his power. Earth endured it with patience and dignity, continuing to provide sustenance for her tenants, knowing that there was little they could do to her of a truly harmful and permanent nature.

Humans, however, suffered much at each other's hands. Great swaths of society were wiped out in wars and exterminations and crusades. Prejudices, superstitious beliefs and greed fueled one conflict after another. Many more scars were left on the land, but they were, in the long run, of such a minor nature, they healed quickly.

Diseases ran rampant, sometimes blooming into major outbreaks, many times perpetuated by man's ignorance. Overall, their knowledge about cleanliness had not advanced much beyond their early days on earth.

And still, the earth continued to turn and to rejuvenate.

The Renaissance was promising. While conflicts still existed, they were often because of a scientific awakening, or burgeoning civic consciousness. So many artistic, musical and literary works of beauty were being produced, it looked as if, perhaps, man was learning from some of his past mistakes and was attempting to make restitution. And the earth, always forgiving, accepted their penance. The hatred and brutality still existed, of course, but *maybe that positive influence could eventually spread to others of his race.*

Instead, unfortunately, ugliness and beauty, good and bad, continued to exist side-by-side, warring with each other. The scales would tip one way for a while, then back the other way. Sometimes it was good and beautiful on one side of the world while simultaneously, on the other side, ugliness dominated.

The second half of the eighteenth century saw the beginning of the First Industrial Revolution in which great advancements were made in manufacturing processes. This marked a major structural change from agriculture to industry and the beginnings of a global economy, and coal-powered factories sprang up in one place after another.

Black smoke belched into the sky, soot rained down on nearby cities, and it was seen as a welcome sign of modern life, and of a healthy economy.

While it was dirty and smelly, it was on such a small scale that the global environment was not permanently harmed.

Still, the earth abideth for ever.

PRECIOUS JEWEL

In the relentless heat, my clothing is oppressive. It's also necessary. The long sleeves and gloves and wide-brimmed hat, the goggles and bandana over my face, all of it protects me from the harsh climate.

Though I've never seen a movie, I have read about them and seen pictures taken from them. Apparently, films from the twentieth and twenty-first centuries that took place in what they liked to call "post-apocalyptic" settings featured costumes of skin-tight black leather and straps and buckles. Some of those costumes were fairly skimpy.

In today's conditions, anyone who went around dressed like that would achieve a fatal level of crispiness in no time, or at least would quickly become riddled with melanoma.

Some forward-thinker a long time ago started developing a variety of hemp that required very little water, and that thrived in heat. Since both of those conditions describe my world, this plant has now taken over and grows among the hardiest of weeds. A fortunate thing for us remaining humans, since we make our clothing primarily from its fibers.

As our atmosphere thinned, the clouds rose higher. For a while, they still performed their assigned duties of insulating the earth, holding in heat to protect earth from the coldness of space.

But the higher the clouds rose, the more heat they trapped and the greater the thickness of the blanket of air they warmed. This was a self-destructive cycle, eventually causing most of the clouds to dissipate altogether.

Because of the earth's equatorial orientation to the sun, weather patterns changed a great deal in the middle latitudes, while the remaining clouds moved toward the poles where the somewhat cooler weather was more hospitable to their existence. Although growing holes in the ozone layer of the atmosphere at both poles have been altering those conditions, as well.

We still have weather patterns that bring rain, but it's rare and inconsistent. I assume there is still rain or snow at higher elevations, as well, since some nearby rivers haven't dried up altogether. The water cycle—evaporation, condensation and precipitation—is, presumably, still taking place, but we have to work a lot harder to get enough water for our daily use.

Still, with more sunlight reaching the middle latitudes, where the majority of the human population lived, the surface is now being heated even more, radiating more heat into the climate, in an unstoppable and deadly cycle.

Therefore, I don't go out much. Not only is the climate trying to kill me, but there might still be occasional people who would do me harm. I tell myself that my own benevolence suggests that there must be others like me out there. But if, like myself, they keep pretty much to themselves, they're not the ones I'm likely to come across.

To be honest, it's been a long time since I've seen anybody out here. Anybody alive, anyway. I've seen the corpse in front of me the last few times I came out. I was alarmed the first time I saw him. Not because he was dead. In our time, skeletons and corpses in varying stages of decomposition are pretty much ubiquitous. We're accustomed to stepping around them or over them to get wherever we're going.

I was alarmed because the motives of corpses can't be known. Living people may give you a chance to know what they're after. But a corpse can't tell you why he was in the area, or if there were any others with him.

Or if they're still around.

There are no visible wounds on the body. Lying in the shade of the north side of the ruins of a granite building, he may have simply sought relief from the burning sun, and peacefully slipped away.

The first time I saw the dead man, I searched the body for anything useful, but either he had nothing to start with, or other scavengers had reached him before I had. I lifted my head and looked all around again, as I frequently do, but as usual, I saw nobody.

The body is still relatively intact. There used to be large animals that would pick the bones clean in hours or days. They may still exist in other regions. I admit I don't know the current condition of the mountains and forests in other parts of the world. But here, I haven't seen any in years. Even the bacterial scavengers seem challenged by the heat and ultraviolet radiation. They are likely still working slowly in this corpse, but for the most part, he seems to just be in a state of mummification, or petrification.

As I trudge back toward home, I can feel the hot, rough ground through the soles of my shoes. It used to be concrete, but generations of neglect have allowed the more tenacious vegetation to take root and slowly break it apart.

I'm going back with little to show for my efforts. The bag swinging from my belt is barely affected by the weight of the sparse fruits I found. Few trees grow anymore. Those I have been able to identify from my research seem to bear little resemblance to their ancestors in the past. Those that have been able to survive have adapted by mutating into little more than scrubby bushes, and the fruit they produce are, generally, unappetizing—tart and chewy, without much moisture. But despite their current state, I assume there may still be some nutritional value in them.

I've also harvested some algae from the slow-moving river nearby. It tastes nasty, but from what I've read, it seems to be nutritious. I wonder if I can incorporate it into my rooftop garden.

I've also gathered a little purslane. Long ago, it used to grow as a weed, and people would pull it out of their lawns, or from the cracks in their sidewalks and throw it out in the trash. As food started becoming scarce, some people started cultivating it as a crop. Now that people are scarce, purslane is back to growing wild, though even it is having a harder time than it used to.

Anyway, I'm not sure if what I've gathered is enough to warrant the potential danger that I'm risking by coming out here. When Frida and I first moved into this area, I came out on long daily foraging ventures, starting in the somewhat cooler early morning hours. Even then, they yielded little so, in time, my expeditions became shorter. Now, I come out about every other day or so.

I don't think there's much left to find.

Early on, I gathered some roots and I now cultivate them, along with a few other hardy plants, in my rooftop garden. Still, I have to shade them a little. Plants that are not weeds do not fare well in the relentless sun that plagues us.

I'm not sure what those roots are. Like the trees, they bear little resemblance to anything I've found referenced in my books from times past. They were probably carrots and potatoes and radishes, or something like that ages ago, but have mutated into something entirely different now, due to our current climate.

I come to a wall that I've stopped at on several occasions. Some of my previous messages are still there, though they're fading, bleaching under the sun, or sandblasted by the occasional windstorm.

I get out a chunk of charcoal I brought with me and find an untouched portion of the wall, and I write the message I have in mind this morning, for any who might come along and be interested in it.

> There is gold and abundance of costly stones, but the lips of knowledge are a precious jewel.
> Proverbs 20:15

HISTORY OF THE WORLD, PART 2

Since the beginning of man's time on earth, the planet has managed to endure his attempts to plunder her resources and tame her wilderness. His ceaseless bickering and bloodletting were tragic and traumatic for man, but in the long run did little that the earth couldn't handle.

The Second Industrial Revolution, also known as the Technological Revolution, began in 1870, roughly a half century after the first one ended. This marked a period of rapid standardization and industrialization that allowed for advancements in manufacturing and production technologies across multiple fields, quickly shrinking the world as humans molded it to their hands.

As a result, telegraph networks and railroad lines quickly linked faraway places, facilitating rapid exchange of information and goods. The development of water and sanitation systems, as well as new technologies such as electrical power grids and telephone communication, were rapidly launching the world into a bright and glorious future.

Then came "the war to end all wars." The Great War was a war unlike any the world had ever seen, with more countries involved, and more individuals affected than any before it. By the time the four-year conflict had ended, nine million combatants and thirteen million civilians had died as a direct result of the war. Countless more perished as nationalistic fervor incited frenzied genocides in several countries.

Before "the war to end all wars" had proven conclusively that its moniker was purely ironic, a great influenza epidemic began. The massive troop movements of the war likely hastened its spread, and the 1918 Influenza Pandemic rampaged around the world, leaving untold millions dead in its wake.

As the world mourned its losses, the planet began attempting to heal its latest wounds. And those wounds were greater than the previous ones, due to the more powerful and destructive weapons employed – airplanes and tanks, rapid-fire machine guns and massive railway guns, and chemical weapons like mustard gas.

After struggling through years of recovery, including The Great Depression, things started looking up, until humans demonstrated that they hadn't learned much from the last couple of decades. World War II officially began in 1939. With more than thirty countries involved, it ended six years later with as many as eighty million dead, and scars unlike any the earth had seen at the hands of man, after fiery saturation bombing and the employment of nightmarish atomic bombs.

Even after that, wars, both hot and cold, continued unabated. Meanwhile, building on some of the sciences developed during the more peaceful years of the previous century, human technological advancement was exponential, but too often with more of a focus on the personal financial gain that could be reaped. Men walked on the moon without having learned how to live peacefully on the earth.

As the twentieth century ended, fossil fuel use was higher than ever, as was the damage being done to earth's atmosphere on a global scale. Holes in the ozone layer had been discovered decades earlier, as had a global warming trend, but aside from a few legislative Band-Aids, and the valiant efforts of the occasional conscientious politician and organization, little was actually done to stem man's lust for oil.

While scientists pointed at rising temperatures and at the dangerous weather patterns that were resulting, growing numbers of opponents argued that it was nothing but a well-orchestrated global hoax. Society in general didn't want to change their habits. Career politicians didn't want to hinder their cash flow. So, they fought efforts to reduce carbon output, seeking new ways to pull *even more oil and coal out of the earth, ripping up formerly pro-tected areas, as the planet's atmosphere became stretched to its limits.*

TUNNEL

The tunnel is dark, but I know the way. When Frida and I first moved in to this pile of granite and marble, we cleared away the debris and the artifacts from its past existence, pushing it all aside to make our trips through the tunnels easier. I usually don't bother with a light, but when my foot strikes something that I know was not there before, I pull the light out of the bag slung over my shoulder.

In years past, family and friends who were still with us thought I was crazy. Whenever I found discarded flashlights on my excursions (rare) or new ones on shelves in the abandoned stores (rarer still), I took them.

"What are you going to do with those?" they asked. "They need a power source."

They had a point. Batteries were even harder to find, and those I did find were usually corroded and unusable. But I had a few rechargeable batteries. I know what you're thinking. I still need a power source to recharge them.

What used to be called the "power grid" hasn't been around for a long time. Power plants needed people to operate them, and often, perplexingly, fuel to run them. Fuel and the people with the necessary knowledge had long since disappeared.

But we still have a power source hanging in the sky. The sun is oppressive and is killing us day by day, but it's still good for providing energy if you have the necessary collectors.

While fossil fuels were the preferred power source for our progenitors for much longer than they should have been, there were many who sought other sources. Cleaner, renewable energy. One of the most common was a system of solar panels on the roofs of their homes. Not much good now if they were connected to the grid, but being dissatisfied with the service or the cost, there were some who had invested in their own in-home storage units.

A few years ago, when we were in a more vigorous condition, Frida and I spent several days taking one of these abandoned systems apart and setting it up in our home. The batteries I had collected were getting pretty old now, hence my frugality with the flashlight. The solar collection cells were also becoming less reliable. The flashlight was getting quite old, as well. As a result, it had gradually changed shape with all the tape I had applied to it to mend cracks, scuffs and dents.

But I need to know if someone has found our home, so I turn on the flashlight to see what my foot had bumped against. Not to worry, though. It's just a chunk of concrete that had broken off and fallen to the floor. These tunnels are not in as good a condition as they were back when they were regularly maintained.

In fact, I see water gathering in places where it hadn't been before. Ever since I found the tunnel, there has been water in it. From what I've read, people had long warned about the consequences of the warming climate. Melting polar ice caps would cause the oceans to rise.

My exploration of our surroundings, combined with the studies I've made of an atlas, has told me that this has happened. The changing shape of the gathered water in the tunnel tells me that it is still ongoing.

It probably won't be long before the whole tunnel becomes completely flooded and we won't be able to use it anymore.

Using my foot, I push the chunk of concrete to the side with the other rubble and debris, and it splashes in the dirty water. Then, I shine the light ahead of me to make sure there are no other obstacles before turning the flashlight off again.

§

Frida is asleep when I return. I'm panting from my climb up the stairs. It would be easier if we had set up our home on the ground floor, but a couple of things convinced us to go higher. We know that the water is rising. I don't know how high it will eventually be, but we didn't want to have to move everything later if it flooded our home.

The second reason is that, if there are others out there, they may not be as kind and humane as we strive to be. We had heard reports, back when there were others in our community, of aggressive people, Raiders, who would kill us without a thought if they decided that they could take something from us. When we were setting up home here, I figured that, if such a circumstance came about, it would be easier to make a defense from the high ground.

I sigh as I look at Frida. Even in her current state, she's the most beautiful thing I've ever seen. Life is not easy on us these days. From what I've read, it wasn't always like this. That's not to say that diseases were not a part of everyday life back then. But most people seemed to enjoy a life free from the most virulent and unforgiving illnesses.

My dear Frida was just unlucky.

Based on my research of materials compiled when extensive writing was made of illnesses, and virtually everything else imaginable, Frida is dying. Cancer, in various forms and varieties, rampaged through society for centuries. For many years, a great deal of "dollars," the currency of the day, was spent on research into the causes of cancer, and on trying to find a cure.

My reading has taught me that their efforts were ultimately unsuccessful.

People in my day often imagined the past as being a time of great enlightenment and wonder, a paradise lost. Still, I have since found that, for a great many people back in what I consider the *Golden Age*, suffering was a way of life.

EXPENDABLE

Jodi Alexander heaved a heavy sigh and looked over her notes as the 737 hurtled eastward, taking her back to New York. She couldn't shake the tightness she felt in her chest. The last few days had been an emotional roller coaster. The tension and animosity of the standoff were an absolute counterpoint to the sweet people, the good friends she had made.

Without thinking, she touched the spot on her ribs, just under her left breast. She winced as she remembered. It was still tender. She didn't need to be reminded about her face. Her eye was still swollen, the skin still tingly.

She thought about when she first arrived a week ago, in her rental car, from Bismarck Municipal Airport. It took her less than an hour and a half to drive along the Missouri River to get to the Sacred Stone Camp in the northeastern portion of the Standing Rock Reservation. It took nearly that long to get from where she had to park to where the Indians were.

Native Americans, she corrected herself. She needed to refer to them properly when writing about the experience. The camp was nothing less than a small town made up of cars and trucks, trailers and tents, and even a few teepees. There were other sympathizers there like herself, with white skin, but the vast majority of the protesters were the Standing Rock Sioux.

They were immediately welcoming, making her feel at home. Despite the tension of the situation, at the camp, everyone smiled a greeting to her.

She fondly remembered her first view of those on the front line of the protest, standing there proudly and resolutely in the face of overwhelming odds. In trying to protect what little land and water supply had been granted to them, they bravely faced down the enemy as their forefathers had a century before, but unarmed this time.

On the opposing side were the white people, the Dakota Access Pipeline construction personnel and the police, the heavy yellow construction equipment standing impotent among them. The Dakota Access Pipeline, or DAPL, had been rerouted near the Standing Rock Sioux Reservation after the original proposed route near the state capitol of Bismarck was denied. It had been determined that it was too risky for Bismarck's water supply.

Apparently, there were no such misgivings about the safety of the Reservation's water supply. The pipeline was to be drilled under Lake Oahe, a long, sinuous recreational site that had been created by damming the Missouri River.

Jodi didn't want to believe that the white man's intentions were blatantly cold and sinister.

But she had seen it too many times

§

"So, you're an environmentalist?" asked Mary Soaring Hawk Cooper as she showed Jodi around. Mary wore a long wool coat festooned with Native American designs woven into it, but Jodi suspected it really wasn't enough. North Dakota in the middle of November was cold.

"That's right," Jodi replied. She felt a little defensive, knowing that, in this battle, the most important thing to the Sioux was their health and well-being. The environment in general was important to them as well, but the basic right to a clean water supply for their people was their primary concern. "I have a theory," she explained, "which has, unfortunately, been proven true far too many times, about a link between racism and pollution."

"Intriguing," Mary said. "Tell me more."

"Well, where are industrial areas located in cities? The more affluent areas don't want them. And the more affluent areas are usually white. Factories and other polluters are located in parts of the city where the poor, usually people of color, live, because rich white folks don't want that ugliness near them."

"Or threats to their water supply," Mary added.

"Exactly. Non-whites usually have to suffer because white people refuse to."

"An admirable position for a white woman to take."

"I can't tell you how frequently I'm ashamed of my skin color because of the poor choices white people make."

"Well, we welcome anyone who wants to join us in our cause, whatever their motivation. There are other white people here, and members of Navajo and other tribes have joined us in solidarity, too. Oh, and we're being joined, today especially, by people around the world."

"Oh, that's right," Jodi said, "the No DAPL Day of Action."

"Right. At last count, people in something like three hundred cities around the world are posting and tweeting their support."

"That's good to know. I haven't had a chance to get online since I left New York."

"Oh, it's overwhelming," Mary said. "We're getting support from so many people, including celebrities like Shailene Woodley, Willow Smith, Rosario Dawson, Mark Ruffalo."

"No shit? You have the Hulk on your side?" Jodi smiled. "There's no way you can lose!"

§

Jodi spent the next few days talking to various individuals in the camp and on the front line. To be fair, she also requested interviews with those on the opposing side, and she wasn't surprised by their arguments.

"These protesters attacked the company's security guards," Morton County Sheriff, Kyle Kirchmeier said, hooking his thumbs into his belt under his rather prodigious belly. "They beat them with wooden posts and flag poles. This has been nowhere near a peaceful protest."

In the time Jodi spent there, she never witnessed violence on the part of the protesters, but her time there was, admittedly, limited.

She did see protesters chain themselves to bulldozers and other large equipment, and subsequently get arrested. She was horrified when she saw, from a distance, several who were arrested get herded into what looked like large dog kennels.

They weren't the first.

Mary Soaring Hawk Cooper pushed her sleeve up and showed Jodi her forearm. She saw what appeared to be a random arrangement of grey marks.

"It used to be a number," Mary said. "It was a couple of weeks ago. I was arrested along with about 140 others for setting up an illegal roadblock to try to keep the workers out. They strip searched me, wrote a number on my arm with a marker and pushed me into a little cage."

"Oh my god," Jodi said as other numbers came to mind.

"At least they didn't tattoo the numbers on," Mary said, echoing Jodi's thoughts.

§

"It's almost always about racism," Jodi said. She sat with a handful of friends she had made over the last few days in the teepee belonging to David Red Oak Jones. Jodi didn't know the hierarchy among the Sioux, but David seemed to be respected by others in the camp.

With the fire burning in the center, it was surprisingly warm. Many of them had heard about Jodi's thoughts on racism and the environment, and wanted to know more. They sat cross-legged on blankets, most with their arms resting on their knees.

"When a factory or a coal-burning power plant is going to be built," Jodi continued, "it's seldom that a white neighborhood is considered for the site, but if it is, there are studies and questionnaires and surveys and elections to determine if the residents are okay with it. Which, of course, they're not.

"If a Black neighborhood or a Hispanic neighborhood are being considered, those same niceties are seldom, if ever, offered. White people don't want the ugliness and the pollution in their backyard, and they have the clout to keep those businesses out.

"People of color aren't given that consideration. They're expected to accept it without complaint. And that mindset goes back a long way.

"Our country was built on the blood, sweat, tears and lives of enslaved Black people, the outright theft of Native land, and the attempted genocide of its Indigenous people. All the way back then, white people got rich off the backs of stolen slave labor, stolen land and property."

There were nods of agreement and soft grunts of approval among all the people in Jodi's small audience.

"Today, the richest people in the world are, for the most part, white. And they still need that white supremacy, that white privilege that so many of them vehemently deny exists, in order to hold on to, and continue building, their wealth. They need areas that can be sacrificed for disposing of their waste and pollution, and those areas happen to be the ones populated by people on the bottom tiers of their imagined racial order of things. So those people can be sacrificed, as well. They're expendable.

"And now, right out here," she gestured toward the sounds of the ongoing standoff, "an oil company has militarized police to terrorize Native Americans because white people didn't want the pipeline going through their neighborhood. And you're expected to just allow it because you don't matter as much as the rich white people who are doing it.

"But what those rich white people don't think about is the fact that increasing water pollution doesn't stay localized. Air pollution doesn't stop at the walls of their gated communities. Greenhouse gases don't recognize borders. Their racism is destroying the earth, and it's going to take us and them with it."

The flap on the teepee was pulled open and a young man stooped in.

"Excuse me," he said as he stepped over a couple of people and whispered something in David's ear. David looked at his watch, nodded and turned to Jodi.

"Jodi, your viewpoints will likely not make you any friends among your people."

"I'm accustomed to holding unpopular views. But I long for the day when we can just be people, rather than my people versus your people."

"Thank you for taking the time to speak with us," David said. "Since you've been here, you've been a good friend to us, and we appreciate your support. I'm afraid I must go now."

Everyone stood up and thanked Jodi before stooping through the flap. Several of them seemed to be heading in the same direction.

"Where's everyone going?" Jodi asked Mary.

"We're going to Cantapeta Creek." She looked at Jodi. "It might get ugly."

§

The creek was wider and slower-moving than Jodi had anticipated. Based on the way it looked, she would have called it a river. The Sioux and their sympathizers were gathered all along the bank of the creek. A rickety wooden bridge that they had hastily constructed across it the night before was being torn down by the people on the other side.

"We built that bridge," Mary told Jodi with tears in her eyes, pointing across the creek, "to be able to get to the other side, and to that hill."

The hill stood, Jodi estimated, eighty to a hundred feet high, but on the side facing them, was nearly a sheer cliff. Lining the opposite bank, and even on top of the cliff, were police officers in riot gear.

"What's so special about that side of the creek, and that hill?" Jodi asked.

"That's sacred ground. The burial sites of our ancestors are over there." Mary's voice cracked. "And they're just walking all over them as if they're nothing! They're scraping ruts in the ground to lay their oil pipeline. Our health is nothing to them. Our history means nothing. Our legacy is meaningless."

The day was chilly but clear, and a bright blue sky hung behind the hill, the grass brown and brittle, as several of the protesters began wading into the water.

"Wait!" Jodi said, grabbing Mary's arm as she started to join them. "What are you doing?"

"We're going to pray for our ancestors, and to protect those sacred sites."

"But," Jodi looked back at the line of armed policemen waiting for them on the opposite side. Mary shook her head as a tear slipped down her cheek.

"No battle is without risk," she said with a gentle smile.

Jodi watched Mary drop her coat to the ground, turn and wade into the water, joining her comrades. A few were in canoes, paddling slowly against the lazy current, but most of them were on foot in water up to their waists.

She heard the clamor of their shouts and chants, about protecting their water and their ancestors, and she saw Mary reach them and join in. She watched in horror as one of the policemen raised his rifle and fired at someone in the group.

Without thinking, Jodi threw off her coat and plunged into the cold water toward them.

"Stop, you assholes!" she shouted, dragging her legs against the resistance of the water. "They're unarmed!" It took her a minute to wade across the river to where the protesters were, and Mary seemed surprised to see her there with them. They weren't attempting to climb up on the bank, but were staying in the water, chanting their chants, clamoring for their voices to finally be heard.

The response of the police on the bank came quickly. One of them, holding what looked like a medium-sized fire extinguisher, began dousing the protesters with pepper spray. Jodi was struck by his casual demeanor as he unleashed the liquid on his fellow human beings in the water.

Some of the protesters had come prepared. They held up tarps or lids from large storage containers to protect themselves from the burning spray, but others were not so lucky. Especially when another cop began doing the same thing, on the side that Jodi was on.

When the liquid first hit her face, it felt as if lava was suddenly flowing down over her. Her skin was on fire, and in a spontaneous involuntary reaction, her eyes immediately slammed themselves shut. In an effort to relieve the intense burning pain, her body responded by releasing tears and mucous. Even though it felt as if she had a year's worth pouring out of her eyes and nose, it wasn't nearly enough to wash away the searing irritant.

Jodi could barely recognize the sounds around her. She was aware of little except the continuing agony on her face and neck. She wanted to scream from the pain, but her throat and lungs felt as if they were blistering.

One sound made it through to her consciousness, though, a loud pop, because it was immediately followed by what felt like a brick smashing into her side. With her eyes swollen shut, the pain in her side was enough to make her lose her balance, and her feet slipped out from under her.

Just before she went under, she felt hands grasp her arm, holding her up. She felt something hard against her back, and she turned, feeling around in a panic. She grabbed on to the edge of the canoe.

"Just hold on," a voice said close to her ear, and Jodi felt the canoe begin turning. With her feet solidly under her again, she fought against the confusion and hysteria, and the searing pain, and concentrated on allowing the canoe to guide her back to the shore.

As she came up into shallower water, she could feel the resistance of the water lessening. Her body was freezing and her face was on fire as she felt hands clutching her, supporting her, and they guided her up onto the bank.

As she sank to her knees, someone wrapped something crinkly around her, one of those silver mylar blankets, she assumed, while someone else lifted her head and began pouring something over her face. She felt a degree of immediate relief. The burning and irritation continued, but she thought she could at least bear it now. And her body was starting to warm up.

"Thank you," she said, although it came out as a hoarse croak.

§

Jodi drove away slowly, wanting to keep her new friends in sight in her rear view mirror as long as possible. As she drove northward, the crowd slowly dissipated, but Mary stayed there, watching her until Jodi couldn't make her out anymore in the distance.

Nearly a day after being sprayed with pepper spray, her skin still tingled, like a body part that had been asleep for a while but was coming back. Her left eye was still swollen, but it was open enough that she had binocular vision again. She had a knot on her ribs from the rubber bullet, the skin purple and scarlet from numerous broken capillaries.

Getting back to Bismarck and the airport was done almost without thinking. Her thoughts were still back at the camp, with her friends and what they were going through. She had been there for a week. They had been there for months, and there was currently no end in sight.

She returned her rental car, went through security and boarded her plane, barely conscious of the stares of others around her, while still thinking about the Sioux's ongoing struggle. And not just *them, but others she had visited in relation to her hypothesis about the link between racism and the environmental death throes of the planet.*

The Black people in low-income neighborhoods in Los Angeles, surrounded by urban oilfields. The Black people in Louisiana, on the Mississippi River, where an overabundance of industrial plants and an extravagant number of cancer patients have given the area the name Cancer Alley. People of different races, but poor, in Ohio, where fracking resulted in air and water pollution, and actually made their water flammable.

And now, the Standing Rock Sioux who just wanted clean water for themselves and their children. She still had their chant, "Water is Life! Water is Life!" going through her head.

Tears came to her eyes at the thought of all the people in the world who were considered expendable. People who were given so little value by those who had some form of power over them, that they were pushed aside as if their needs and wishes didn't matter.

She now had tons of research put away, stacks of notebooks, boxes of recordings. She had more than enough material to write an extremely comprehensive book on the subject. She didn't know if it would spark a movement, make a difference in the world. Other books she had written on the environment hadn't made any noticeable difference, but she figured if it helped just a few people, it would be worth it.

Nobody should be expendable.

REMINISCE

As I sit in my threadbare chair and watch Frida sleeping, I remember, as I often do, happier times. Now, my mind has drifted all the way back to when we met.

My parents, Bookman and Valencia, had been intrepid explorers. They had bravely struck out on their own in hopes that they could find a new home that could support them better than the place they had come from, having left all of their friends and family behind. When they reached the great water, they stopped and settled there.

Why they came south, I don't know, though, in their defense, they did not have access to the voluminous information that I have now.

Frida's family had made a similar journey, but not alone, as my parents had, from the south and west, from a place they called Kay-nox-VIL-lee. Admittedly, we do not know for certain the pronunciation of certain place names from the past, but that is what they called it, and having seen the place in an atlas, it seems to me to be as good a label as any other. Their group accepted us into their settlement.

My parents had taken their time on the journey, spending several days at each camp, scouting in all directions before moving on. Mountain ranges made this process take that much longer, as did my mother's pregnancy. Thus, my first several years were spent in a nomadic lifestyle.

Frida was only five years old when I met her, having been born toward the beginning of her family's journey. I was seven at the time, having taken my first breath near a place my father called El-MI-ra.

I became fast friends with Frida, or Goldie, as her parents had named her. She took the name Frida a few years later.

When she was ten, her parents died, as parents do, and my parents took her into our family. I don't know if her family's friends allowed it because she and I were such good friends, or because none of them wanted the extra mouth to feed. It really didn't matter to me. I was able to be with the person I was closest to, after my parents.

But my parents died only a few years later.

To me, Frida only became more beautiful the older she grew. And eventually, she became the primary focus of my life. My parents were gone, and gradually, those in her group, our whole community, died as well. It was just Frida and me.

She is my wife, although we had no formal union. In the past, marriages were joyous affairs that involved friends and family, and a clergyman or a civil officiant. We did not have access to such things, being practically alone by that time.

But we love each other. Our union is engraved in our hearts, even though it is not blessed by the particulars of the past.

Frida has such vision! My love of expression through words is matched by her love of expression through the visual arts.

I have placed some of her artwork within view of the bed. The place where we live is full of faded but beautiful artwork. But I wanted Frida to be surrounded by familiarity. Canvases with expressive swashes of color, paper with bold strokes of charcoal. One is a beautiful—but somewhat embarrassing—portrait that she painted of me not long ago. I have that one directly in front of her so she can see it if I don't happen to be here when she wakes up.

She stirs, and she makes a sound that reminds me of a kind of sigh she used to make when we made love. We had mixed feelings about bringing a child into this world, though those feelings were, admittedly, heavily weighted on the side of not doing so.

People in the past could make love without fear of getting pregnant, if a child was not desired or convenient at the time. Nowadays, people do not have access to the medications and devices that were common back then, so we are, to an extent, at the mercy of our passions.

When Frida never got pregnant, though, we were not disappointed. We could make love to our hearts' content without worry, and we did. There were times when we spent almost the whole day in bed together.

Those were good days, the best days, when nothing in the world existed except the two of us.

BLACK LIVES

James buried his face in the soft cushion of Ashanti's thick afro and inhaled. The scent of her hair and the softness of her warm body pressed against his sharpened his already intense arousal. John Legend crooning softly from the boombox on Ashanti's dresser didn't hurt, either.

A master of multitasking, James nuzzled her neck and her earlobe while he slipped his hand up her dark umber belly. When it reached her breasts, he cupped his hand around one of them, softly running his thumb in a circular motion around the dark charcoal areola surrounding her nipple.

Ashanti moaned, pressing his hand hard against her breast. With her other arm under his neck, she leveraged James into an angle that was more convenient for her. They ended up on their sides, face to face.

James stared into her eyes, her pupils black as obsidian. She was breathing hard, staring back at him. The intensity on her face reminded him of when he first saw her.

Yesterday.

§

It was the first time James had ever joined in a march. He had never been one to get involved in political protests. He had his opinions, of course, and he was sometimes vocal about them. Still, he had always tried to be a live-and-let-live kind of person.

But too many black men had died at the hands of white policemen, brutalized because of the color of their skin. It was becoming much too common, almost as common as school shootings. James always strove to be a law-abiding citizen, and he had never had a negative encounter with a police officer. He knew they weren't all bad, but it seemed there were too many bad ones.

He finally realized that it was time. It wasn't just a political issue. It was a moral issue, a human rights issue. Black men shouldn't have to wonder if they'll be able to make it back home every time they venture out.

So, when he heard that a Black Lives Matter march was going to be held in Philadelphia, James showed up. He even made a sign.

ALL LIVES MATTER IS NOT TRUE
UNTIL BLACK LIVES MATTER

James had no idea how many people were there, but he knew it must be thousands. They filled the streets in all four directions from the intersection where it started. He couldn't hear the speech that was made at the beginning, but once everyone around him started marching, he did, too.

It was about twenty minutes into the march when he first saw her. She was beautiful. Poised and dignified, but with an expression on her face that said, "Don't fuck with me." She carried a sign that had the words "Black Lives Matter" printed vertically with their initials "BLM" in big, bold letters across the top.

She was dark and fine, with an afro that could have come from the early seventies. And that intensity! The determination on her face only made her more magnificent.

He could barely take his eyes off of her.

§

Face to face was good. Seeing her face an inch away from his, James pulled her closer, pressing their naked bodies together. He kissed her, and as their lips parted and their tongues probed, their hands explored.

James caressed the soft skin in the small of her back, feeling the curve flare back out again into her buttocks. He grabbed one and pressed their groins together, and Ashanti responded by tilting her hips forward, grinding against him. She lifted the leg that was on top and wrapped it around his legs, trapping him in an incredibly erotic bond.

Giving in to the need he was feeling, he wrapped his arms around her and held her tightly against him. Holding each other, they found the rhythm they were both searching for as Ciara began singing on the boombox.

§

James didn't want her to think he was stalking her, so he walked alongside her for a bit, within her view. The street was so crowded, she couldn't blame him for walking near her. He glanced at her, and when she looked at him, he smiled at her.

She nodded at him, but she never lost that fierce expression. A couple of minutes later, she saw what his sign said, and she nodded again, but this time, she allowed the fierceness to soften just a bit with a smile.

The group chanted through the streets, "Hey, hey, ho, ho, these racist cops have got to go!" After a while, James stopped to cough and clear his throat. She noticed, and she smiled at him, a real smile this time.

"You should have brought some water with you," she said, speaking loudly enough for him to hear her over the chanting. He nodded, seeing the water bottle in her other hand.

"It's my first time," he replied.

"Ah, a BLM virgin."

"Yes, be gentle with me."

"I don't have to be gentle with you. You're on the right side. You already have my approval."

"That's a relief," James said. "You look pretty damn intense."

"I am intense. We're fighting for our lives."

James nodded.

"I'm Ashanti," she said.

"Ashanti. Cool name."

"My father's from Ghana."

"I'm James," he shrugged. "My father's from Chicago."

Ashanti smiled again.

A new chant began, "No justice, no peace, no racist police!" With a glance at each other, James and Ashanti joined in.

The march snaked through Philadelphia, ending up on Broad Street, in front of the police station. At least that's where James had read that it was going to stop. He and Ashanti were blocks away when the crowd in front of them came to a stop.

As a counter march came to a halt nearby. Angry white people bearing slogans, some patriotic, some racist, were shouting "All lives matter!"

One of them, a particularly combative-looking man was wearing a T-shirt with the word "DEPLORABLE" stenciled across it. He was looking at James and Ashanti as he said something that they couldn't hear above the growing clamor.

James glanced to his side at Ashanti. He was impressed by her composure. She was standing her ground, not making any moves against anyone, but solid in her firm determination.

§

Lying on his back, James looked up at Ashanti. He caressed her dark chocolate thighs as she straddled him. Her hands on his chest, she was still rocking back and forth, even though the climax had come and gone, swaying to the rhythm of Usher playing in the background.

James allowed his eyes to slide up and down her body. He appreciated every curve and shadow, every sinuous motion of her torso. He admired the determination and conviction that seemed to adorn her face no matter what activity she was engaged in, whether marching for civil rights issues or making love.

She was looking at him, too, and while he couldn't be certain of what she was thinking, that bit of softness in her gaze and the smile on her lips was encouraging.

§

"Why don't you go back where you came from?" the man shouted at Ashanti, as he stepped closer.

"Wilder Street?" she replied with a confused look on her face. Despite the charged atmosphere, James couldn't help but laugh at her smartass response. Deplorable Man didn't laugh, though. He was briefly distracted by James' reaction, but he turned his attention back to Ashanti.

"I'm talking about Africa, bitch!"

"I know what you're talking about. I was simply correcting an apparent misunderstanding you seem to have about my point of origin."

"Why are you even here?" the man demanded.

"Because Black lives matter."

"All lives matter!"

"Including Black lives?"

"ALL lives!"

"Do white lives matter?"

"Hell yeah!"

"What about Black lives?"

"ALL lives, goddammit!"

James was impressed with Ashanti's calm demeanor in the face of such blatant racism, but he could see that the man was growing more agitated, and he stepped up and tried a logical argument.

"Excuse me, sir," he said, "if your wife had breast cancer and you were trying to raise money for breast cancer research or treatment because it mattered to you particularly, what if someone shrugged off your efforts and said, 'All cancer matters.' How would that make you feel?"

The man screwed up his face as he looked at James and ignored his question.

"What the fuck are you even doing here?" he asked. "Look at you. Blond hair, blue eyes, perfect white skin. You're a fine Aryan specimen. Why are you marching with a bunch of niggers? You're on the wrong side."

"No, I don't think I am," James replied, recoiling from him.

"You're a fucking embarrassment to your race!"

"More and more, these days, someone makes me feel embarrassed about my race or my sex or my nationality. I can see now that you're one of them."

The man sneered at him, but then turned his attention back to Ashanti, taking another step toward her. James watched him warily as Deplorable Man looked at Ashanti's full lips, her generous afro, her dark brown skin.

"All you fuckin' chimps need to get back to the jungle!" he shouted.

"Alright, that's enough!" James said.

"And nigger-lovers like you need to go with them!"

James felt his heart pounding in anger, and his righteous indignation for Ashanti and all the other people of color he had been marching with. He hated confrontations, and this feeling was the reason why. He knew that Deplorable Man was just trying to incite them to react, to strike out in violence.

"Come on, Ashanti," he said, "let's see if we can get any closer to the police station."

Deplorable Man, though, didn't seem to want them to get away from him so easily. He reached out and grabbed Ashanti's arm. James didn't wait to determine his intentions.

"Back off, man!" he demanded, pushing him away from Ashanti.

Deplorable Man fell back against another angry white man, who helped steady Deplorable Man. Others around him saw what happened and joined him in his verbal attack against James and Ashanti.

The shouting was getting intense, not only from the herd of white supremacists, but from the African Americans who had gathered behind James and Ashanti. The commotion was growing so loud that James couldn't even pick out anything that was being said. It was all combining into one great roar.

James could see that Ashanti, despite her fierce determination, seemed frightened by the threats, and James wanted to get them both away from the instigators. He took her hand and started to work his way through the crowd of BLM protestors, but he felt resistance. He looked back, thinking that Ashanti didn't want to come with him.

Instead, he saw that Deplorable Man had grabbed her other arm, the one holding the sign, and was yelling something into her face. She swung her sign downward, hoping to hit him with it, but the angle of her arm and the location of his grip impeded her movement. The lightweight stick it was mounted on wouldn't have done any real damage anyway. Still, the stick grazed his face, leaving a small cut on his forehead, further angering him. He pulled back his other arm and slapped Ashanti hard across the face.

It all happened in a moment, and when he saw it, James dropped his sign and swung his fist, catching Deplorable Man in the side of his jaw. He fell back again, this time taking down a couple of others standing behind him. One of Deplorable Man's supporters balled up his fist and took a step toward James, but Ashanti was able to swing her leg, catching him hard in the groin with her knee. James turned, pulling Ashanti with him, squeezing through the crowd.

The last he saw was a group of police in riot gear who had apparently witnessed the confrontation. They pushed their way through the crowd toward the agitators, taking Deplorable Man and a few others into custody. That was a bit of a relief to James, that they weren't after him or Ashanti.

§

"Is it hot in here, or is it just you?" James asked with a wry smile. Ashanti smiled back as she leaned forward, lying down in James' arms, still straddling him. He encircled her body with his arms, caressing every inch of her back, as the weight of her afro pulled it down on the sides, enclosing their faces in shadow.

47

She kissed him, long and deep, before she rolled off of him to his side, her head resting on his shoulder. James pushed her hair back as he gazed into her eyes.

Ashanti took his hand and looked at it. His knuckles were still a little bruised.

"How does it feel?" she asked.

"It'll be fine," he said, flexing his fingers a couple of times. Ashanti brought his hand to her lips, kissing his knuckles.

"You're not bad for a white boy," she said, smiling again, and James smiled back. "It's too bad you lost your sign, though. That was a good message."

"It's okay," James replied. "I still remember what it said." He caressed the side of her face and kissed her. "Besides, in the end, I got so much more!"

CONNECTED

According to twenty-first century scientists, everything was connected. In fact, that was known as the First Law of Ecology. Numerous biological systems might seem completely unrelated, but when one was taken out of balance or eliminated, the results showed otherwise. The earth's natural balance was delicately affected by the connection of seemingly unrelated systems and species.

When we were younger, before we had even begun to discover our deeper feelings for each other, Frida and I often shared long discussions about things that interested us. I had recently read about this First Law of Ecology, and about a similar dogma called the Butterfly Effect, and these figured into a conversation we had when I was twelve and Frida was ten.

Frida's father, Hunter, had died a few weeks before, and her mother was absolutely despondent. Frida was sad, too, though she did not yet truly appreciate the significance of her father's absence. I initiated the conversation to, hopefully, transfer my enthusiasm about a subject to her, as often happened, to get her mind off her loss temporarily.

"Butterfly effect?" Frida asked, her eyebrows scrunched together.

"Yes!" I replied enthusiastically. I remember being absolutely fascinated by scientific studies. "Mathematician and meteorologist Edward Lorenz was running a computer model of a weather prediction, one that he had already run before." We had already discussed this sort of thing, so I didn't have to stop to explain. "This time, he entered .506 instead of," I closed my eyes to recall the full number—accuracy was important to me— ".506127, and he got a completely different result."

Frida's eyebrows raised, and while I figured that, from her reaction, she understood the implication, I couldn't restrain myself from plowing ahead.

"Doctor Lorenz later wrote that, 'one meteorologist remarked that if the theory were correct, one flap of a sea gull's wings would be enough to alter the course of the weather forever.'"

Frida's eyebrows lowered again at this.

"Lorenz later changed it to 'a butterfly's wings,' thinking that it sounded more poetic."

Knowing from her already extensive study of art what a butterfly was, since they didn't exist anymore, at least where we lived, Frida understood the theory. The flap of a butterfly's wing might be enough to cause a series of previously non-existent air currents, tiny, seemingly insignificant alterations which could accumulate, eventually resulting in a tornado in another part of the world later.

I remember the look on her face after that. She smiled, but then, the smile faded. She looked intently at me, her lovely face now very serious.

"Can you imagine the butterfly effect when someone you love dies?"

I became very serious myself after that. My plan had been foiled, and I realized how significant a thing death was in the lives of the survivors. I would discover for myself a few years later when my own parents died.

BUTTERFLY EFFECT

Catharine McAdams looked around disoriented. Covered with mud and bits of debris, there was no way to determine if the blood was her own, from some, as yet, unseen wound, or if the source was someone else.

Slipping on the mud, she struggled to maintain her footing as she wandered around, looking for something familiar. Monte Cristo, Colorado seemed completely foreign now. She could barely remember what had happened.

She and Joe had just been relaxing, watching TV, when suddenly the house began trembling. A deafening rumble surrounded them, penetrated them, as she felt as if her internal organs were shaking. This was quickly joined by higher pitched noises as glass, ceramic and china from innumerable sources shattered.

The next thing she knew, she was outside, covered with mud, and a piece of a wall, next to a ski lift chair and a tangle of cable.

There were a few other people now, some wandering in a daze like Catharine, some moaning in pain from wounds or broken bones. Her heart went out to them, but she needed to find Joe.

And at that moment, she thought she recognized the particular shape of the turned spindles of her front porch. Joe had turned them himself a few years ago in his woodshop out back when he was redoing their porch. The porch was gone, but a length of balustrade was there with a few of the spindles. Using her hands, she dug through the mud and debris. After what seemed like hours, she uncovered the sign that Joe had hung beside their front door. "Joseph and Catharine McAdams."

Tears began washing white streaks through the mud on her face as she continued her search. Catharine was exhausted by the time she uncovered a hand, as cool as the mud that had been encasing it. She recognized the ring, the distinctive Celtic design that encircled it.

Feeling the sadness and panic building inside her, she grasped the hand, tugging on it, trying to pull Joe out from under the mass of mud and house parts and broken tree limbs. But he wouldn't budge. Nor did he move. She hoped that she might feel his hand grab on to hers and hold it tightly.

But there was nothing.

Catharine sat down in the mud, holding the cool, lifeless hand, and she cried desperate sobs, wondering how something like this could happen.

TWO YEARS EARLIER

The Sierra Nevada is a range of mountains that cuts across south-central Mexico. Not to be confused with the mountain range of the same name in California, it is also known as the Trans-Mexican Volcanic Belt due to the number of volcanic peaks that rise from the high plateau.

In the forests surrounding the mountains, the oyamel trees, or sacred fir, were quivering and orange, their branches drooping under the weight of the wintering Monarch butterflies covering them. There were fewer of the butterflies than there used to be in years past, but it was still a sight to see.

The butterflies had no knowledge about how several major countries, including the United States, had allowed their economies to guide whether they work to control carbon emissions or not. The butterflies didn't know that the carbon output of these countries far exceeded earlier commitments they had made.

They didn't know anything about the polar ice melting, to the point where North Pole cruises had actually become a common thing in the last several years. They didn't know that the decreasing ice surface reflected less sunlight back into space, nor that the greater water surface absorbed more heat, further raising the temperature of the atmosphere. They knew nothing about the resulting changing weather patterns which affected their own migration routes.

The butterflies only knew, after a fashion, when it was time to begin their long journey north, to feed on the milkweed back in the States and to lay their eggs.

One of them let go of the branch it was hanging from, fluttering its wings upward, disturbing a few others which also lifted off from their roost. A large cluster of them suddenly let go of their branch and took off, their delicate wings beating against the warm air. If anyone had been there to witness the exodus, they might have thought that the sound of the swarm resembled a light rain.

Rising up through the trees, their movement stirred other clusters. Traveling separately, without any kind of formation, the butterflies turned toward the north and began their long pilgrimage.

§

Peregrino was a small town. Nothing exciting ever happened there, despite its proximity to Santa Fe, New Mexico, formerly a popular travel destination. Currently, the topic occupying the minds of virtually all of its inhabitants was how to get rid of the infestation of Japanese beetles.

They had battled the iridescent green and copper beetles in the past, but usually, the infestation didn't begin until June or July. Now that it was barely spring and temperatures had already risen dramatically, the beetles were wasting no time in stripping the roses and other plants of their leaves, leaving behind just a lacy network of veins.

Based on the research of a couple of local horticulturists, one pesticide had been recommended that was supposed to be especially effective on Japanese beetles. The residents of Peregrino had purchased every bottle and jug of the product they could find, leading a few cynics to posit that it had simply been a clever marketing ploy by the manufacturer.

In fact, though, it proved to be effective, and the Peregrinoans had spent a day celebrating their victory over the pests when, shortly before dusk, their little town was suddenly blanketed with

Monarch butterflies. Usually, the butterflies' northward migratory path took them miles to the east, through Oklahoma, Kansas and Nebraska. That they stopped to spend the night in Peregrino at this time of victory was seen by many as a good omen.

It seemed as if their biological luck was finally improving.

§

The common grackle was once, as its name implied, a common bird. Years ago, the National Audubon Society estimated a population of nearly two hundred million birds. Somewhat omnivorous and opportunistic, they benefited in decades past from the growth and expansion of human populations, so much so that they began to be looked upon as pests by the agricultural community due to their fondness for seeds and grains.

City dwellers often saw them as pests, too, since grackles would often bully and crowd out 'desirable' birds from bird feeders. Their raucous calls were annoying replacements for the melodious songbirds that they had displaced.

As weather patterns and economic situations changed, farmers either went out of business or adapted to different crops. In the cities, as food for humans became less abundant and more expensive, bird feeders eventually became something of a luxury. In time, grackles followed the food. Some still thrived in cities, but several populations also grew in the wild.

The weather caused gradual changes in their migratory habits, as well. With winters becoming milder, on average, some grackles began staying in their home locations, while others continued wintering in northern Mexico or the southern United States.

Flying northward one warm spring morning over northern New Mexico, a flock of grackles were surprised by the appearance of thousands of Monarch butterflies in their path. The feast was too good to pass up.

Monarch larvae, gorging themselves on milkweed, absorb and metabolize cardenolide glycoside from the plants. While toxic to many creatures, the glycoside remains in the caterpillars' bodies without harming them. This toxin survives their metamorphosis into butterflies.

A few birds prey on Monarchs, but have learned to leave the wings and abdomen, where the glycoside is most concentrated. Other species have adapted to the point that they can consume the entire butterfly without adverse effects. However, combined with the pesticide that the butterflies had picked up on their overnight stop in Peregrino, the effect on the grackles was, unfortunately, a fatal one.

§

Heat is one condition that often encourages the rapid increase in the populations of destructive insects like locusts, at least as long as there is food for them. Due to rising average temperatures and sweltering heat waves in Africa and the Middle East, locusts were stripping their already ravaged food sources, and taking food out of the mouths of starving people.

In America, particularly in the south, locusts were proving to be a plague, as well, though on a smaller scale. That's not to say that other parts of the United States were given a reprieve.

Dendroctonus was a genus of bark beetles that made a career out of destroying forests in North America. Several species of this beetle ranged across the United States, leaving reddish-brown coniferous forests in their wake.

In Colorado, the forestry service had all but given up on their battle against the beetles. There were now more dead pines than live ones, and forest rangers were actually considering pesticides, something they had shied away from before, to protect other denizens of the forest.

As with the locusts, the mild winter and early heat had contributed to the pine beetles' increase. This spring, they were back in force and were already indulging their voracious appetites for the pines.

The beetles did have predators, but in recent years, the balance was too precarious to really call it a balance. In one area, a population of common grackles had been keeping them somewhat in check.

But, for some reason, the grackles hadn't returned. Taking advantage of their opportunity for unhindered gorging, the beetles continued their feast unabated, consuming the bark of the pine trees, until the entire hillside was brown and dry.

§

Climatologists have long claimed that climate change would make storms stronger. Much study has been done on storms of all kinds, with the results confirming the scientists' predictions.

Massive storm clouds were building now, churning over the mountains of Colorado, casting a deep shadow over a once healthy and thriving forest that now consisted of one brown pine after another. The beetles had moved on now, looking for more live trees to devour.

The interior of the storm was active, as air rapidly moved upward through the center of the cloud where the temperature was below freezing. This produced a mixture of super-cooled cloud droplets, ice crystals and soft hail called graupel.

The cloud droplets and ice crystals rose on the updraft, while the graupel, being heavier, tended to fall, or at least be suspended in the rising air currents. Collisions of these particles in the cloud caused the rising ice crystals and the falling graupel to produce electrical charges. As a result, the entire upper part of the storm eventually received a positive charge, while the lower portion became negatively charged.

The immense storm cloud began dropping rain in some places, but the building electrical charge within it sought outlets for discharge. Following circuitous routes through the air, streaks of lightning cracked loudly between the ground and the cloud, the shock waves spreading outward in the form of thunder.

As the lightning blasted to earth four and five times per minute, several of those electrical bolts found the trees. The pines, dead and dry, exploded as the pulsing current superheated them, flash boiling any sap or moisture that might have remained inside them and, in several cases, igniting the deadwood.

From multiple sources, flames spread outward, eventually joining to form a monstrously destructive fire that consumed homes, a ski resort, and forest, living and dead.

§

Catharine McAdams looked out between the slats of the blinds as the storm brewed outside, the rain falling in sheets. She could feel the goosebumps rising on her arms. It was all too familiar. And there was a prickly feeling on the back of her neck.

"Honey, come on," Joe pleaded. "It's going to be fine. It's just a storm."

"Yeah," she replied shakily, "you remember what 'just a storm' did last year? It burned up the whole mountain and put the ski resort out of business, along with most of the town."

"Exactly," Joe said, in a tone that, he felt, proved his point. "The mountain's bare. Nothing but dead, charred trees up there. Even if lightning strikes again, so what? What's there to burn?"

He had a point, she admitted to herself.

"Come here, Cathy," he said, patting the cushion next to him on the love seat. "Let's find something fun on Netflix and just relax."

She looked at him and sputtered, slapping a hand over her mouth. He had pushed his jeans down around his ankles.

"Or," he added, "we don't have to relax."

"I'm not sure Netflix is going to do it," Catharine said, as she let the blinds fall back into place and went toward Joe. She dropped down on the love seat next to him, snuggling under his arm and resting her hand on his thigh, nestling her elbow gently against his crotch.

"Yeah, I know," Joe replied with a mock macho tone. "You'll probably need something stronger to coax your attention off of me." Catharine smiled, but she felt him move his head toward hers, and his tone became softer. "Just don't let your attention go too far."

Catharine turned her head up to him and kissed him.

§

The rain fell for hours. Up on the mountain, the desiccated ground soaked up all the moisture it could, until it couldn't hold any more. The forest had been dead for a couple of years, and burned for the last one. Grasses had started sprouting again, but any major root systems that had been there before had weakened and died.

The ground, now little more than mud, couldn't support the weight of the gallons of water that it had absorbed. Sections of it began slipping away, soggy cracks forming here and there.

Tons of mud, huge slabs of it, began slipping, as gravity pulled at it, tugging it downward, toward the town of Monte Cristo.

When my parents and I first arrived, and after we endured a few days of suspicious questioning, we were accepted into Frida's community. We settled in a red brick house that faced east. While the sun was already trying to kill us by this time, the western sun was the *most* oppressive, so delaying that heat buildup just a little bit helped, we thought, to some degree.

The house had indoor bathrooms, but without water pumping into the house, the toilets wouldn't work. Even if we were to use water from the river to flush the toilet, with no power or people running the sewage treatment plants, the toilets would quickly back up.

So, one of the first things my father did, with the help of a few others in the community, was to dig a deep toilet hole in the backyard. By scrounging wood from unused houses nearby, they constructed an enclosed platform over it.

My father said that, in the past, these were called outhouses. I learned later, when my father helped a neighbor move theirs, that these last a few years until the hole fills up and needs to be covered with dirt and a new one dug.

As I mentioned, there was a river that ran through the community, though saying it ran is a bit of an exaggeration. The source of the river, I suspected, didn't have much water feeding it. The water of the river tasted, well, not quite brackish, but not quite fresh, either. There was, apparently, still *some* fresh water coming down from the north, but the closer it got to the sea, the worse the water tasted.

Since it had been my way of life from the time I was born, or at least from the time we came to existing settlements, I thought little of the fact that we were living in the previous homes of people who were, most likely, long dead. Being naturally curious, though, it didn't take me long to start exploring.

One of the first things I found in my bedroom was a book, *Where the Wild Things Are*. I knew that it was old. But from the amount of wear on it, I decided that, even at the time of my room's previous occupant, it was already old then.

My father was delighted to see it when I showed it to him. My parents had made certain that I was able to read. It was not considered a necessary ability anymore, but my father, especially, recognized the many doors it opened, even if those doors were only internal.

It was at that point that my love of books was truly kindled. Frida's parents had felt similarly, though admittedly to a somewhat lesser degree. Frida was, at her tender age, already a reader, and had collected a small library of books, particularly art books, by the time we met.

When I showed her *Where the Wild Things Are*, her dark eyes lit up. The artwork was different than anything she had seen before then. It hadn't taken her long to introduce me to her own little library. The pictures, though they seemed a little faded with age, were beautiful. I could understand why she appreciated them so much.

At this time, I only had access to my father's books, the two that he had chosen to bring with them on their journey. *The Holy Bible*, long and confusing, and *Harry Potter and the Philosopher's Stone*, a fun story, but at the time, I wasn't sure I understood the concept of fiction. I think I believed that life back in that *Golden Age* was very much like it was depicted in the story.

Where the Wild Things Are was not as difficult for me to understand, possibly because of the illustrations. They were recognizable, but not realistic. It was at that point that I began to understand fiction, or to distinguish it from real life.

Frida primarily appreciated the artwork, pushing her golden hair back over her ear as she studied it.

And it was at that point that we became good friends.

BIRDS AND BEES

Billy took a long pull from his glass. The beer went down real smooth. Billy generally wasn't too particular about his beer, but with the approach of autumn, he did lean a little more toward a malty brew.

The weather was still warm, though. That was weird. But the beer was cold, so that was good. He looked across the table at his friend, Tony, who was nursing an oatmeal stout.

"How can you drink that shit?" Billy asked.

"What?" Tony replied with an indignant tone. "It's good."

"I just can't drink nuthin' I feel like I hafta chew."

Tony shook his head, but didn't reply.

"I tell ya," Billy said, as if the previous exchange had never even taken place, "I ain't never seen a time when there ain't no ducks in duck huntin' season."

"No ducks at all?" Tony asked, trying not to seem too distracted. "That does seem odd."

"Well, I mean there was a few, but none in range. But I was in a place where I used to come home with more'n my limit. I usually had to stash a couple under the seat o' my pickup in case a ranger stopped me. This time, I didn't shoot a single duck!"

He had to take another swallow of beer to slake his disgust at the situation.

"Hmm," Tony replied ambiguously. Billy narrowed his eyes at Tony.

"Hey, sump'n's eatin' atcha," Billy said. "What's up?"

Tony looked up at Billy, then frowned and shook his head.

"It's no big deal, compared to your he-man activities," Tony replied, aware that his life was quite different from his friend's. Unlike Billy, who was a native, Tony had only moved to Georgia a few years before when his company transferred him. Fitting in to the lifestyle had been something of a challenge.

He realized too late that his remark sounded a little caustic.

"Sorry," he said. "Maggie's just been upset lately."

"She been takin' it out on you, huh?"

"Well, she hasn't been talking it out on me, but still, I'm aware of it. It's really bothering her."

"And if it bothers her, it bothers you." Billy saw Tony's face harden a bit, and he put his hand up in a placating gesture. "Don't get me wrong, buddy, I envy ya. I mean me an' Helen, we're at each other's throats more often than not. She even gimme shit about goin' duck huntin', which she knows I do every year. But I told her to back off and leave me be."

Tony looked at Billy a little skeptically. Billy saw his expression and fessed up.

"Well, okay, I didn't say it directly at her. I said it later, under my breath. In a different part o' the castle I'm king of."

Tony managed a bit of a smile.

"So, what is it?"

"Well, it's nothing, really," Tony said, shaking his head. "But our garden hasn't produced much of anything. Maggie's had a green thumb all her life and, well, frankly it's kind of freaky."

"Huh," Billy replied, "it's interesting you should say that. Our garden ain't produced much, neither. But we did have a purdy hot summer. Seemed like it dried up as fast as we soaked it."

"We've been thinking about something else," Tony said. He looked up at Billy. "What was your windshield like when you got back from hunting?"

"My windshield?" Billy said, cocking his head back in confusion. "Wuddaya mean?"

"When I was a kid," Tony said, "I went on road trips with my folks, and my dad was constantly cleaning the windshield from all the bugs that smashed onto it."

"Oh yeah," Billy nodded, "I 'member that, too. My old man kept a jug of washer fluid in the car 'cuz he always run out."

"So?" Tony persisted. "What was your windshield like after your hunting trip?"

"Ya know, now that I think about it, there was maybe a coupla' bugs on it, but nuthin' like the mess that used ta be on my dad's windshield."

Tony nodded, leaning forward as if that made his point.

"Most of the vegetables in our garden flowered, but they never got beyond that."

"Whut's my windshield got to do with yer garden?"

"There aren't as many insects around as there used to be."

"Are you shittin' me?" Billy asked. "Don't you 'member my Fourth o' July barbecue? We was almost eaten alive by all the mosquitoes."

"I'm not saying there are no bugs. I mean insects constitute the vast majority of life on earth. But I think their numbers are dwindling. And if there are fewer insects, then that means there are fewer pollinators. Which would explain why our vegetable garden produced flowers, but not many vegetables."

"But what about them giant swarms of locusts we been hearin' about?"

"Again, I'm not saying that all bugs are gone. I'm saying that the environment is out of balance. There may be more bugs in some places and fewer in others, just like climate change causes flooding in one place and drought in another. It's out of balance. That's probably the way it will continue until, for better or worse, the earth finds some kind of equilibrium."

"Ya know," Billy replied, "I kinda 'member back when I was a kid, folks was talkin' about savin' honeybees. I didn't think much about it back then, but I know honey's purdy much a delicacy now. Only rich folks can afford it."

Tony raised his eyebrows and nodded.

"And you know what?" he asked. "That could be part of why you didn't get any ducks, either."

"Wuddaya mean?"

"Well, what do ducks eat?"

"Oh, ducks eat lotsa stuff. Plants and algae, fish and tadpoles, bugs and – oh, yeah."

"And now that you mention tadpoles, I haven't seen or heard frogs around here for some time, either." Billy was quiet while Tony took a drink of his beer. "So if there are fewer bugs, the frogs either die off or move on. And if there are no bugs, and no frogs to lay eggs and hatch tadpoles, the ducks are going to move on to where there's more plentiful food."

"Well damn, son, that pisses me off. I was lookin' forward to havin' some duck this fall."

"Sorry, Billy, but it's not just duck. While you were away on your trip, I was doing some research online. Scientists have been predicting an 'insect apocalypse' for a while now. That affects more than just your ducks. More than a third of our food depends on insect pollinators."

"So, professor, what can we do?"

Tony sat back and shook his head.

"I don't know if there's anything we can do. It's been linked to climate change and pesticides and numerous other things that we've been doing for decades. A lot of people have said that we've passed the tipping point. If it's already to the point where we've actually noticed the obvious reduction of their number on our windshield, I'm afraid it might be too late to reverse it."

"Damn!" Billy said as he picked up his glass and took a drink. He looked appreciatively at the glass as he set it back down. "Purdy soon, there ain't gonna be nuthin' much to do around here except drink beer." He looked at Tony and his countenance fell. "I suppose barley and hops need to be pollinated, too?"

"Actually, they're both self-pollinating."

Billy perked up.

"Well finally, there's some good news!"

Billy drained the last of his beer, then he raised his glass when he got the waitress' attention.

CHANGES

Frida's mother, Blue, died a few months after her father. We didn't know why. We seldom did.

Some people, like Frida's father, display external signs of the cause of death. He was constantly busy, making forays out in all directions, looking for useful items. His wife had urged him to cut back on his hunts. When he started getting sick, he did, but by that time, the damage had been done. He had spent a great deal of time outside, and was not always as careful as he should have been about covering up.

When Hunter died, he was covered with black splotches of melanoma. Cause of death was a simple enough matter to determine.

When Blue died, there was no visible cause. She had displayed no symptoms that any of those around her were able to see, aside from the sadness of losing her husband.

But that was often the way with us. After thirty or forty years, our bodies just give out. That's not to say that there weren't warnings. But the warning signs, the symptoms, were ones that, back in the *Golden Age*, didn't show up until thirty or forty years later. In Blue's case, she just didn't wake up.

§

"So, am I your sister now?" Frida asked. My parents had just taken her into our home, and the transition was a little confusing for her.

And for me.

"I'm not sure," I replied. It was confusing because, at twelve years old, I was feeling stirrings which, I learned later, were completely normal, but felt entirely foreign to me at the time. Frida was my friend, but this sensation I started feeling for her was different.

We sat on the floor in the bedroom that my parents had designated would be hers, the old worn fibers of the carpet providing little cushion. The curtains were pulled tightly across the window, but it was still bright, and very warm.

Leaning my back against the bed, I looked at Frida. Sadness seemed to be ever-present in her eyes, now, threatening to well up and overflow at a moment's notice.

I felt this overwhelming desire to protect her from bad feelings, including the sadness she felt about losing both of her parents. I wanted to hold her in my arms and make the sad feelings go away.

But holding her in my arms brought about other feelings. Feelings that didn't seem as magnanimous or charitable. I actually felt afraid of these new feelings, yet I craved them.

"I'm glad you're here, though," I ventured.

"I am, too," Frida replied, moving toward me and snuggling her face against my chest. She sniffed back the tears, and I held her a little tighter, the stronger, protective instinct taking the fore.

There were no other children in our little community, and my mind had been pondering it for a while.

"Do you realize how amazing it is that we met?" I asked. It seemed like a worthy distraction. I enjoyed pondering such flights of fancy. Frida turned her head to look up at me.

"How do you mean?"

"Think of all the things that you and I have done, and that our parents have done, that led to you and me meeting here."

Mentioning her parents was a risk, and I saw the momentary flicker, but her eyebrows scrunched together as she pondered what I had said.

"Every day of exploring," I continued, "looking for food, water, shelter, signs of other people. I was born after my parents had already started their expedition, and that had to change their routines, too. Virtually anything could have happened to alter their daily habits. The slightest change in any of those routines, on any day, in any year, could have sent us in a different direction, and you and I never would have met."

Frida raised her eyebrows as she looked at me.

"Or, maybe something *did* change," she suggested, her voice taking on that excited tone that always expressed her enthusiasm about learning something new. "Maybe the way they chose turned out to be blocked by a landslide, and they had to turn a different way, and *that's* why you ended up here."

"Maybe," I smiled and nodded. "Or maybe they came to a cliff and decided that it wasn't worth trying to climb down."

"Maybe they saw a mountain lion—were there still mountain lions?"

"I don't know." I squinted in a regretful expression, sorry to foil her contribution. "I don't think so."

"Well, maybe they saw the last one," Frida continued unperturbed, "and were scared to go that way."

Having heard stories of my mother's prowess, I doubted that one, but I gave it to Frida.

"Maybe," I nodded.

Frida snuggled her head into my chest again and relaxed.

"Or maybe a butterfly flapped its wings," she said softly.

RETIREMENT

Amy slipped her hand into Jack's as they sat together on the sofa. She heard him sigh, felt him squeeze her hand gently. The last of the guests had gone. All of the leftover food had been put away, except for some of the non-perishable items that still sat out on the table, in case they wanted a quick snack. Amy didn't feel like doing anything with it yet.

She looked down at their hands resting on the sofa, their fingers entwined. Their hands had been finding each other frequently lately. They sat like that for a few minutes in silence. When Amy heard Jack sigh again, she knew he was going to get up. He leaned over and kissed the side of her face and got to his feet.

"I need to get busy," he said. "I think I'll clean out the garage."

Amy nodded and watched him walk away. She sat alone for a couple of minutes, but she knew she should be busy, too. She pushed herself up from the sofa and went into her office. Unfortunately, it didn't have the desired effect.

The first thing she saw was the collage photo frame hanging on the wall behind her desk. She couldn't resist looking at all the photographs of happy moments frozen in time. There was her and Jack in front of Mount Rushmore, with little Tony, seven years old, but tall for his age, standing in front of them.

He looked a little more his age when the picture was taken at the Grand Canyon, when he was ten.

In front of the Capitol Building in Washington, D.C., he looked grumpy, but he was a teenager. They were supposed to be moody.

Looking at the reminders of family vacations through the years, Amy could remember what was going on with them at the time. When they were at Disneyland, their house was being shown by the realtor, and they would move a few weeks after they got back. Tony didn't like his new school, and he began acting up and his grades began to falter.

As they stood in front of a giant redwood tree, she could see the somewhat gnarled expression on Tony's face. The new anti-depressant had some side-effects, and he often felt nauseated. By the time they went to New England, though, he was on a different one, and was doing much better. He actually smiled for that picture.

Feeling the grief overtaking her again, she sat down at her desk and grabbed a tissue, pressing it against her eyes as she cried. For several minutes, the tears kept coming, her body convulsing with violent sobs as, time after time, she replaced one wet tissue with a new dry one.

After the past week, she was amazed that she could still produce that many tears. She gathered the wads of wet tissue and tossed them in the trash can. Her body continued twitching as her diaphragm continued the involuntary jerks that had begun with the sobbing.

She sighed as she looked at the mess cluttering the top of her desk. She hadn't done any actual work since she made the awful discovery, but her business had already been suffering for a while. There just weren't very many people getting married anymore, and those who did were often enduring severe financial hardships.

The climate change that people had been arguing about for decades seemed to actually be happening, causing a number of unforeseen problems. In addition to that, the economy was going to hell. She didn't know if the two issues were related or not. At any rate, her catering company had mainly been doing simple, low-cost events, while she watched her business account dwindling.

She picked up a number of papers and began sorting them, based on subject-matter and on the attention needed. After a half hour of focused immersion in the activity, she had the top of her desk cleared off. Except for a file folder that she hadn't seen in a while. She opened the folder and looked at the paper on top, and immediately, she felt a longing, a deep yearning. It was several sheets she had printed from a web site and stapled together.

She and Jack had been dreaming about that for years. She remembered talking about it with her parents. They had considered it themselves many years before, when the cost of retiring in Italy was closer to four thousand dollars a month. Over the last two or three decades, the economy had plummeted. These papers were a few years old, so the cost of retiring in Italy was probably closer to eight or nine thousand now. Still, cheaper than here.

But Amy began reading through them as if they were brand new. She looked at the pictures that had captured their hearts, of towns and villages with ancient stone architecture, glowing golden in the sun, and she felt that old feeling growing, building in her chest as she read it.

What better time than now to start considering it again?

§

Jack apparently hadn't been able to focus as well as Amy had. A few items had been moved to the center of the garage, things, Amy saw, that they hadn't used in a long time. She hoped those were things he was planning on getting rid of.

But Jack was sitting on a lawn chair holding an old baseball glove. It had been his as a teenager, and he had given it to Tony years ago. But Tony hadn't been interested in baseball. It stayed, unused, in a closet in the house until, a few years later, it found its way to a shelf in the garage, where it stayed ever since.

Jack looked up at Amy as she quietly approached him. The tears were still wet on his cheeks.

"I said some mean things to him when he didn't want this," he said sadly. Amy placed her hand on his shoulder and shook her head.

"Jack, that was a long time ago," she said quietly. "He knew you loved him. Don't beat yourself up about things in the past."

Jack looked back down at the glove, but didn't say anything.

"Look what I found," Amy said, holding out the file folder, hoping a change of subject would help. Jack placed the baseball glove palm down on his knee, not ready to put it aside yet. He reached for the folder a little listlessly and opened it. The top page caught his attention, as it had Amy's. He scanned the page and looked at the picture, and he looked up inquiringly at her.

"Do you remember how badly we wanted to do that?" Amy asked. "To just sell most of our stuff and move to a little town in Italy?"

"Of course I do," Jack said, looking back down at the picture of the happy older couple enjoying their retirement among their classical surroundings. The stone buildings were absolutely glowing in the golden Italian sunlight. "It was practically all we could think or talk about for a couple of years."

"I know," Amy said quietly.

"Then Tony started getting worse, and we decided we couldn't leave."

Amy nodded, remembering it vividly. Moving Tony out of his apartment and back into their home. The visits to the doctor. The search for a psychiatrist that Tony liked. The night in the emergency room after he attempted suicide when their attention lapsed.

It was grueling, but now it was over. She didn't regret the help they gave him, but if she was completely honest, it was a relief to be done with it. Agonizing and heartbreaking, but still a relief.

"Let's do it," Amy implored.

"But," Jack said, turning back to her, "they always say you shouldn't make a major life change right after a traumatic experience."

"That's the thing," Amy replied, "we won't be making the change right after. It'll take us at least a year to get our affairs in order and to do all the necessary research before we can actually do it. That will give us time to consider the pros and cons, and to know whether or not we're being impulsive."

Jack looked back down at the file and started leafing through the pages. He started reading one of them, an article written by a couple who had moved to Giovinazzo, a town on the Adriatic coast of Italy.

As he became engrossed in the article, Amy quietly turned and went back in the house.

§

"Oh god," Jack said.

"What?" Amy lifted her WebVisor and looked at him. She had been perusing real estate listings in and around Giovinazzo. Jack lifted his own WebVisor and looked at her, sighing.

"The average summertime high temperature in Giovinazzo is 104°."

Amy raised an eyebrow his direction.

"We figured that would be the case."

"I know, but—" Jack shook his head. "Don't you think that might just be a constant reminder?"

"Honey, the reminder's going to be there pretty much wherever we go," Amy replied, "when he's not with us." Jack nodded.

"Yeah, I know." He sighed.

Dr. Robbins, Tony's psychiatrist, had tried to help them with their feelings of guilt. And what he said, Amy later found through her own research, was correct.

"A long time ago," he had said, "it was discovered that suicides seem to peak in the summertime. When there's a heatwave, especially one of an extended duration, suicides spike. The elevated temperatures that we're experiencing, I'm afraid, are only heightening that effect."

"You're telling me it was inevitable that he was going to kill himself?" Amy asked incredulously, scrubbing away another tear.

"I'm telling you that, if someone is already inclined toward severe depression and suicide, there's little anyone can do to prevent it when the circumstance presents itself."

"We shouldn't have let the circumstance present itself," Jack murmured. "He was living in our home. There was only one of him and two of us."

"You're human," Dr. Robbins said. "You have your own needs to care for. Short of tying him to his bed, you couldn't watch over him twenty-four hours of every day."

"So—" Amy started.

"I'm saying that, given Tony's condition, his predilection, this outcome was," he paused and took a breath, "unfortunately, very likely."

"We're dealing with the heat here," Amy said now, looking across at Jack. "I think we might be able to deal with it a little better in Italy."

Jack looked at her for a few moments, then he smiled, sort of, and pulled his WebVisor back down.

§

Jack and Amy wandered hand-in-hand along what used to be a river. They breathed deeply of the fresh air near their new home in Piccola Antica. In the past, it had been heavily-forested, though the trees had thinned out quite a bit in recent decades.

They had spent the last year and a half researching locations, while going through their possessions, selling and donating what they hadn't used in years. They were thankful for Jack's pension. It wasn't as much as they would have liked, but at least here, it would last longer than it would have in the States.

The grief was still their constant companion, sometimes interrupting their activities with more tears, but the shared focused attention on a goal helped them work their way through it together, and actually drew them closer.

After all their research, they had settled on a tiny village in the Piedmont region of northern Italy, at the southern portion of the Alps, in the hills literally just a few yards away from the French border.

"Tony would have loved this," Jack said. Amy looked up at him warily, but was happy to see a bit of a smile on his face.

They had decided that a village built up around a monastery founded in 600 A.D., while not in the middle of the popular culture of Italy, still had the age and history that they craved. And being sheltered by the hills at the base of the Alps, the temperatures were not as high as elsewhere. It wasn't as much of a reminder.

"Yes," she nodded, "he sure would have."

watched curiously as Frida pried the top off of the big clay pot. Even from where I stood several feet away, I could smell the acidic aroma wafting out of it.

She reached into the pot and pulled out a flat greenish object. It was shaped like a plate, but I had never seen one of such a strange, unsightly color.

"What are those?" I asked as Frida pulled one after another out of the pot.

"They're copper dishes," Frida replied. "My father made it a mission to find some once he learned how to make green paint."

She was about eleven years old now. Several weeks after her parents' death, she could talk about them with a smile instead of tears.

"Paint?" I asked, not expecting such a response.

"He learned that, centuries ago, they collected green pigment by soaking copper plates in vinegar. The acid causes the copper to rust, and copper rust is green."

She placed the last of the plates on top of the stack and dried her hands.

"Where did he find vinegar?" I asked.

"Apparently," she replied, smiling at the adventure of sharing knowledge, "a lot of people used to have what he called wine cellars. Most of the bottles he found were almost empty. They were sealed with some kind of stopper that rotted, and after so many years, the wine dried up.

"He said that some used some kind of synthetic stopper, and they kept better. But he said that, even in most of those, the wine wasn't good to drink anymore." She smiled at me. "When wine rusts, it makes vinegar."

I was fascinated.

"The acid in the vinegar reacts in some way with the copper," she continued, "and it makes this green coating. I just have to scrape it off every now and then, and I have my green pigment."

She looked at me, her eyebrows raised once again.

"The algae on the river?" she said. I nodded, scrunching up my face. Mother said it was good for us, but she couldn't make it not taste nasty. "I can make a different color of green from that."

"And then you paint with it?" I asked.

"Well, no," Frida replied. "That's just the color. To make paint, I need something to hold it together, something called a binder. But Father taught me how to collect starch from root vegetables. The starch binds the color so it stays in place."

"Forever?"

"I'm afraid not. Paints they made centuries ago were mixed with some kind of oil, and when that dried, it was a lot more permanent. With mine, I'm just happy that it stays in place when the painting is upright."

She smiled, but I was still entranced by this new knowledge.

"How did your father learn all this?" I asked, astonished. Frida looked at me as if she couldn't believe what she was hearing.

"From books. Whenever he found a library, he would spend hours inside, looking for art books for me." Her eyes threatened to fill up, but she blinked and pointed to the books on her shelves. "He learned that they were placed on the shelves by some kind of numbering system. Art books were all in the seven hundreds."

I couldn't believe I didn't know this. My father loved books so much, and yet this information was new to me. He had found a few new books in his inspection of this and other houses, but I had never heard of these libraries.

I had seen Frida grinding different soils and even rocks to make various color pigments. This green pigment marked the moment when I realized how extensive her knowledge of art really was. And she had learned about it through books!

"Do you know where these libraries are?" I asked.

"I know where a couple of them are," she replied, "but they're in pretty bad shape." She knew of my love of books, and her face expressed her chagrin at telling me this. "The buildings are falling down, and my father said that most of the books have rotted."

"I want to see them," I said decisively. Frida smiled and nodded.

ADAPTATION

George looked at his hands. Correction, paws. They weren't hands anymore. He didn't know how long it had been. Time was losing meaning to him. But his fingers had become unrecognizable sometime in the past, he couldn't say when. He had slept several times since then. That's all he knew.

He hadn't seen his wife in a while. Penny had been rather aloof lately. But he vaguely remembered one of the last times she had been with him, when some friends, the Cooksons, had come over for a visit. He recalled how Janine Cookson had looked down at him and smiled, saying something unintelligible, and she bent over to pet him, cooing at him.

He didn't know what had caused the transformation. At first, he had been alarmed. His slender, human fingers had begun shrinking, turning stubby, the nails pulling away and becoming cylindrical, like claws.

To see his dexterous, human hands gradually change into paws, covered with snow-white fur, was rather unsettling. At the time, his only consolation, if it could be called that, was the fact that his feet were undergoing a similar metamorphosis. At least his appendages would match.

The change was occurring, not only on his hands and feet, but his whole body. He had noticed the cottony fuzz sprouting from his arms, his chest, his belly. Before his arms shortened, he could reach back and feel, with the pads on the bottom of his paws, the fur growing on his back and shoulders.

Even stranger, he was shrinking. He used to be able to walk up to his bed and sit down on it. Now, the bed was higher than he was, and he had to jump to get up on it. Fortunately, he had also acquired a particular spring to his step that allowed him to do that.

In time, he found that standing upright felt unpleasant. He tried walking around on all fours, and decided that that was much more comfortable, more efficient. He discovered that he had developed a certain grace that he had never possessed walking upright. He had also developed a long, bushy tail which helped with his balance, likely contributing to his new-found grace.

But George's home had become foreign to him. All the man-made furnishings, the clothing, everything. It all looked and smelled strange to him. Outside was where he felt most at home. The clean smell of the freshly-fallen snow, the natural feel of the tundra under his feet. That's where he felt at home, at peace.

§

George sensed something in the air, not tangible, but electric. He lifted his head from where he had been curled up in the snow, his tail covering his paws and his nose. He looked around, his nose now exposed to the currents. In the cold-stilled air, he caught the hint of something. Something familiar. Something dangerous.

He cautiously stood up on all fours, scanning the snow. That's when he saw one of the dunes of snow move.

Knowing he was found out, the polar bear lunged. George took off in the opposite direction, his tail streaming behind him, sometimes reacting and balancing his moves, sometimes anticipating them. The polar bear loped after him, quickly gaining speed.

George knew that the polar bear was an agile runner, the big pads on his paws gripping the snow and ice. His mighty muscles could push him to speeds around fifty miles an hour. George could only top out at about thirty.

At least, George used to know these facts. Now, it was mainly just instinct that guided him.

His little legs pumping as fast as they could go, he bounded over the snow. He could hear the exhalations of the bear gaining on him. He could feel the vibrations of the bear's heavy footfalls on the ground. He could almost feel the heat of the bear radiating out away from him.

But he dared not look behind.

George's lungs were about to burst, his heart battering his ribs. The vocal huffing of the bear was immediately behind him. He heard the bear take a greater breath, as if preparing for something, and George didn't want to think about what that was.

Suddenly, he saw it – the opening to his den. He had ventured far in search of food, and almost became food in the process. Plunging into the darkness, he went deep, knowing the bear wouldn't give up so easily.

He heard the frustrated roar of the polar bear behind him, followed by an abrasive sound as the bear attempted to enlarge the hole, trying to scrape out huge pawfuls of snow, ice and tundra. George didn't stop to watch, but continued deeper, following a shaft that branched off the main tunnel.

The tunnel ended at a cozy den, and he curled up there, his back against the wall. He was safe here. He couldn't even hear the bear anymore. Either he was far enough away from it that the sound couldn't reach him, or the bear had given up and gone off in search of other prey.

After a while, George caught his breath, and he sighed and laid his head down, wrapping his tail around himself again.

§

The heat was torturous. The sun beat down on a front lawn that, in better days, had been green with cool, lush grass. There were still patches of grass here and there, but they were all brittle brown. Ivy still clung to the sign, though the leaves had become sparse. Those that remained had been dried to a crisp, and it no longer concealed any of what the sign said.

Cascade County Psychiatric Institution

Penny looked through the window into the room where her husband was curled up on his bed, naked, in an unnatural-looking position, sleeping. He twitched, then lifted his head, sniffing the air. Penny thought his actions looked like those of a wolf or a big cat in the wild, catching a scent of dinner. Then, he lowered his head and looked around the room.

He got up on his hands and knees and stretched, with his head down and his butt up in the air, much like an animal would do. He shook himself a little, then crawled around in a circle on his bed, finally curling up as he had been before, but in the other direction.

With tears in her eyes, Penny turned toward Dr. Huson. She looked at him for a few moments, seemingly at a loss for words.

"What's wrong with him?" she finally asked.

"I can't say for certain," Dr. Huson replied, "since he refuses to talk, but my best guess at this time is that he's suffering from clinical lycanthropy."

"Lycanthropy?" Penny exclaimed. "You think he's turned into a werewolf?"

"No," Dr. Huson said with a half-smile, but seeing Penny's reaction, he quickly retrieved a serious expression. "Lycanthropy is the mythical condition in which a person turns into a werewolf. But clinical lycanthropy refers to a rare but very real psychiatric condition, the delusion or belief that one is an animal of some kind."

Penny looked through the window. George twitched again and brushed his hand over his face in a downward motion, like a dog, half-asleep, brushing away some irritation.

"I don't understand. Why is he like this? There's no history of mental illness in his family."

"I'm afraid mental illness is becoming much more commonplace," Dr. Huson replied. "Depression, particularly, has skyrocketed lately, and as an offshoot of that, various delusions have been cropping up. During sustained heatwaves, suicides often escalate, so we're very fortunate that that's not an issue in George's case. But people are desperate for relief, an escape of some kind."

"Is —" Penny huffed, glancing through the window again, "is there any hope for recovery?"

"I'm very sorry to say that there's no way to know for sure. He doesn't seem to have any lucid moments when he talks, so that's not very encouraging. And the fact that the higher temperatures are expected to continue, well, I'm afraid your guess is as good as mine." Dr. Huson seemed to realize that he wasn't making the Institution look very good, and quickly added, "At least in here, he can't harm himself or anybody else."

"Well, can't he at least have some clothes?"

"Oh, he has clothes," Dr. Huson said, pointing toward a little pile of something near the far wall. "Whenever an orderly dresses him, George manages to get the clothes off within a couple of minutes. He's obviously more comfortable that way, so we don't press the issue. Especially considering that our old cooling system can't keep up with the heat."

Penny nodded. It really was warm. She looked through the window again.

"I hope wherever he is, he's happy," she finally said under her breath.

§

The little arctic fox cautiously stuck his nose up through the opening of his den. The opening had been enlarged somewhat by the polar bear, but the bear seemed to have given up and left for easier prey.

The fox emerged from the tunnel, looking around in all directions, sniffing the air. Satisfied that he was safe, he stretched and shook, fluffing his fur out as protection against the subfreezing temperature.

Suddenly, he caught a whiff of something upwind. He lowered his head and went into a crouch, stepping softly through the snow. As he came around the curvature of a low dune of snow, he saw it, a plump lemming just ahead.

The lemming was unaware that he had been seen, and was happily munching on moss that was clinging to a rock protruding up through the snow. The fox moved slowly, patiently, barely breathing, as he inched toward the lemming.

A change in the breeze carried his scent to the lemming, and the rodent took off, plunging into an unseen hole in the snow. The fox lifted his head when he realized he had lost out on this meal. But there would be more. The tundra was crawling with them.

The sky was violet as the sun leisurely dipped toward the horizon, and the fox bounded through the snow seemingly aimlessly. He didn't have any place he had to go.

He was just happy to be.

KNOWLEDGE

Mother made certain that Frida and I were both dressed properly, covered from head to foot in our white hemp clothing, including our face coverings. We had been doing it all our lives, but Mother still had to be sure.

Walking out the front door was always the most unpleasant part of going out. The heat was unbearable at any time, but that first blast of intense sunlight was always a shock to the system.

Frida led the way, heading west. We walked over old concrete that was being reduced to gravel by the relentless weeds. In places, the hemp was nearly as tall as we were. Mother would, likely, be out here soon to harvest the stems for their fibers.

Father had built her a loom shortly after we arrived here, based on what he remembered reading about in a book he had read years before, in their previous settlement. Besides our clothing, she now had the added responsibility of making canvases for Frida to paint on.

Which she assured Frida was no trouble at all.

The river on our left, where we got our water, moved sluggishly, slower than we did. Frida led me through the old neighborhood, as it used to be called. Though there had not been any neighbors for quite a long time.

The library didn't look like much. As Frida had warned me, the roof had caved in, and we had to climb over rubble to get inside. Considering the state of what was left of the building, "inside" didn't seem that safe.

But once I was there, it didn't matter. I looked around at the shelves of books, and I sighed. As Frida had also warned, the books were in bad shape, as well. The first few books that I pulled off the shelves crumbled under their own weight.

After I went farther into the building, under the part of the roof that was still intact, I found books that actually held together as I handled them.

I can't describe the emotions that swept through me as I held ancient wisdom in my hands. Knowledge that was readily available to the common man ages ago. All they had to do was drive their vehicles, their cars, to the library.

There were some of those in the area outside the building, dirty and corroded. There were also, I must add, dusty, crumbling remains of some of those past denizens of the world in the library. But Frida and I had become inured to seeing them, stepping past them, or over them, whenever necessary.

I have no idea how long we spent in the library, but my arms could not hold any more books than I had collected. Books on gardening and history and popular entertainment figures of the past. Fictional stories and biographies of people in various moments in history.

I found Frida, not surprisingly, in the section that contained books on art, and she had gathered several, as well.

Despite the burden weighing down my arms, I couldn't help just standing there and watching her as she leafed through a book on chiaroscuro—which she explained to me later.

She really was the most beautiful thing I had ever seen.

CRUISE

David looked up at Jenny straddling him. Stroking his hands up the sides of her body, he traced her hourglass shape as she slid up and down on top of him. Supporting herself with her hands on his shins behind her, Jenny looked down at David through blissfully narrowed eyelids.

As the moment arrived, David began pumping upward harder, and Jenny panted as she diametrically matched his movements. Grasping her hips, David gave one last thrust, pushing his hips up and holding the position as he made it a point to keep his eyes open so he could watch her face as he throbbed inside her.

Jenny was the prettiest thing that David Lennox had ever seen. The fact that she had, just a few days before, become his wife, was the most amazing and gratifying thing he could imagine.

As the spasms subsided, Jenny leaned forward and lay down on top of David. She kissed him, long and deep, as David studiously traced with his fingertips the shape of her body, now damp with sweat.

"So, did we make it?" Jenny asked breathlessly.

David lay still, concentrating, and pondered for a few moments. He looked at her and nodded.

"It feels like we're still rocking a little. I think we made it."

§

The Naiad, flagship of the Atlantis Cruise Line, was approaching the dock at Georgetown, Guyana, on the northeast coast of South America. Passengers crowded on deck to watch the proceedings. Pushing through them was David Lennox, his arm stretched behind him, holding Jenny's hand as he pulled her through the crowd.

Jenny was still adjusting her clothing with her free hand.

David was a journalist for the Kansas City Times. A lot of newspapers had gone out of business over the last few decades.

Those that still remained had to adjust to not being papers anymore, since most people got their news online. While he had dreams of working for the big guys, the New York Times or the Washington Post, still, he was particularly thankful for the job he had. It was his assignment for a fluff piece that introduced him to Jenny.

Wanting to do hard news, David had originally balked at the assignment, a series about local caregivers. But it was when he was working on the segment about a local veterinarian that he met Jenny, the veterinarian's assistant. He silently thanked his editor for the assignment, and he had a hard time focusing on the questions he had for the veterinarian. Being the kind of person that would attract the attention of a city newspaper doing a piece about caregivers, though, the vet didn't mind.

Since Jenny fell for David just as quickly, they were married six months after they met, just last week. They both agreed that a South American cruise would be the perfect way to start off the rest of their lives together.

January had typically been the rainy season in South America, but they figured that being stuck in their cabin together wouldn't be the worst thing in the world. As it turned out, though, there hadn't been a drop of rain on the entire trip. Too bad. It was considerably hotter than usual, and they thought a little rain might help cool it off.

The Naiad's ropes pulled taut, the ramps were opened up and the passengers began filing down to see Georgetown.

§

The market on the streets of Georgetown was crowded, but nothing like pictures that David had seen of the markets in Buenos Aires or Rio de Janeiro. That was why they had chosen this particular cruise. David would have found the bustling markets of the bigger cities exciting, but Jenny, being more of an introvert, would have been tense the whole time.

Even here in the marketplace, though there was room to move among the stalls, there were still a lot of people, and David could sense that she was a little anxious, though she made light of it when he asked her about it.

"I'm with my handsome and thoughtful new husband," she said, leaning into him. "What would I possibly have to be anxious about?"

David smiled at her as they wandered aimlessly. The stalls seemed a little barren compared with what he remembered from the brochures. He wondered if the global warming that everybody had been fighting about for so many decades was affecting the produce. It certainly seemed to be affecting the weather.

And on their approach to Georgetown, David noticed a lot of dead trees and other vegetation, ominous considering that Guyana was part of the once mighty Amazon rainforest. So much of it, in years past, had been cleared for farming, while millions of acres were lost to fire, pollution and changing climate conditions. It appeared that the so-called lungs of the earth were dying.

Suddenly, Jenny's attention was captured by something at one of the stalls. The stall was sponsored by a local wildlife conservation organization.

"Oh my god!" she gushed as she knelt down beside a baby animal. "Is this a tapir?" she asked the woman at the stall.

"Yes," the dark-skinned woman replied. "Its mother was killed by a poacher." The woman spoke English with a bit of an African-sounding accent.

"Oh, the poor baby." Jenny petted the little animal, cooing over it. It was shaped somewhat like a piglet, with short, dark brown fur and whitish stripes and spots. Its downward sloping trunk-like nose, though, was one of its most distinctive features. As Jenny petted and talked to it, it looked at her, raising its prehensile snout to smell her, licking her with its long pale pink tongue.

"Isn't it adorable?" Jenny asked, looking up at David.

David stood there, smiling and nodding, as he watched Jenny. It was usually her long and shapely brown legs that captured his attention, but at the moment, it was her love for other creatures, and her empathy, that particularly held his consideration and admiration.

Jenny fished a couple of twenty-dollar bills out of her purse and gave them to the woman, to help with her organization's work. David smiled and shook his head at her altruism, and he knew he was the luckiest man in the world.

By the end of the day, they had purchased several souvenirs, some for themselves, and some as Christmas gifts for friends and family. They each sighed when they were finally able to deposit their burdens in their room.

"I need to get cleaned up before we go to dinner," Jenny said, holding the sides of her soaked shirt away from her body for emphasis.

"I do, too," David replied, tossing his hat on the bed. Even with sunscreen, people didn't usually go out without a hat anymore. "We probably shouldn't do it together, though, or we'll never get out of here."

"Hmm." Jenny raised her eyebrows as she twirled a lock of her hair between her fingers and looked David up and down as if she was seriously considering it. "I'm actually not really hungry," she finally said. "We snacked all day. But maybe a drink or two. Then we can come back here." She smiled suggestively and went into the bathroom.

§

They decided to try a lounge that had a more casual atmosphere, with TVs around the perimeter, like a sports bar.

Except that several of the TVs were showing coverage of the escalating conflict in Algeria.

"Shit," David said. "I was doing pretty well for the last few days without any reminders."

"For a journalist," Jenny said thoughtfully, "that's kind of significant." David responded with a sort of facial shrug with his eyebrows and a roll of his eyes.

"Do you realize," he said, hooking his thumb over his shoulder toward the TV, his face expressing more feeling than the previous shrug, "that the United States, as of now, is currently involved in military actions with ten different countries?"

"There's never enough money for education, housing or health care," Jenny replied, "but we can always afford another war."

"Yeah, I know," David said before taking a gulp of his Jameson on the rocks. "I'm constantly amazed that America isn't completely bankrupt yet."

"I guess it helps to have your own money presses."

"I wish it was that easy," David scoffed. "Of course, if it was, we'd probably be involved in even more, because we could always afford it." He looked up at the TV again, and Jenny could see the darkness descending over his face.

She loved his sensitivity. She thought it made him a good journalist in a lot of ways. In some ways, though, she knew he felt it was a hindrance. With some subjects, he had a hard time being objective.

"Okay," Jenny said, taking on an authoritative tone, "we're still on our honeymoon. This is the first cruise I've ever been on in my life, and I don't want anything to spoil it. So, no more talk about war, alright?"

David looked at her and smiled. He couldn't help it. He lifted his glass toward her.

"To us, and to our happily ever after," he said.

Jenny smiled warmly at him and sighed, as she lifted her wine glass and clinked it against his.

§

The sun was nearing the horizon to their right as they stood at the rail at the stern of the ship. It had been hot that day, hotter than it was supposed to be this time of year. But with the ship now underway northward, the breeze their journey created, while still warm, made it a little more comfortable. They watched the waves spreading out behind them as David stood behind Jenny, one arm on each side of her.

Despite the sticky heat, Jenny leaned back against David, appreciating the sense of protection and contentment she felt in his arms. She felt him gently kiss the back of her head, and she smiled. The yearning was building, and she knew they would have to go back to their cabin soon.

She sighed and looked down at the waves.

"Oh my god!" she suddenly exclaimed, her body tensing, her grip tightening on the railing. David leaned forward and looked over her shoulder to see where she was looking.

Spreading out behind the ship in its wake was a greenish-brown cloud in the water.

"I sure hope that's not what it looks like," Jenny said, feeling her stomach turning.

She looked around and saw a member of the crew a short distance away.

"Excuse me," she called to him, and she motioned to him to join them.

"Yes, ma'am," he said as he came alongside them, "what can I do for you?" Jenny pointed down at the discoloration in the water stretching out in the distance behind them.

"What is that?" she asked.

He looked down at the water, and couldn't seem to hide the embarrassment on his face.

"That's nothing to be concerned about," he said. Jenny couldn't tell if he believed what he was saying or not. "Cruise ships, as you might imagine, generate a lot of waste products every day.

"To handle the waste from thousands of guests and crew members, the ship has its own wastewater treatment plant. It's only after going through several rigorous stages of cleansing that it's finally discharged into the sea."

"That's clean?" Jenny said, wrinkling her nose.

"Yes, ma'am. It's nothing to worry about." He glanced at his watch. "If you'll excuse me." He quickly walked away.

§

Back in their cabin, the intimacy and passion that had been building earlier was temporarily forgotten. Having kept their clothes on, they decided to follow up on their ecological indignation. They were each doing some independent research on their WebVisors.

"Well," Jenny said from her position on the bed, "what he told us was, at least, partly true. Cruise ships do have their own treatment plants. There's some disparity between cruise lines and ships concerning the effectiveness of the treatment, and concerning their adherence to the laws."

"There always have to be noncompliant troublemakers," David said shaking his head, as he flipped his WebVisor up. He was sitting in a chair, leaning on the table next to it.

"There are other issues, too," Jenny continued. "Oil contaminated bilge water is also supposed to be regulated. Way back in 2002, the Carnival Cruise line was found guilty of dumping theirs in the ocean over the course of five years. They were fined $18 million and ordered to perform community service."

"Back then, that was probably a lot of money for a corporation to pay for a little water."

"Apparently, not so little. In 2013, the Caribbean Princess discharged 4,227 gallons of contaminated bilge water into the sea off the English coast." David whistled his surprise. "It was only found out because one of their engineers on the ship turned whistle-blower. Apparently, this ship, and four others in the Princess fleet had been doing this for at least eight years. The Princess line, also owned by Carnival, was fined $40 million.

"And it still seems to be an issue. Most of the big-name cruise lines, generally, follow the rules. But in international waters, there really aren't any regulations, and some ships have been known to do only the minimum treatment, or even to dump raw sewage in the ocean."

"Damn!" David exclaimed. "Well, sweetheart, you're not going to like this, either." He flipped his WebVisor back down. "This article lumps all shipping together, but it acknowledges that cruise lines are a major offender in the group where air pollution is concerned.

"The two major air pollutants from shipping are sulfur oxides and nitrogen oxides. They're both greenhouse gases and play a large role in climate change. Most ships burn low-grade fuel oil with high sulfur contents which add to the problem.

"Again, as with the water issues you mentioned, international waters have relaxed regulations. Ships can use fuel with an even higher sulfur content. This is an old article, but back then, the EPA estimated that an average cruise ship on the open sea emitted the same sulfur oxide contaminants into the air in a single day as 13 million cars."

"Oh my god," Jenny said, her voice barely more than a shocked whisper. "Can you imagine the kind of impact just these two issues had on the sea life and their environment?"

"I doubt the average person knows anything about this," David said, studying the page on his WebVisor, and Jenny could see the wheels turning. "I should write a story about this."

"My hero," Jenny said with an admiring smile. She put her WebVisor down on the night stand. "Well, honey, you better take your clothes off." David lifted his WebVisor and looked up at her, raising an eyebrow. "I think after this cruise, it might be quite a while before we can make love on the waves again."

BLOOD

From what I've read about the past, the body's natural functions were considered by many to be private and mysterious, and not to be discussed with just anyone. The workings of certain parts of one's body were simply not shared with someone of the opposite gender, which Frida and I, of course, were.

Since we were not a part of that past civilization, though, this particular constraint held no sway over us.

"Press," Frida said one morning, panic showing in her dark brown eyes, tension in her voice, "I'm afraid!" She had rushed into my room, waking me up, and was sitting on the edge of my bed, her hands pressed between her legs.

"Why?" I asked, mirroring her concern, "what's wrong?"

"I don't know," she said as tears filled her eyes, "but I'm bleeding!"

I looked down at where her hands were pulled tightly up against her body, and I could see the blood spreading out on her tunic.

Suddenly, I was afraid, too. Frida was the person who was competing for first place in my life. My parents had always been the first two, but Frida was, somehow, working on displacing them, in my mind, at least.

The thing is Father had never mentioned bleeding like this, nor had I ever experienced it, despite being two years older than Frida. Somehow, I decided to suggest what turned out to be the correct course of action.

"Let's go ask Mother," I said.

I jumped out of bed and grabbed Frida's elbow, as she kept her hands clamped tightly against herself.

"Mother," I gasped as I came into the kitchen, "Frida's bleeding!"

Mother looked in a panic at Frida, but then, as she took in the situation, her face calmed.

"Frida," she said calmly, smiling, "it's nothing to be alarmed about." She looked at me. "Press, maybe you should go get dressed."

I looked at Frida, then back at Mother. Despite the horror that I'm sure was showing on my face, my mother nodded and included me in her smile.

"Go on, it's fine."

I looked at Frida and reluctantly let go of her arm. I frowned at Mother and turned toward my room. I couldn't believe I was being excluded from this. Frida, the—possibly—most important person in my life, was bleeding for no apparent reason. How was that 'fine'?

After I had thrown on some clothes and returned to the kitchen a few minutes later, Mother and Frida were not there. A few minutes after that, they emerged from Frida's room. Both looked at me as calmly as can be. Frida, wearing clean clothing now, smiled demurely at me.

*G*ood evening. I'm your host Darren Scott. Thank you for joining us for Foreground, on the Independent News Network."

The red and blue INN logo appeared on the lower right of the screen, and to the left of it, under Darren Scott, was a banner containing the words, "War in Algeria?"

"First up tonight, tensions escalated today in Algiers as American naval forces in the Mediterranean moved closer to the capitol. Algerian President Ben-Jazar denounced the move as imprudent and provocative.

"Joining me tonight are Dr. Robert Finney, professor of anthropology and political science at Columbia University, and Secretary of State John Lawson." Dr. Finney's face appeared in a box next to Darren Scott, from a remote location, probably his office at Columbia. Secretary of State Lawson's face appeared next to it in a similar box, with the seal of the Secretary of State behind him. "Dr. Finney, what are your thoughts on this?"

"Well, Darren, I'm afraid President Ben-Jazar definitely has a point. The history of the People's Democratic Republic of Algeria has been a rocky one, but I believe that the last several decades have shown that their intentions are good. Theirs is a hard-earned democracy. The country's motto is 'By the people and for the people,' which sounds hauntingly like a philosophy that the United States used to live by."

Lawson was shaking his head, putting forth little effort to hide his annoyance.

"Mr. Secretary," Scott said, "you seem to disagree."

"I do, Darren. Despite their official name and motto, Algeria is no democracy. I believe their history sets a number of precedents which, when considered together, casts a very different light on their actions and their intentions."

Now, it was Finney's turn to shake his head.

"No democracy?" he asked. "What do you call free and open elections, and the fact that everyone automatically has the legal right to vote at age eighteen?"

"Their elections are a sham," Lawson replied dismissively. "Yes, they elect people into representative positions, but those representatives have no official power. The country is actually ruled by a shady group of unelected people, civilian and military, known as 'The Power.' They're the ones who ultimately make decisions concerning the country, some feel even to the point of deciding the outcome of their elections. This has been the case for a long time now."

"Dr. Finney," Scott said, "what do you think about this latest development in the Mediterranean?"

"I think it's a childish example of saber-rattling. America is trying to provoke Algeria to make the first move so we feel justified in striking back."

"That's a very simplistic conclusion," Lawson said with a demeaning tone. "Ben-Jazar has a history of aggressive and antagonistic actions and language toward the United States."

"His language," Finney interrupted, "has not been against the United States, but against President McCauley. He's taken no action against America, whereas President McCauley has slapped multiple tariffs and embargos on Algeria."

The discussion raged heatedly for a few more minutes, with neither side backing down, and neither being determined the winner. The show cut away for commercials.

§

"In our next story," Darren Scott said as Foreground returned from its commercial break, "growing concern about the so-called Severe Hemorrhagic Pulmonary Failure, or SHePF virus, is causing widespread panic in many places in America and elsewhere.

"Joining me now is Dr. Sonya Warren, spokesperson for the World Health Organization." Dr. Warren's worry-worn face, complete with dark shadows under her eyes, now appeared in a box next to Darren Scott. "Dr. Warren, what can you tell us about this virus? Where did it come from?"

"The symptoms of this virus, which primarily attacks lung tissues, began showing up simultaneously in Kansas City, Missouri, Miami, Florida, and Dallas, Texas. But other reports almost immediately began surfacing in other cities around the country, and in fact various other countries around the world.

"From what we've been able to determine so far, the incubation period seems to be fairly long, as much as two weeks before any symptoms appear. Unfortunately, that has made it difficult to contain its spread, since people have been able to move around freely and spread the disease before they even knew they were carrying it. Once the virus takes hold, though, and symptoms appear, it moves quickly and aggressively. But we've been able to trace the contagion's introduction into America to the Naiad, an Atlantis Cruise ship."

"As I understand it," Scott said, "you received some helpful information from an unexpected source."

Dr. Warren briefly closed her eyes and took a breath.

"Yes, a journalist for the Kansas City Times apparently recognized that he wasn't going to survive the illness. He and his new wife were on the Naiad for their honeymoon. Immediately after his wife died, he was at home when he recognized that he was starting to experience symptoms himself.

"Having witnessed the aggression and devastation that the virus had already wreaked on his bride, and recognizing that it was a new and as yet unknown contagion with no known treatment, he self-quarantined in his home and regularly documented his vitals and the progression of symptoms. He also wrote down anything that he could remember about the cruise, and their activities since then, that he thought might prove helpful. He recorded this information at least every hour, until he no longer had the strength."

"Amazing," Scott interjected.

"Yes, he stated that the activity helped him deal with the tragic loss of his wife. But this man's heartbreaking heroism helped us a great deal as well, not only in tracing the rapid progression of the illness, but also in narrowing down its origin. We now believe that this novel virus originated in Georgetown, Guyana, with a South American tapir."

"Dr. Warren, what is it about this virus that makes it so virulent, and what can you tell us about its symptoms?"

"Well, when a contagion originates in another species, in this case a tapir, and then mutates to infect a human, even a relatively mild affliction for the tapir can be extremely serious for us, since humans haven't had a chance to build up a resistance to this virus. We have no antibodies against it, so the genetic makeup of the agent is something that our immune systems have never seen, and therefore don't know how to fight.

"We've seen this numerous times over the past century, with pigs being the infecting agent with swine flu, birds with avian flu, bats with COVID-19, and so on."

Scott waited a moment, to make sure she was finished, before repeating his second question.

"And the symptoms?"

Dr. Warren closed her eyes and took a breath again. Darren Scott couldn't tell if she did that because she was nervous and relatively inexperienced as a spokesperson, or if it was because she had seen horrendous things.

"Initially, it seems to present as a simple cold. Several patients reported sniffles and a mild fever. But these symptoms passed after a day or two, and they dismissed them and went about their business.

"The next symptoms resembled a chest cold, with apparent congestion and difficulty breathing, accompanied by a severe cough. The virus attacks pulmonary tissues, causing bleeding in the lungs, so coughing up blood is common, until–" She paused and took another breath. "Until the victim essentially drowns in their own blood."

"Oh, my goodness," Scott said, shaking his head. He took a longer pause than usual, as if trying to hold on to his composure. "You mentioned that the illness was quick and aggressive. What kind of timeline are we talking about here?"

"Well, again, it could take as much as two weeks for any symptoms to initially appear. The head cold symptoms pass, as I said, in a day or two. Within a couple more days, though, the chest congestion and coughing will start. Once that begins, it progresses very rapidly. From that point, death comes within twenty-four hours."

"What kind of recovery rate are you seeing?"

Dr. Warren tried to surreptitiously wipe away a tear.

"Not what we would like, I'm afraid," she said ambiguously. "Some have been able to fight it off from the earlier, milder symptoms, and we are studying blood samples to determine if we can create a vaccine from whatever antibodies they have been able to develop. While we've been unsuccessful, so far, in isolating a usable antibody, still, we're very encouraged by this, because it's proof that the battle can be won. Unfortunately, though, it will take time. I'm afraid, however," her voice became quieter, "that at the onset of the chest symptoms, the respiratory distress, there seems to be no chance of survival."

Darren Scott was looking worried.

"What do you recommend Americans do to protect themselves?"

"Stay at home!" she said firmly and without hesitation. "If you suspect you have symptoms, avoid contact with others. Again,

stay home and call your health provider to get their recommenda-
tion."

"Thank you, Dr. Warren," Scott said, visibly more shaken than
he had been at the beginning of the show.

PERFECTLY NORMAL

I couldn't put my finger on it for sure, but something had changed. A few months after "The Blood Incident," which Mother and Frida had both assured me was *perfectly normal (!)*, I was noticing certain changes. If someone had asked me what those changes were, I couldn't have described them, but I could sense them.

Frida seemed a little different. She was still beautiful and perfect, but maybe a little more so. I was drawn to her in a way that seemed almost mystical, a word which I knew from reading, but which had no bearing on my real life, until now.

There was no natural reason that I could discern why Frida should seem any different. She still looked pretty much the same. She acted the same, except that, okay, maybe there was a certain maturity that I hadn't noticed before.

Her brown eyes held me in their gaze a little longer at times, and I found myself studying her features, trying to determine what had changed. I couldn't figure out what it was. She was still the same sweet, beautiful Frida that I had known for the past few years.

But there was something about her, some strange, unknowable quality that managed to hold my attention when we were together, and pervaded my every thought when we weren't.

If there was any consolation, it was that she seemed to view me differently, as well. Her attention toward me was more ubiquitous, her smile more ready.

Perhaps someone with her artistic eye, her ability to really see tangible details, might have spotted physical changes, if indeed they were present when I was puzzling this out. In my case, words were what spoke to me, and they were failing me. It took a few weeks before I recognized any physical changes.

By then, I was beginning to notice that she was rounder. Not in the sense of being fat. Nobody in our time is fat. But the little girl angles and corners were softening into more graceful contours.

In all fairness, I should state that I could sense my own body changing, as well. Hair was growing on my face. Not nearly as thick as Father's beard, but it was starting. It was also growing elsewhere. When pressed about it, Father assured me that it was *perfectly normal*. Those words again.

There were times when Frida and I were together when she touched me. Not as if she made it a point to do so, it just happened. Just a casual touch. But it seemed as if she did so more readily, more often.

And I began to notice that my reaction to her touch was, well, noteworthy.

On our next trip to the library, I brought home a few books on human physiology and biology.

And I realized that my reaction was *perfectly normal*.

WATERCOURSE

Pushing a button on her washing machine, it dispensed a premeasured dollop of detergent as it began filling up. She watched for a moment as the suds started forming.

She was spooked about that virus going around. Some people were in an outright panic, while others acted as if there was nothing to it. She felt as if her viewpoint was balanced, somewhere in the middle. She was doing what she could to kill germs and avoid infection, without being hysterical about it.

So many people were suddenly so obsessed with washing their hands. It occurred to her that if people were even half as concerned about cleanliness when there wasn't a health scare going on, there would be fewer health scares.

Satisfied with the suds in the washer, she picked up the pile of dark items and began dropping them into the machine, arranging them evenly.

She closed the lid and left the laundry room to go about her business, giving it no further thought.

§

The washing machine stopped filling, and the agitator began moving, spinning back and forth, performing its distinctive dance with its multiple partners, pulling the clothing down through the water in the middle, then pushing the items back up on the outside, to start it all over again.

Mixed in with the other clothing was a fleece hoody. People still loved their fleece hoodies. As the agitator beat against it during the course of the wash, thousands of microfibers, nearly microscopic strands of plastic, washed out of it.

As the wash cycle ended, many of the fibers were pumped out, others clinging to the clothing remaining in the washer. Then, the rinse cycle began, pumping clean water in, re-suspending the remaining fibers, before finally pumping them out, too.

By the time the load was done, there were as many as 250,000 of these tiny bits of plastic, 100 times finer than a human hair, that washed down the drain.

Some of these fibers, inevitably, get caught in rough sections of sewer pipe, or snagged by goo and hair clinging to certain portions along the line. But the vast majority of the fibers succeed in reaching the water treatment plant where, due to their miniscule size, the bulk of them slip right through the filters, continuing into the waterway.

Insect larva, small fish and other tiny water creatures mistake the plastic fibers for food. As a food source for larger fish, these little creatures are consumed in larger numbers, and the fibers increase exponentially in their stomachs the higher up the food chain they go.

Still, a great many of them eventually make it to the ocean where a similar chain of events occurs with the saltwater creatures. Those that aren't consumed right away may get swept up in ocean currents and tides, absorbing whatever they soak in. Some may absorb oil or refuse expelled from ships, or pesticides and other chemicals that wash down from industrial or agricultural areas. These pollutants, again, increase and compound as more small creatures eat them, and larger creatures eat the smaller ones, and so on. Some fibers ultimately sink to the ocean floor, to be consumed by the bottom-dwellers.

These plastic microfibers have found their way into seafood from the Arctic to the California coast to the Great Lakes. They are particularly prevalent in oysters and mussels, and have even been found in table salt in China.

Some years back, it was estimated that laundering 100,000 fleece jackets over the course of a year releases enough plastic into the waterways to make nearly 12,000 of the kind of plastic grocery bags that stores used to use, before they were phased out.

§

She came back into the laundry room when the load was done. She pulled the wet garments out of the washer and tossed them into her dryer. She selected the settings she wanted and turned it on.

Turning to the next load, she picked up the pile of sheets and pillowcases. She couldn't help rubbing her fingers over them. These microfiber sheets were the softest she had ever felt!

As she stuffed them into the washer, she reminded herself to take some fish out of the freezer for dinner.

RELATIVITY

O ur community was not large by any means. Certainly not compared to the enormous cities of the past. I can only imagine what those were like because of the endless expanse of structures that those people left behind. Imagining them filled with people, actual living people, though, was beyond the capability of my imagination, even having seen photographs of the cities in the history books I've collected.

According to those books, world population peaked around the end of the twenty-first century. Nearly twelve million people filled the planet before changing views of reproduction finally tipped the scale. Even then, there were still those who felt that it was the responsibility of every family to produce offspring, to continue the family's genetic line. But the popular view of that time was that adding more mouths to feed and lungs to breathe was just overtaxing our world.

Many felt, though, that the views changed too late. They thought that the damage was done and that there was no coming back from it.

Because of a megavirus, though, we'll never know if they were right or not.

My parents, Frida, and I live in one of the structures, houses as they were called then, left behind by those people of the past. A few houses away, there was an older couple in their forties. In all, there were twelve people in our community, double the size of the one that my parents left before I was born.

I remember my father wondering if this area could support them. There were few animals about, and most of our food came from weeds, trees and other plant life in the area.

I had read a little about nutrition, and I knew that, by this time, we were not ingesting enough protein to nourish our bodies as they needed.

Father died before our next move could be decided on.

The others in our community rallied around us after this. Mother was disconsolate. I was, too.

My father, Bookman, had been the guiding light in my life. He had been the one to cultivate my love of books and history. The stories he told of the past, while, obviously, nowhere near first-hand, had shaped my love of finding out details of what had come before us.

Others in our community had helped, as well. Alphonse, for instance, had given guidance in the best places for gathering food. Alphonse was the oldest person in our group, at forty-five, and he died a few weeks later.

A few months after this, when I was fifteen, my mother, Valencia, died. I couldn't believe how alone I suddenly felt.

§

"Come on, Press," Frida said, "we need to go on."

Lying on my bed, I looked at her. I knew that she had grown close to my mother, in particular, after her parents died, but I was too ensconced in my own grief to comprehend hers.

"I'm an orphan," I replied, having learned that word only recently.

"I know," Frida replied, pain creasing her face. "I am, too."

I looked at her, at the tears filling her eyes. Of course, she was. She had already endured this, and was enduring it, now, for the second time.

I placed my hands against her face as I looked at her. I can't say, now, what I felt at that time. I was barely present then.

But I remember Frida's eyes. They looked into me, peering deeply into my soul, if such a thing exists. I remember feeling the slight percussion of her tears falling onto my chest.

I pulled her face to mine, and I kissed her. It was the closest I had ever felt to her. To be entirely honest, it was the closest I had ever felt to another human being.

Frida's tears were loosed at that point, and she laid her head down on my chest, and we cried together. With my arms wrapped as far around her as they would go, I held her tightly against me, feeling the trembling as she wept.

We fell asleep in each other's arms.

LIFESAVER

Bill sighed and got out of his car. As he walked toward the front door of 5280 Label Company, he wondered, as he did every morning since the virus began, if today was going to be the day.

5280 Label, located in Denver, was named after the famous mile-high elevation of Colorado's capitol. Bill had worked here as a prepress artist for twenty-five years, nearly half his life.

The moon shone brightly on him in the dark and cloudless sky but it was still hot. He approached the front door and swiped his fob across the electronic scanner beside the door. The immediate click told him the door had unlocked, and he went inside and walked toward the prepress department.

Tom, the owner of the company, ran the business well and generally took care of his employees. That's why Bill had stayed here for so long, even after they became so busy that they phased out design, which was his main love. Bill needed a creative outlet, and he missed being able to do design work.

Otherwise happy with his position, though, he found other means of expressing his creativity, and still came in every day to do his relatively mindless job. Queueing one job after another to the digital presses didn't take much brain power, only an awareness of where he was in the routine so as not to leave out a step.

He opened the door and went inside the prepress room, waking up his computer. He selected a little packet from the drawer beside his work station and tore it open. The first step in his daily routine now involved his WebVisor, his phone, and other items that he used every day. Unfortunately, others sometimes used them too, after he left, and he had no way of knowing their level of commitment to fighting off the virus. Hence, he made it a point to diligently swab everything down with an alcohol wipe first thing in the morning. He wished he had a mask to wear, but people had been buying them up faster than stores could keep them in stock since SHePF began, and he hadn't been able to get any. So, he wore a bandana tied around his face. Better than nothing, he thought. Nobody else bothered to wear masks here. It was all just a hoax.

Bill was always the first one in the building. He had woken up early for so long, it had been months since he had heard his alarm. Since he automatically woke up early, he opted for an early start time, and was able to leave early, still having a great deal of the day ahead of him.

Of course, since the self-quarantine began, that meant staying home, in his free time, anyway, which was okay with Bill. After all, that's where Sheila was. He smiled briefly as he thought of her.

They had been lucky. Finally. After each enduring difficult marriages and painful divorces, they had found each other. Bill often remarked to Sheila that, while he knew she wasn't perfect, she was absolutely perfect for him. That always elicited a smile and a sigh from her. And often a lingering hug.

He never liked leaving his happy home to come to work. But that feeling had changed from a mere irritant to a very real concern since the SHePF virus became such a big deal, and especially after the governor had issued a statewide stay-at-home order, as had several other governors. Only "essential employees" were allowed to go to their places of employment, although Bill had never been stopped and questioned about his destination, nor had he heard of that happening to anybody else.

Still, Tom had supplied everybody in the company with an official letter designating them as essential employees. Bill kept his letter on the passenger seat of his car, always ready to present "his papers" in case he ever got pulled over and questioned about why he was out and about.

Since a sizable number of 5280's clientele were in the food, drink and pharmaceutical industries, which the governor had deemed essential businesses, and since stores couldn't sell their products without labels, 5280 was, by extension, an essential business, as well.

Bill felt guilty about that, though. He understood the logic, and it made sense to him. Still, it's not like he was a doctor or nurse treating sick people, or a fireman or EMT, risking his life to save the lives of others. Even a grocery store employee, providing food to the general public, seemed more essential than Bill. Just that one degree of separation from the grocery shelf seemed to make a difference to him.

He was grateful for his job when so many others were losing theirs. But he felt guilty that, in the face of so much financial hardship, his life hadn't really changed much at all.

Bill sighed and sat down and slipped his WebVisor on. From what he had heard, the printing technology really hadn't changed much in decades. Everything was computerized. Back in the old days, printers used to have to make flexible printing plates, but that had been pretty much eliminated in the past century. The jobs went directly from computer to press. They just needed Bill to send them.

But that was the part that could really use a change, he thought. He knew Eric, the early-shift pressman, would be coming in soon for work. He picked up the first job on the stack and got started.

§

"I know you've been wanting, for a while now, to stop coming in here and start working from home," Tom said as Bill sat in front of his desk.

"Well, yeah," Bill replied, hoping he could make it sound a little less petty. "But it's not that I just don't want to come here. I'm grateful for my job. But my wife has asthma and other respiratory issues. She's right in the middle of the target demographic of this thing."

"I know," Tom said, nodding. Bill couldn't be sure, but he thought it looked as if Tom caught himself just before rolling his eyes. *And he seemed to look with a little scorn on the bandana tied around Bill's face.*

To his credit, Tom had instituted a number of safety measures within the company. Posting signs in the restrooms and the lunch room about washing hands, limiting the number of people in the lunch room at a time, even keeping the front door locked during business hours. Customers coming to pick up labels had to ring the bell, state who they were with, and wait outside for their order to be brought out to them.

Still, sometimes it seemed to Bill that Tom looked with a little disdain on those who were truly worried. A lot of people thought that SHePF was a hoax, and Bill wondered if Tom was one of those.

"Sheila hasn't been anywhere outside of our home except the back yard since this thing started," Bill continued. "And I haven't been anyplace except here. If she gets SHePF, it will be from my job."

"I understand," Tom said. "And I just wanted to let you know that we're close. Amalgam is almost ready to go."

Amalgam was a system that would electronically tie all their departments together. It, and systems like it, had been in use by other companies for years. Decades, in fact. It's about time, Bill thought.

It was touted to be a revolutionary upgrade to their current system, eliminating the need for paper. All jobs would be entered online, starting with the customers themselves, along with all pertinent information. From that point on, each department in the company would subsequently be able to access each product from their computers, to do their part in completing the job, without anything having to be printed out until it reached the press.

Bill had seen bits and pieces of the system in action, and it really did look like a game-changer. But he had been hearing about it as they worked on it for over a year. Bill had almost given up on it. He looked at Tom, while trying to hide the doubt he knew was showing on his face.

"Really," Tom said, apparently seeing what Bill was trying to obscure. "We're working on ironing out the last couple of bugs, but it looks like it'll be ready to roll in the next day or two. You'll be able to access Amalgam from your WebVisor at home and have everything you need online to do your work."

"That's great!" Bill said, allowing himself to feel the first hesitant pang of hope. He won't have to worry that he might have picked up the virus from one of the hundreds of sheets of paper he handled each day, or from a shopping cart at the grocery store, or from any number of other potential sources that would be eliminated if he could just stay home with Sheila.

One of the electric variable message signs that hung over the highway on his way to work, which usually gave warnings about road closures and such, had lately been saying, "Save lives. Stay home." He felt conscience-stricken, and worried about Sheila, every time he drove under it, on his way to or from his "life as usual." This news about Amalgam was the glimmer of encouragement that he needed!

§

The prepress department door opened and Bill felt the usual awareness of potential impending death whenever someone came in. It was Eric, the early press operator, and Bill sighed. Eric was an unhappy person. If he spoke, it was usually to bitch and complain about someone or something. If he didn't speak, Bill could at least count on him exhaling heavily at least once — he didn't know what to call it, but it was bigger than a sigh.

"This color's not right," Eric said as he sniffed and handed the job jacket to Bill. "Last time we ran it CMYK-OVG."

Most of their color work was printed with cyan, magenta, yellow and black ink, or CMYK, as it had been for decades. But some of the more critical jobs, where the color was especially important, were printed with the addition of orange, violet and green ink, thus expanding their color gamut.

Bill took note of the job number and looked up the file in the application that linked the prepress department with the digital pressroom, as Eric stood behind him, waiting. It was an easy enough matter to re-RIP the job as CMYK-OVG. Bill did it quickly to get Eric out of there as soon as possible. His sniffing and sneezing today had more deeply impressed on Bill his need to stay home, although Eric had insisted it was just allergies.

The job finished processing and Bill picked up the job jacket, turning around to hand it back to Eric, just as Eric sneezed suddenly, bathing the job jacket, and Bill, with a pinkish mist.

"Oh, shit," Eric said quietly, horrified, wiping the blood from his mouth. He turned and ran out of the prepress department, leaving Bill sitting there holding the sticky job jacket. And he could feel the blood against his face through the saturated bandana. He could smell the infection.

Realization settled quickly over Bill. He was surprised that he didn't feel panic. In fact, it felt almost like a relief of sorts. He knew that was stretching it a bit. It's not that he was looking forward to leaving Sheila, by any means, or to getting sick and possibly – probably? – dying. But still, this latest development constituted the end of the incessant dread he'd been feeling.

He untied the bandana and reached over, pulling a tissue out of the box beside his work station. Taking a deep breath, he calmly wiped away Eric's sanguinary spray from his face.

As he sat there, he saw Sheila's face in his mind, smiling sweetly at him. It seemed to be the expression that came most easily to her. While Bill knew he would miss her immensely, and that she would miss him, he felt good knowing that, by not going home, he would actually, finally, be saving a life. The life. The life most precious to him.

SHRINKING

Our community was shrinking. King and Rose, a couple who lived a block away from us, died within two weeks of each other. In the past, people spoke of someone dying of a broken heart. That concept was, long ago, scientifically disproved, but there have been enough examples that many people throughout history have rejected the science and accepted it as fact.

Under the shadow of our shrinking society, Frida had become, in a very short time, the primary focus of my life. Knowing that we had the prospect of, maybe, twenty to thirty years together, I decided that I didn't want to squander a single one of them.

I announced to the remaining ones in our community that I wished to take Frida as my wife. She responded that she agreed to the union.

Nobody seemed at all surprised.

That night, Frida moved into my room. As I held her in my arms, in my bed, it felt as if we had finally found the place we were meant to be. While the general location hadn't changed, certain details had finally altered to the point that we felt as if we were home for the first time in several months.

When Doc died a couple of blocks away, Frida and I found solace in each other's arms. When Greta, the adopted mother of our colony, died, Frida drowned her sorrows by engulfing me inside her beautiful body.

Within a couple of years, Frida and I were the only ones left. Since we had each other, we didn't feel lonely, but we did feel abandoned. And knowing our situation as I did, from my reading, I felt as if we might be in a certain amount of danger.

We had never come across any other people outside of our little community. It was tempting, in a way, to believe that we were the last. Of course, it was daunting, as well, but by then, we had no illusion that we were going to be relied on to repopulate the earth. Nobody we knew had ever had a child during our lifetimes.

It was just my beloved wife and me.

PARTY

The throbbing of the bass and drums vibrated the street. Inside the house, it was nearly deafening. However, none of the twenty-something partiers seemed to mind. They just talked louder, directly into the ear of their intended listener.

The music was loudest in the family room, where the bulk of the speakers were, pumping out throbbing dance music from the global network. There were several couples who were dancing, writhing together, leaving little to the imagination as to what was on their minds. Others stood around the periphery in little clumps, drinking, laughing and posturing.

And looking defiant. It was a SHePF party, after all.

Still, some of the party-goers sought out more distant rooms where the music existed simply as a generic and otherwise unrecognizable thumping. One of the upstairs bedrooms was one such room.

§

"Why are we doing this?" Janice asked, tossing her bra on a chair.

Trent stopped in mid unzip and looked at her. She was so hot downstairs when they were dancing, dry humping to the music. Their hands were all over each other, and it only took a few minutes for them to agree to move upstairs. Now, her bare breasts caught Trent's eye, and he decided she was even hotter naked, but he made it a point to focus on her face when he replied.

"I thought you wanted to fuck." He narrowed his eyes at her. "You're not going to pull a 'Me Too' on me, are you?

"A 'Me Too'?" she asked, puzzled.

"A long time ago, there was a, a movement, I guess you could call it. It was to call attention to sexual harassment and rape. Women, and some men, too, would say 'me too' to let others know that they had experienced it, to indicate that they identified as

120

members of the club. You're not planning on that, are you? We came up here consensually."

"I'm not talking about that," Janice replied, pushing her jeans down, to Trent's relief, and he was happy to see her briefly check out the bulge in his underwear. "Why are we here, at this party?" she asked.

"I'm here because I live here."

Janice stopped and looked up at him, surprised.

"This is your house?"

"Yeah. Well, my dad's. But he's away in Washington."

"Washington?"

"D.C." Trent looked piercingly at Janice. "Representative Jim Covington?"

"Jim Covington is your father?" Janice rubbed her nose and sniffed, and she looked around for a moment as if she had become disoriented and was trying to regain her bearings. "Damn, I didn't realize you were Jim Covington's son," she said.

"Well, that makes me feel good," Trent smiled.

"Why?"

"Because it means you're up here because of me, not because of who I am, or who I'm related to."

Janice draped her jeans over the chair with the other items she had taken off.

"Still," she said, "this SHePF sounds like some serious shit."

"Come on, Janice, it's just another fucking flu. There's a new one every year. I mean, I get it. Older people are more susceptible to it. That's the way it always is. But why do they have to order all of us to isolate and self-quarantine? That's bullshit! The old people should stay inside. They're cool with that anyway."

"I guess." Janice slipped her panties off and dropped them on her jeans, unconsciously brushing her hand down over her pubic hair, smoothing it down. "And I do feel safer in here alone with you than out there in the crowd."

"As you should," Trent smiled, dropping his shorts on the floor. He pulled down the covers and sat down on the bed, patting the space next to him. He was chagrined at the turn their conversation had taken. He had been menacingly hard downstairs when they were dancing. A couple more minutes of that and he thought he would cum in his pants.

But this serious talk about SHePF was having a negative downward effect on his erection. He hoped that a little naked snuggling and rubbing would bring that back.

Janice lay down beside him and took him in her hand. As her fingers stroked him, he could feel his cock surging up again. He thought there was a noticeable lack of passion, but still, a hand job was a good start.

He leaned forward and kissed her on the top of her head, willing her to go down on him. She looked up at him, her eyebrows bunched together.

"Still," she said, "what about what they've said about the possibility of being a carrier? We could bring the virus to someone in our families, even if we aren't sick."

"Janice," Trent said, exasperated, "come on. It's the fucking flu."

She thought for a few moments, then nodded.

"Okay," she said, "you're right."

She sniffed and wiped her nose with her wrist. With a sigh, she turned back to the business at hand.

MY WHOLE WORLD

After a while, Frida and I had focused our attention on each other for long enough that we settled into a certain routine. Our daily life involved waking up and greeting each other with a kiss, then having a brief breakfast together. I left after that to forage for food and other goods, while Frida stayed at home to clean, to prepare food, and to weave hemp for clothing, and for canvases to paint on.

I remembered reading in some of my history books about people in the past spurning gender-defined roles. Apparently, in the centuries leading up to what I call man's more enlightened *Golden Age*, the women were expected to stay at home and carry out their domestic duties—cooking, cleaning, raising the children—while the men went to their jobs in some other location to earn the money that was necessary at the time to support the family.

It occurred to me that Frida and I had fallen into those roles, ourselves, and I mentioned it to her one morning as she worked in the kitchen.

Which is where some of those people in that distant past said a woman's place was.

The kitchen was kind of strange when I thought about it. Without electricity or gas powering the appliances, and without running water, the kitchen was just like any other room in the house.

I had to tote tepid water from the river every morning, for drinking and for food preparation. Our food was seldom cooked anymore, unless I happened to bag a rat or a squirrel, in which case they were cooked over a fire I built on the front porch. And we never had so much food that there were leftovers that needed to be kept cold.

But the countertops in the kitchen just seemed like the perfect place for food preparation. It was also a good place for making paints. So, this is where Frida primarily worked while I went out and foraged.

Frida looked at me for a few moments as she thought about my question concerning gender roles. Finally, she frowned.

"Do you *expect* me to stay at home and do these things?" she asked.

"I don't *expect* you to do any particular thing," I replied, "unless it's something that you were willing or wanted to do."

"And I think that's the difference," she smiled. "From what you've told me, women in the past were forced into those roles, or were put down if they strayed from them. You never force me to do anything, and you never put me down."

"It helps to have the perfect wife," I said. I was only partly joking.

She smirked at me, then made a show of looking around.

"I'm the *only* wife. It's not like you ever had much of a choice."

At that, a shadow descended over her countenance, and she looked at me.

"I do miss having other people around."

I nodded understandingly. It was a subject that we generally tried to avoid, since there was nothing that could be done about it, anyway. But occasionally, it came through, either ambiguously or directly. Today seemed to be a direct day.

"I know, my love," I said.

I placed an arm around her shoulders, but she came in for a full hug. We held each other silently. How do you talk about possibly being the last two living people on earth? How do you consider that, within twenty years or so, you're going to die, and there will be no more humans left to carry on?

How do you think about the impending literal end of the world without driving yourself crazy?

Governors of nearly every state in the union have issued orders to their citizens requiring some level of isolation," said Jackson Lightner, Deputy Director of the CDC. He stood somewhat stiffly behind a podium with the big blue and white CDC logo on the front, under a canopy shielding him from the relentless sun overhead. His features, though, were mostly hidden by the mask he was wearing. "We appreciate their cooperation in this matter," Lightner continued, "but due to leniency in some cases, and the dire severity of the threat of the SHePF virus, the CDC is considering taking more drastic measures."

"Deputy Director," began a reporter, her eyebrows cocked in alarm, "what kind of measures are you referring to? And does the CDC have the authority to actually issue and enforce direct orders of this nature?"

"The CDC was granted authority by the Secretary of Health and Human Services, under section 361 of the Public Health Service Act, first enacted about a century and a half ago, back in 1944. That authority includes the ability to issue quarantine orders for individuals known to be displaying symptoms of the disease.

"In addition, we are currently considering the issuance of widespread orders of isolation. Such large-scale isolation and quarantine have not been enforced by Health and Human Services since the Spanish Flu pandemic of 1918 and 1919, but we feel that, having surpassed 300,000 deaths in the United States alone, it may be time to take such drastic action."

"Deputy Director," another reporter asked, as he was acknowledged by Lightner, "does President McCauley's reluctance to take such action have anything to do with your consideration of this step now?"

"Well, I don't wish to get into the politics that has, unfortunately, crept into this situation. The fact is, though, that Mr.

McCauley, as President, has a number of political matters that he needs to consider, but he's not a doctor. The CDC, on the other hand, employs a number of physicians, epidemiologists, research scientists, and so on. This is our field, and of all those who have contributed to this dialogue, it has been their unanimous decision that we absolutely must be doing more to protect the health of the American people."

"Many individuals and companies are already suffering from the voluntary shutdowns that have taken place," asked another reporter. "What kind of effect would such a drastic action as you're talking about have on the economy?"

"Now that is one of the matters resting squarely on the shoulders of the President. I'm afraid I'm not in a position to make any comments or suggestions about that.

"I can, however, strongly urge everyone to adopt and continue such practices as avoiding large gatherings, such as this one." There was a little scattered nervous laughter. "Also, wearing gloves and masks when it's necessary to be out in public, maintaining a safe distance of at least six feet from others, frequent and thorough hand washing, and so on. A complete list of safety practices can be found on our website."

A number of the reporters gathered in front of him looked sheepishly around at each other. Several were wearing masks, but some were not.

Lightner pointed to another reporter.

"Sir, you mentioned wearing masks out in public. But what about those who have been unable to acquire masks?"

"Yes, certain materials, including professionally-made face masks, are being reserved for health-care workers. But anyone can make a mask using instructions found on our website. Some of them don't even require sewing ability."

"What about those gathering in protest of the local and state-ordered self-quarantines? Do you think that these may increase in number and size if indeed federal action is taken? And what about riots?"

"That is a concern that we are taking into consideration, but the CDC can and will enlist law enforcement agencies to aid in implementing this order. Anyone breaking this law will suffer hefty penalties, including fines and jail time. This is a serious health matter, and anybody willfully breaking the order will be arrested and charged with terrorism."

Several reporters appeared shocked at that revelation. One of them spoke up when Lightner pointed to her.

"Sir, I noticed that you're speaking about this order now as if it's already in effect."

"It's simply a matter of time," Lightner replied simply. Then, he put his hands up. "Thank you. That's all for now."

THREAT ASSESSMENT

Everything changed one morning.

Actually, nothing changed except for our mental state, but what caused it was profound enough to make everything change.

I had left Frida to her activities in our home, and I went out to do my daily foraging. When everything including the weather is the same for days, weeks, months, it's truly disconcerting when something changes.

Which it didn't, but it sure seemed like it did.

Judging by the size of the bridges and roadways crossing the river, I had long ago assumed that it used to be pretty wide. An old atlas in my library confirmed that assumption.

Now, it was only a few yards across, and most of those bridges looked to be in bad shape. The ground between the old crumbling roadway and the water's edge, which the river at one time likely covered, was dry and cracked. But closer to the water, there were patches of damp, muddy soil.

In one of those muddy patches, I saw what looked like a footprint. In fact, it looked like there were a lot of them.

It was hard to say for certain, since there were so many, overlapping, running together. It was difficult to determine for sure what they were.

I looked around, hoping to see more people, and at the same time, fearing it. My parents had warned me about Raiders. Apparently, they had a run-in with Raiders in their old camp, before they struck out on their own. Before I was born.

I had never encountered any, but Hunter, Frida's father, had, years ago. However, when years pass without seeing any threats other than the ones you're regularly accustomed to, it's easy to become complacent.

My attention was fully engaged, now.

On my way back home, I thought about those (potential) footprints. When I had brought the big buckets down to the river earlier to gather water, I hadn't seen any footprints except for my own. But that was a different location, several yards upstream.

I went home by way of that location, to see if there were any footprints besides mine there now. To my relief, there were not. Whoever it was had not seen evidence of my presence.

I realized that the flicker of hope I had originally felt of seeing more people was now pretty much routed by the dread of that very thing.

With my head turning back and forth, constantly scanning in all directions, I made my way back to our house. I was a little dismayed at how easy it was to open the door and come inside. I couldn't help but notice the open windows, the crumbling bricks and mortar around them. This place would be impossible to defend against a concerted attack.

Frida was surprised to see me back so soon. Her surprise turned to concern when she saw my face.

"Press, what's wrong?"

"I saw what looked like a lot of footprints down by the river."

Despite her recent wishing for other people in her life, Frida's eyes immediately reflected the sense of danger that I felt. She remembered the distressing stories her father had told about his encounters with Raiders. She was instantly ready for whatever action was necessary.

"What should we do?" she asked.

I shook my head. That's what I had been puzzling on my way home.

"I don't know," I admitted. "I haven't actually seen any-body, only the footprints."

Frida nodded. I could see her working it through in her mind, and I felt so fortunate to have an intelligent partner.

"And you don't know if they're hostile or not," she said. It wasn't a question.

"No. But I can't help thinking about when we came here. What if you had turned us away?"

"Yes, but there were a lot more of us then. We could have defended our community if you had turned out to be ene-mies. It's only you and me now."

"What if they were only passing through?" I asked.

"What if they weren't? What if they were scouting out the neighborhood? If we wait until we actually see them, it could be too late."

I nodded, looking around the house again.

"And this house is not much of a fortress."

Frida looked around, too, a look of sadness in her eyes. I understood. For my entire life, this had been the only home I had ever known. For the last few years, it had become more than a home. With Frida here, it had become a haven.

"We should go," Frida said, echoing my thoughts.

"Yeah," I agreed. "Now, we just need to figure out where."

Mandatory lockdown?" John said in response to the announcement on the news. He pointed the remote at the MicroThin VidScreen embedded in the wall and angrily pushed the power button. His face was contorted in an expression of anger. "That's bullshit!"

"Why is it bullshit?" asked Harley, his wife of twenty-five years. Her face wore a similar expression, but the emotion behind it was different. "It's for our protection. Over 300,000 people have died so far. I don't want to be one of the next to go."

John sighed and shook his head.

"You never understand, Harley. It's not about saving lives, it's about government control."

"You think the government is in control of the virus?"

"Oh my god," he said, exasperated. "No, the government's not in control of the virus, but they have to try to control everything the people do."

"Well, if people were smarter, maybe the government wouldn't feel the need to do that. Look at seatbelts," she said, gesturing for emphasis. "Over a hundred years ago, when they finally started installing them in cars as standard equipment, and when they finally passed laws to make it mandatory to actually use them, traffic deaths and injuries went down."

"If people don't want to take reasonable precautions," John retorted, "I say let 'em go. That's natural selection."

"It would be natural selection if only the idiots died," Harley fired back. "In the case of this virus, the idiots can carry it to innocent people and infect them, too."

John grimaced at the now blank video screen, as if the offending person was still there.

"Besides," Harley continued, trying not to sound as angry as she felt, "they're not even declaring a mandatory lockdown, yet.

They're still just urging individuals to not be the selfish idiots we usually are."

John dropped the remote on the coffee table with a little more force than he meant to.

"The fact that they're even considering it is bad enough. It's goddamn government overreach, plain and simple," he said. "Nothing good can come from this." With that, he stood up and left the room.

§

John sat in his office where he had retreated from the family room a few hours before. He had tried different things to occupy his mind, but everything seemed to bore him. What was he going to do if they did actually declare a mandatory lockdown?

Finally, he got out his guitar and was painfully trying to pick out one of the songs he used to know. It had been over a year since he had attempted to play it, so any calluses he once had on his fingertips were long gone. He sighed, knowing that it was just a distraction, and if the last year was any indication, one that wouldn't last very long.

He and Harley just seemed to get on each other's nerves so much lately. Ever since the kids moved out, they eventually found that they just didn't seem to have many mutual interests anymore. Although, if he was honest, he suspected it had probably been longer than that. Maybe that's why the kids had been so anxious to leave.

He couldn't pinpoint when they had started pulling away from each other. It had probably been such a gradual thing that the transition wasn't even perceptible without some kind of specialized relationship technology.

Or intense scrutiny in couples therapy.

Before his fingers became too sore, he managed to pick out a couple of Harley's favorite songs from when they were falling in love. It seemed like such a long time ago. Strangely, though, as he *thought about it now, he still loved her. That hadn't gone away. It had just gotten buried by everyday life.*

He couldn't even remember the last time he had told her he loved her. He knew he did, though. They had just sort of gone their separate ways.

The sex was still good, when they found time to have it. Harley had complained that it had become a little routine, but it was still satisfying.

Well, for John, anyway.

"Shit," he said under his breath. The mood passed and he didn't feel like playing his guitar anymore. He sighed and put it back in its dusty case.

§

Harley pondered the assortment of pieces in front of her. She had set up a card table in the living room and dumped out a 1000-piece jigsaw puzzle of Frank Frazetta's Egyptian Queen.

After the harsh exchange that she and John had, she tried reading to get her mind off of it, but she couldn't focus. After a half hour spent futilely attempting to follow what she had been reading, she decided it wasn't meant to be.

As a distraction, she got up and went rummaging around in the basement. That's when she came across the puzzle. She had given it to John, a fan of Frank Frazetta, a twentieth-century illustrator, years ago for his birthday, and it hadn't found its way out of the basement since then.

Harley had been at it for a couple of hours and had the perimeter of the puzzle done. She found it interesting that assembling jigsaw puzzles was an activity that she enjoyed. It was such a seemingly mindless pursuit, yet she could keep it up for hours at a time and only get up when she realized that parts of her body were feeling stiff.

"Watcha doin'?" John asked. Harley hadn't heard him enter the room.

"Just giving credence to the malicious voices in my head," she replied in a monotone, the sarcasm emerging before she could stop it. John, though, acted as if he hadn't even noticed. He stopped at the edge of the card table and looked down at the pieces for a couple of minutes before picking one up and slipping it into its place just inside the border.

"Smartass," Harley said with a hint of a smile. "I forgot how easily you could do that."

"Sometimes," John shrugged. "It's just a matter of color comparison and spatial recognition." A minute or two later, he had located and placed another one. He pulled another chair up to the card table and sat across from Harley, studying the pieces scattered across the table top.

Harley knew about the benefits to a person's visual acuity that John had mentioned. They used to assemble jigsaw puzzles fairly regularly years ago, and she knew that it also helped to improve memory and coordination, critical thinking and creativity, and even increased the brain's dopamine production.

"Why did we stop doing this?" Harley asked as she found three pieces that she could tell went together. They didn't attach to the border, but she went ahead and assembled them and put them aside, to put into place when the time came.

"I don't know," John replied. "I guess we had too many other things that needed to be done to find the time to just sit and stare at a table."

"Hmm," Harley replied noncommittally. "I wonder how many of those things really needed to be done."

"Hmm," John echoed. He looked up at her, watching her face as she continued searching for the puzzle pieces she needed, unaware of his perusal. His recent thoughts still in his mind, he suddenly felt an overwhelming sadness. And he was surprised that it wasn't only sadness over what he felt he had lost over the years, but also an empathetic sadness for Harley.

"I'm sorry," he said softly. Harley looked up at him, an almost startled expression on her face.

"For what?" she asked.

"For blowing up earlier," he replied. "And for screwing up the last several years."

Harley tilted her head and, as was usually the case when she did that, she reminded John of a confused puppy. He tried not to smile, but to stay focused and serious.

Harley was a little surprised at the mutually introspective moods they seemed to be in. She was sure they still had differing opinions about the government's handling of the virus, but this was a good start.

"The last several years aren't just on you," she said. "I'm just as much to blame. I've been distant and cold. I've been resentful. Sometimes I've been downright bitchy."

"I knew it wasn't just me!" John said, poking his finger at her, but he smiled to show that he wasn't being serious. Harley returned the smile. "You know what I just realized that I miss?" he continued. Harley shook her head. "Making love to you, and then just lying in your arms. We used to hold each other for so long afterwards, just talking about anything, or nothing. Sometimes we'd just lie there staring into each other's eyes. It was as if we had nothing else in the world to do."

"I remember that," Harley said as tears rippled in her eyes. "Nothing was more important than our time together." She sighed. "Of course, I was much younger then, and the mirror didn't show as many wrinkles."

"You're still a beautiful woman," John said, sitting back in his chair and regarding her. "And I'm not just talking about the way you look."

"John," Harley said, nearly choking on the whispered syllable.

John studied her for a few more moments, then he stood up, holding his hand out toward her. Harley looked at John for a few *moments, puzzled, and she took his hand. She stood up as she felt the gentle pull. John kissed the back of her hand, and he looked briefly into her eyes, guiding her toward the stairs.*

EXPEDITION

The footprints, as I recalled, seemed to be heading west, so Frida and I headed east. That's not to say that we were overconfident in our choice. We were wary and watchful the whole way.

We had only taken a few things. Depending on where we ended up, I figured I might be able to make another trip or two back for more, if it was not too far, or dangerous. Still, we brought more than my parents did when they had struck out on their own.

It's not as if we had much, anyway. The largest accumulation of things we had were each of our collections of books, plus Frida had several paintings that she had done through the years.

I had a rusty little wagon that my father had found at a neighboring house years ago. Still, following my parents' example, we traveled light. I chose two of my books, though sentimentality may have actually made the choice. I took the *Holy Bible* and *Harry Potter and the Philosopher's Stone*, the two books that my father had brought from their starting point.

I must confess, though, to a bit of a deception. It wasn't, really, but I still felt a little guilty about it. I brought a third book, an atlas, which I asserted might be helpful in our search for a new home. That was entirely truthful, but still it felt a little duplicitous.

Frida chose two of her paintings, one of her earlier ones and one that she had painted just a few weeks before. They were of similar subjects, and they beautifully showed her growth as an artist.

We brought several yards of hemp fabric that Frida had woven, a few changes of clothing, our two water buckets, and what little bit of food we had on hand, along with tools that my father had used to dig the "outhouse." I also brought the bow and arrows that my father had been armed with on their journey, and the spear that was my mother's.

Though it was not a necessity, I also insisted that Frida bring the paints that she had already made. It may have been partly my guilt about the third book, but I felt that Frida's gift was one that needed to be cultivated and encouraged. The past paintings were good, but I wanted her to continue, to make more.

Besides all the books and paintings, the thing I chafed most about leaving behind was the loom that my father had built.

We didn't want to stray far from the river, but with the wagon, I needed a surface that was a little more flat and hard, so we followed city streets for a few blocks, winding our way between crumbling brick and concrete buildings. The road was lined with dusty rusting hulks of old automobiles and trucks. There were also the occasional human remains, usually not much more than skeletons draped with faded whisps of clothing and bits of mummified skin.

We had lost sight of the river by that time, so we turned toward the south whenever we could, and ended up on an old pathway that looked as if it had, long ago, been covered in some kind of paving stones. Like elsewhere, the hemp and other weeds were growing from every possible bit of exposed soil, so even here, pulling the wagon was a challenge. But we could see the river, such as it was, on our right. And, looking behind us at the broken weeds we were leaving in our wake, I felt a little safer knowing that nobody else had traveled this path before us.

But seeing the trail we were leaving, I was a little concerned about anyone who might come after us.

But the roads were fickle, and we found ourselves in the shadows of the old buildings and towers, in various states of decay and collapse. The shade was welcome, but we were aware of all the areas that could offer a hiding place to possible marauders. So, we were happy when the buildings spread apart and the roadway widened.

We were on a road called, according to a green sign mounted at an intersection, VIRGINIA AVE NW. I don't know if the capitalization was significant or not, but that's what was on the sign.

As we continued toward the southeast, we could see a strange shape ahead of us, something which I knew, in ancient times, was called an obelisk. We had lost sight of the river, but that shape intrigued me. A glance at Frida confirmed that she felt similarly, so we continued along that route.

Pulling the wagon through the weeds growing through the pavement in the stifling sun, it took us, I think, nearly an hour to reach the thing. Our curiosity, though, went unsatisfied. We walked all around the thing, but there was no marking to tell us what it was.

After a few minutes, I thought of the atlas that I had brought and pulled it out of the wagon, happy to feel a little less guilty about having brought it.

We sat down on one of the benches that encircled the tower. There was a small structure sticking out of the base that looked as if it might be a portal to enter the tower, but parts of it had collapsed sometime in the past, blocking entry.

I flipped gingerly through the pages of the atlas until I reached our location.

"The Washington Monument," I said as I found the spot where we sat.

Frida looked at me with her eyebrows drawn together.

"What's that?" she asked.

"I don't know," I replied, shaking my head, feeling no closer to a revelation than before. We each took a sip of water, then sighed and stood up. I glanced around to be sure we were not being watched, then took the lead, continuing eastward.

What appeared to be very long, straight, parallel trails led directly toward the east. These paths had either broken down more quickly, or had never been paved except in gravel, but they were strewn with the ubiquitous hemp plants. In the distance, I saw the remains of a large rusty-looking dome.

It took us the better part of the early afternoon to travel this path, pulling the wagon through the weeds, and altering course for barriers such as, according to the atlas, the Capitol Reflecting Pond. Needless to say, there was no water in the pond, and the concrete that had once lined it was little more than gravel, having been broken up long ago by the invading plant life.

We were getting quite weary by the time we finally reached the domed structure, and neither of us felt capable of climbing the great flight of steps that led up to what appeared to be its entrance.

Parts of the dome had collapsed, as had some of the pillars of the building that supported it, and we decided that, based on how we were feeling, our curiosity would remain unsatisfied about this place, as well. The atlas told me that it was called the United States Capitol Building, but the descriptor meant little to me.

Having spent so many hours in our journey under the cruel and lethal sun, we made our way around this building to the eastern side, an endeavor that still took, I think, nearly an hour, and we were quite exhausted by the time we reached a little shade from the relentless killer above us. We found some arched doorways, and we decided to make our camp here.

FACEOFF

Vince stared intently into his WebVisor, reading a news article. The more he read, the more frustrated and angry he became.

Vince considered himself an armchair political expert. He lived in Los Angeles, and he had strong opinions about what the politicians in Washington were doing, or not doing, as the case may be. And he had a lot more time for this perusal now.

"Millions of Americans are out of work," he said into the headset connected to his WebVisor, the words appearing on his interactive blog page, "as the SHePF virus rampages across the country. Those who are fortunate enough to be able to work from home are doing so, but the rest of us are screwed.

"And for the longest time, all Congress could do was sit on their collective asses and argue and criticize the other side. Republicans denounced Democrats for not moving quickly enough. Democrats raged at Republicans for not being generous enough. To the American people, anyway. Republicans were plenty generous to their rich corporate cronies.

"But when they finally did pass SHePF relief legislation, it turned out to not be nearly enough. And now that SHePF has taken out a number of senators and representatives and other politicians, I can only imagine how slow subsequent aid is going to be in coming. If it comes at all!

"Makes me wish I had stockpiled supplies when I had the chance. Maybe the survivalists were right."

It didn't take long to start receiving responses. His page had a lot of followers, and likely a lot of them had more free time on their hands as well.

"Pretty much what I've come to expect from you," said George in Kentucky. "Always quick to get your digs in on Republicans." Vince had a lot of followers who didn't share his views.

"Just stating the facts, George. They're out there for anybody who cares to look at them."

"Republicans are too cheap and corrupt to be trusted with any kind of fair relief legislation," replied James in New Mexico.

"Just another example of the rich taking care of the rich, and to hell with us unworthy little guys," said Terry in Colorado.

"We're fighting a war, asshole!" Randy protested from Idaho. "It's not like we have unlimited resources. President McCauley is doing everything he can to get relief to those who need it, but all the Democrats can do is stand in his way."

"Randy, I don't understand why you still follow my page," Vince replied. "You're militant and belligerent, and you never agree with anything I post. I'm beginning to wonder if you just like to fight.

"We're actually fighting wars in TEN different countries, the majority of which, I suspect, few people can even remember why. If a conflict ever comes up in any country, we just charge right in without even questioning how much it will cost. But if there's an issue that involves taking care of our own, suddenly we're so very concerned about the budget."

A few more responses appeared, either praising Vince's wisdom concerning the situation, demeaning him for his stupidity, or adding insults about Randy's comments. Vince glanced through them as he waited for Randy's response, which he knew would come.

"We have to be careful," Randy replied, "because so many able-bodied people are draining the nation's coffers dry. Half the people on welfare and unemployment, maybe more, are able to work but are too fucking lazy."

"Kind of a moot point now, don't you think?" Vince said. "As I stated in my original post, millions of Americans are out of work. I don't know if you've heard about it or not, but there's this virus going around, and non-essential workers are urged to stay at home instead of possibly infecting others.

"The United States is the biggest contributor to the global GDP, so when America's economy suffers, it causes a drag on the rest of the world. I can't think of anything that would make the economy suffer more than mass unemployment. Except, possibly, mass death from a killer virus.

"So during this time, maintaining the purchasing power of America's citizens should be job one, instead of spending countless trillions of dollars bombing and shooting up countries on the other side of the world from us. But Congress' response to the financial hardships caused by SHePF turned out to be little more than a Band-Aid, and a little one at that. Unless you happen to be a corporation."

"Corporations are job-creators," Randy replied. "Without corporations, there would be no jobs."

"If consumers don't have money to buy their products and services," Vince shot back, "there will be no corporations."

"It's only been a few weeks. How many times have financial experts urged people to have three to six months' worth of money on hand in case of emergency?"

"Yes, it's only been a few weeks," Vince replied, "but SHePF isn't showing signs of letting up any time soon. Current projections are recommending non-essential workers remain under self-quarantine for at least another couple of months.

"Wages haven't risen to match cost of living in years. When people can barely pay their rent and buy groceries, how are they supposed to save up extra money for emergencies?

"And while we're on the subject, why doesn't that advice apply to banks and airlines and automobile manufacturers? Under that philosophy, our hard-earned tax dollars shouldn't be used to bail out corporations that didn't bother to plan ahead.

"Besides, corporations have proven on too many occasions to be job destroyers rather than creators. When they get bail-out money from the government, or annual subsidies, they don't use

this windfall to help their employees. Too many times, they've used it for stock buy-backs or for fat bonuses for their CEOs, while the employees continue suffering under the hard economic times, often even getting laid off because the company supposedly can't afford them."

"Typical of you and your corporation-bashing."

"It's not just me, Randy. Americans in general don't agree with the government's preferential treatment of big business. Congress' aid package being so top-heavy toward corporations is only going to further fuel their resentment toward the corporate world and their distrust of the government. If the government doesn't respect its citizens, why should the citizens respect the government?

"If they don't trust the government, they won't listen to the government's advice, for instance about dealing with the current health crisis. With citizens rebelling against the government's urgings and refusing to comply with social distancing and self-quarantining, that will only prolong the emergency, increase the number of deaths, and require more drastic measures. President McCauley has already been hinting at martial law."

"Well, McCauley won't be doing that," said Robert in Virginia. "He's just been diagnosed. He tested positive."

HOMECOMING

awn arrived, as it is wont to do, waking us from our restless slumber. Lacking any kind of portable pallet, our sleep on the stone flooring was less than comfortable. We were pleased, though, to have not been disturbed by anything—or anyone—other than our physical discomfort.

We wanted to get started before the sun rose very high in the sky, so we made quick work of our breakfast. Within a few minutes, we set out, continuing our eastward trek. Our journey was slowed, as it was the previous day, by the relentless hemp and other weeds which grew through every crack and crevice in the paving.

By the time I pulled the wagon through it and reached the street, my clothing was already soaked through from head to foot. A street continued straight ahead of us, "East Capital ST NE," according to the sign. But an enormous grey building to my right caught my eye.

We crossed and walked past a few broken tree stumps, and a couple of skeletal trees still standing. One of them had the remains of a person under it, likely having sought shade from the merciless sun, never to rise again.

A number of steps led up to the entrance to the building, but being, at least, a little better rested than last night, I felt more able to make the climb. I looked at Frida. I'm not sure what it was that attracted me to this building, and I can't say for sure that Frida felt it herself, but she shrugged in response to my look.

I checked all around to make sure nobody was watching us, then I started trudging up the steps, Frida at my side, leaving the wagon below. After a flight of steps, they turned to the right, and we continued pushing ourselves up.

On our left, yet another flight led up to three arched doorways, each one flanked by classical-styled columns, and with carvings in the curves of each arch. As we summited the last flight of steps, I was surprised to see that each glass double door in each doorway was still intact. I wondered if they were still locked.

The first one I came to was either locked or rusted. It didn't budge. The second one, the center one, creaked open a little. I inserted my shoulder for leverage and pushed against the door. It opened a little more, but not without protest. It was just enough for us to squeeze through, though.

As we came inside through one of three great interior arches, the grandeur of the place reminded me of a glorious church from man's *Golden Age*. In fact, it made me think of the Sistine Chapel, which I had seen pictures of in one of Frida's art books.

Looking up inside the great entryway, the vaulted ceiling high above was supported all around by eighteen pairs of classical columns, their bases on the next floor up and surrounding the entry hall. The ceiling had what looked like six stained glass skylights. Three of them, sadly, were broken, the bits of glass lying scattered on the dusty floor at our feet.

Surrounding those skylights, though faded, was an elaborate tableau of frescoes. Visible between all those pairs of columns on the floor above us was similar artwork covering every inch of the vaulted ceiling over the hall that wrapped around this entry.

On the left and the right, elaborately carved marble staircases led up to that second level. Straight ahead were three more beautifully carved marble archways. Beckoning us forward even more than the archways themselves were the words carved into the lintel above the central arch:

I had no words, and I looked at Frida. She seemed similarly affected, her eyes glassy behind a sheen of tears. But she was still looking at all the artwork surrounding us. I didn't know if she had even seen the words yet.

I looked back at my surroundings, feeling a lump in my throat. That such an enormous, beautiful building was used as a library, a great temple of knowledge, took my breath away. How wise those people must have been!

"So," Frida said quietly, "Congress was the name of this city?"

"No," I replied, "the city was Washington. I don't know what Congress was."

Answering the call, we both walked through the arch, going deeper into the building, leaving the grand entry behind. Here, we saw some display cases. One contained a large book.

"What does that say?" Frida asked, squinting at the tarnished gold text at the top of the wooden case. It was written in a text known as, if I recall correctly, Old English.

"The Gutenberg Bible," I replied. It was open to a page in the Psalms, and I recognized it from the copy that I brought with me, the one that my father brought, though the wording seemed slightly different. And the printing was a work of art in itself.

I don't know how many hours we spent exploring this building, but in nearly every part of it we entered, we were greeted by more artwork and more evidence of our forebears' reverence for the written word.

§

"What do you think?" I asked Frida. We sat on a sofa at the back of the building on the upper floor, in a room that was lined with bookshelves and filled with tables and chairs.

Frida sighed and shook her head.

"I could spend the rest of my life in this place," she said.

I can't even describe the feeling of relief that coursed through my body at hearing that. I felt, myself, as if I never wanted to leave.

"There are a number of logistical issues that will need to be addressed," I replied.

Frida nodded. She knew how little this world of the past was adapted to our life now. But she seemed to be willing to make the attempt.

Tyler remembered how hot and oppressive the Kansas summer sun was when he was a boy. He remembered how he welcomed the cool, rainy days, despite how rare they were. That was why, after he grew up, he resettled in Seattle.

But even then, it was not the Seattle that he had heard about from so long ago, the overcast city with more rainy days than sunny. It was somewhat cooler than Kansas, likely from its more northerly latitude, but the rainy climate just wasn't a thing anymore. Tyler could remember hearing all his life about how 20th and 21st century climatologists had warned about the changing weather patterns. Despite proclamations primarily in favor of limiting carbon output, most developed nations still did pretty much what their politicians and business owners demanded.

Tyler couldn't figure out how they had managed to keep finding petroleum for so long. Well into the twenty-first century, gasoline had still been used to fuel cars. How had the planet not been sucked dry? He thought it should look like a giant raisin.

Finally, hybrids and fully-electric cars became more commonplace. Unfortunately, they, like many other things nowadays, were so expensive as to be out of reach for most folks, especially in this economy.

Until then, though, because petroleum products had continued to be de rigueur for so long, the buildup of greenhouse gases, primarily from fossil fuel exhaust, as well as livestock production and numerous other sources, had trapped the sun's heat inside the atmosphere, gradually raising the temperature and changing weather patterns. It wasn't the post-apocalyptic wasteland that the old Hollywood movies had predicted. Not yet, anyway.

But it was definitely different.

As he walked westward along North 155th Street, Tyler felt a burning on the left side of his neck. He adjusted his hat to lower the brim on that side, and pulled the collar of his shirt up. The classic button-down shirt was now made with a tall collar meant to be worn standing up instead of folded over as it had traditionally been worn in times past.

That wasn't always enough, though, and since he hadn't thought to wrap a bandana around his neck, he tried to stay in the shade, what little shade there was.

Helen used to complain about always needing to remind him to dress properly, or about applying sunscreen, or any number of other things that he didn't seem to remember. She complained about him a lot. That's why they weren't together anymore.

There had been others since Helen, but they hadn't worked out, either. For different reasons, but all of them could be traced to one distinctive problem.

Tyler.

He sighed. That was the trouble with not being able to afford a car. Whenever he had to go anywhere, he had to walk. And that meant that he had plenty of time to think while walking, and sometimes, the thoughts were less than pleasant.

During a particularly contemplative walk a while back, Tyler had made a discovery about himself. During most of his adult life, he realized that he had been a shallow asshole, where women were concerned, at least. He had always placed so much emphasis on a woman's looks that other, more meaningful qualities were seldom considered, until the relationship was already underway and they were both in the process of becoming miserable.

A breakup inevitably occurred, after which he found another woman based solely on her looks or some other superficial characteristic rather than deeper qualities that might or might not be compatible with him. As his failed relationships mounted, he told himself that the law of averages implied that, given enough attempts, eventually one of the good-looking women he took up with would be a good match.

But he had gotten tired of the hunt. The law of averages had taken a lot longer than he had expected, and he just didn't have it in him anymore. And it's not as if he was anything special, himself. He knew he was a pretty average specimen. He didn't feel that he had that much to attract a woman with. Or maybe that was just a result of the recent reflective self-contemplation.

Of course, current situations, particularly the SHePF virus, had rendered the dating scene pretty much non-existent anyway. Bars and restaurants were closed, and people were urged to not mix recreationally.

Just as well. Tyler had become tired of hiding behind his façade, trying to appear deeper than he actually was.

§

RubyLeigh adjusted her mask as she looked at herself in the mirror beside the door to her garage. Happy enough with the result, she put her hat on and pulled her sleeves down. They were long sleeves, and she wore them pushed up over her elbows to be a little cooler while inside.

Some people refused to wear masks, or at least did it begrudgingly if there was no way around it. It was the law, after all. Others, while they didn't care for them, wore them because of their desire to protect themselves and others, and to prevent the spread of the virus.

RubyLeigh was glad to have an excuse to wear it.

She pulled the door closed behind her. The garage was hot, really sweltering, but at least it kept the car a few degrees cooler than it would be out in the sun, and prevented the second degree burns she might get from touching some of the blazing surfaces.

She had never liked her face. She acknowledged that she had individual features that were fine on their own. She had been told she had a decent figure, even though she always thought it was thinner than she wanted it to be. She generally liked her hair, thick and shiny red. Even her eyes, she knew, were pretty.

Other features, though, she felt, just weren't attractive. She had spent her life being self-conscious and critical. When she was still working, it was a little better. At least then she had something to occupy her mind. And she had actually enjoyed her job. But by now, spending every day at home by herself, she had emptied the "to be read" list on her reader, and had started over on books she had already read. She had watched everything that interested her on TV, which, admittedly, was not that much.

Now, she was looking forward to going to the store, just for a change of pace, and for a little human contact, even if it was from six feet apart. She pressed her thumb against the pad on the dashboard, her thumbprint was instantly scanned, and the motor hummed to life. The garage door rose silently on its track, and the navscreen lit up on the dashboard.

"Safeway, Aurora Avenue," RubyLeigh said, enunciating carefully, and the navscreen beeped its acknowledgment.

She caught a glimpse of her face in the mirror, and she adjusted her mask. She remembered an old saying, that we are often our own worst critics. That's probably true, but in her case, she knew her criticism was valid. She had even had a couple of boyfriends who had fixated on her looks. When you have a flaw, it's as if that's the only thing anybody can see.

Wearing a mask actually made her feel better about being seen by others.

The car backed out of the garage and the garage door closed. With the price of electricity rising, she mused, she would probably forego the use of her car soon. Not that she ever went anywhere anyway. The grocery store was pretty much the only place she ever went. Dressed properly, she could walk there. If she had to.

§

Tyler had heard old-timers talk about the selection of groceries that could be had back in the old days. Multiple brands of the same item, but with somewhat different features. Even in the produce department, they spoke of six or eight different varieties of apples with slight variations of flavor.

Tyler couldn't even imagine that kind of selection. He also couldn't imagine how people ever got out of the store. How could they ever decide?

Grocery shopping nowadays didn't call for nearly as much decision-making. If they had what you wanted, there was generally one variety or brand. Shoppers were only restricted by whatever allotment limit the store might have placed on the item. And there was usually a restriction since fertile land was in such short supply now.

Tyler picked up a basket and looked around once he was inside. It didn't take him long. He headed into the produce area. He pulled a paper bag from the dispenser and, with his gloved hands, began placing handfuls of green beans in it.

"You ever wonder why we have so many beans, but not much else?"

Tyler looked up and saw a statuesque redhead, picking up beans from the other side of the bin, wearing a mask that coordinated nicely with her hair. Tyler's was basic white.

"Actually, no I don't," he replied. "I grew up in Kansas where there were still a few farms. I know that legumes grow quickly and don't need much water."

"Really?" the woman replied, her head tilted a bit. "Very interesting." She looked around at the nearby displays. "What about tomatoes?"

Tyler looked at the bin of tomatoes, a cheerful dash of color among a grouping of shades of green.

"Tomatoes develop deep root systems pretty quickly. They need a fair amount of water to get started, but after they have, and after the surface has dried up, they can pull moisture from deeper in the ground. Same with squash and melons," he added, pointing to other bins.

"Huh," she replied thoughtfully.

"Just in case you were going to ask," he smiled.

Most of the woman's face was hidden behind her mask, but her eyes were smiling. And they were such pretty eyes! Tyler felt himself being drawn toward her, once again attracted to a woman based solely on her physical features. He couldn't let that happen again.

He looked in the bag and was satisfied with how many green beans he had. He took a deep breath as if it was a major decision, and he folded it up and put it in his basket.

§

He had smiled at her, but then he suddenly stopped and looked away. RubyLeigh couldn't believe it. Could he actually sense what she looked like through the mask? Maybe it didn't hide as much as she had convinced herself it did.

"Well," she said, "I see you're busy. I won't bother asking you about the horticultural history of purslane." She smiled as she started to walk away.

"Actually, I'm not," he replied, still looking down at the paper bag in his basket. "Busy, I mean." Then, he glanced at the purslane in the display nearby. "Funny thing about purslane. It used to be considered an invasive weed." He stole a glimpse up at her. "People used to pull it out of their lawns and their gardens and throw it out in the trash. Now, like so many other plants, it seldom grows naturally and it has to be cultivated by professionals."

"How do you know all this?" RubyLeigh asked. "Just from growing up in Kansas?"

"Partly," he said as he looked away again, and the sides of his mask moved outward, following the contours of his face as he smiled. But then, his eyebrows went down as if his expression had changed to a frown. "And partly just because I'm curious. I've heard stories of what it used to be like. I've wondered how we let the world turn into such a shithole."

"So, you've made a study of the past?"

"More like an intermittent perusal. Not really an applied study."

RubyLeigh smiled.

"Ah, a kindred spirit," she said. "I, too, am a pertinacious seeker of knowledge."

"Pertinacious!" he said, raising his eyebrows at her. He attempted a whistle, but with the mask pressed against his lips, it came out more like a weak sputter. "I'm afraid that word's not in my vocabulary, but I'm impressed that it's in yours, and that you were actually able to use it in a sentence." He lowered one eyebrow at her, hoping his critical expression showed despite the mask. "Assuming it's a real word."

"Are you accusing me of neologism?" RubyLeigh asked with an offended tone.

He laughed

"Okay, now you're just showing off." RubyLeigh shrugged but didn't deny it. Tyler's eyes warmed toward her. "I'm Tyler."

"RubyLeigh," she replied. They made a point of not shaking hands, even with their gloves on. "That's spelled with an e-i-g-h, not a double e."

"Interesting," Tyler said.

"My parents were into weird names. Just ask my sister Steve."

Tyler snorted at that.

"Oh my god," he said abruptly, "I snorted. You're not supposed to hear that until we've known each other for at least a couple of weeks."

Again, he suddenly seemed nervous and looked away, although RubyLeigh acknowledged to herself that it was likely just embarrassment about the snort. She was surprised at how chatty and, apparently, outgoing she was today. Even when she used to be at her job, she generally kept to herself. The mask really did seem to give her a measure of self-confidence.

Of course, it couldn't last. Eventually the pandemic will end and the masks will come off. Her face will be visible again, and men will be repelled by her hideousness. But as long as the mask was on, she was enjoying her new-found boldness.

§

Tyler couldn't help it. He kept stealing glances at RubyLeigh. She was pretty and his eyes were just drawn to her. That gorgeous shiny red hair, and her soft, beautiful eyes. And the long, delicate dress she was wearing only seemed to enhance the willowy shape of her body instead of hiding it.

He tried to use what he could see, her hair, her eyes, her figure, to extrapolate what the rest of her face under the mask must look like. But then, he mentally shook his head. That's exactly what the old Tyler would have done. The old Tyler would have been wowed by RubyLeigh's external features and not bothered to delve much deeper.

The thing is he liked what he was seeing and hearing, even if he couldn't see all of her. She was poised, confident and intelligent, with a subtle, understated sense of humor. In the short time they had spent together so far, with him making a point of not staring at her but exploring deeper than her physical features, he was completely comfortable with her.

And he had learned a couple of new words. He made a mental note to look them up later. But he felt as if it would be a pleasant thing to spend hours in her company.

And given his recent determination to do better, to look deeper, to see below the surface, that made him feel as if he might actually have a chance at, someday, making a good match. A match that might last longer than weeks or months. A relationship that wouldn't end in disappointment.

"Well," RubyLeigh said, glancing around, "I need to get a few more things. I should leave you alone and let you finish your shopping."

"Oh, I don't mind," Tyler replied quickly, feeling a sudden urge to keep her near. "I need to get a few more things, too. I'm enjoying your company."

He suddenly wondered, nitpicking what he said, if he sounded too desperate. Did he object too quickly? Should he have said he was enjoying the company instead of hers specifically? But still, he continued.

"I'm okay with shopping together," he continued, "I mean unless you're in a hurry to leave."

"I'm not," RubyLeigh replied, her eyes crinkling a bit with her otherwise unseen smile.

§

She was happy to stay. She liked Tyler. His suggestion that they shop together helped to ease the misgivings she had felt about him earlier, that he found her repulsive. It seemed as if he didn't want her to go, and it warmed her heart. And she was surprised to realize that she already felt the same about him.

At the same time, she couldn't help but wonder if he would have been so quick to suggest shopping together if she hadn't been wearing her mask.

"So, RubyLeigh," Tyler said, "tell me about yourself. How is it you know such prodigious words?"

"Well, as I said, I'm a seeker of knowledge."

"Yes, pertinaciously so, apparently."

"Indeed," she smiled. "In my previous life, before SHePF struck and changed our way of life, I was a librarian."

"Nice," Tyler said. "I used to love going to the library. Sometimes I'd go, even if I wasn't looking for anything in particular. I'd just walk around and browse, looking for anything that caught my interest."

"I did that, too," RubyLeigh smiled. "I discovered a couple of my favorite authors that way." She looked away as she smiled again, knowing that, with her mask, her eyes would be showing only the sadness behind it. "I used to love my job. I mean there were some aspects of it that were actually work, but for the most part, it was like a pleasant dream."

"Wow," Tyler replied, "I don't think I ever felt that way about my job."

"What did you do?"

"Inventory and stocking at a warehouse store that has since gone out of business."

RubyLeigh looked at him for a moment.

"It's so surreal, isn't it?" she asked. "This virus has been going on for months, but it still feels like a weird nightmare. Millions of people dead, countless companies out of business, bankruptcies at a historic level."

They were quiet as they wandered around the end of an aisle. In the bread aisle, Tyler picked up a loaf off the shelf.

"Did you know that wheat flour used to be the main ingredient in bread?" he asked.

"Now you're just showing off," RubyLeigh said. The upper part of Tyler's face flushed.

"Yeah, maybe I am," he admitted.

He glanced briefly at her and RubyLeigh's heart almost melted over the embarrassed little boy look he seemed to exude.

RubyLeigh looked down, smiling, but with a conflicting emotion competing for dominance, perhaps fear of being 'found out.' She felt like a fraud revealing only her best features.

"I'm sorry," Tyler said. "I like you. I guess I'm just trying to impress you."

"You don't have to impress me, Tyler," RubyLeigh said. "I like you, too." Then, an attempt to lighten the mood. "Assuming you don't do something stupid." She hoped she hadn't gone too far.

"Well, I'm afraid that's a little more likely than I might hope." He sighed. "Anyway, I'm sorry if I seem to be moving too fast."

"You are," RubyLeigh replied, "but I think I understand it."

Tyler looked up at her again, and this time, he held her gaze.

"I think it's just because, on some level, you know how little time we have." Tyler frowned his confusion at her. RubyLeigh took a breath, then continued. "This is something that I've studied. It just seems fairly rare anymore that a couple of middle-aged people meet and really like each other."

Tyler pulled his head back, looking pointedly at her.

"Excuse me?" he replied, an offended expression in his eyes. "I'm only thirty-two."

"And I'm thirty," RubyLeigh said. "How many people do you know who are sixty years old?" Tyler raised his eyebrows in concession. "You know, as recently as just a century ago, the average life expectancy was about seventy-two years. And it wasn't terribly unusual for people to live ten or twenty years beyond that. Some even lived as long as a hundred years!"

"What happened?"

"We happened. Humans have a long reputation for fucking up their lives and the lives of other living things. We've polluted the air, thinned the atmosphere, and by cutting down and killing the forests, we've ruined the earth's ability to generate more. As you said earlier, we've turned the earth into a shithole.

"Add to that the wars, crime, riots, economic collapse, and just everyday apprehension and fear for our health and general well-being, and we've diseased and stressed ourselves out of decades of lifespan.

"So maybe your 'moving too fast' is just recognition of how short our lives are now. I think a lot of things nowadays are more accelerated than they used to be."

Tyler looked at her, fighting the longing he felt. Hearing the passion in her expression, seeing the distress that had suddenly appeared on her face, he felt that feeling of a kindred spirit that she had mentioned. He wanted to hold her, to do the typical guy thing and try to fix it.

But he knew he couldn't. He had to keep his distance. And he couldn't fix it. He looked down at the loaf of bread he was still holding.

"Okay," RubyLeigh said, opting to change the subject, "so tell me about this fabled wheat bread you mentioned."

Tyler snickered as he looked at the loaf.

"In the central part of the United Stattes, there used to be acres and acres of wheat fields. Amber waves of grain stretching from one horizon to the other. Wheat was probably the most-consumed grain in the world. It didn't require a lot of water, but it grew best in a climate of around seventy degrees. As the atmosphere thinned, though, and the temperature rose, wheat became too difficult to grow.

"Amaranth, though," he hefted the loaf and then placed it in his basket, "grows well in an arid and hot climate. So, over the course of a hundred years or so, amaranth gradually replaced wheat as our main cereal grain."

"So, do you believe in love at first sight?" RubyLeigh suddenly asked, surprised at her fearlessness.

Did she really just ask him that? Tyler stopped abruptly and looked at her, and RubyLeigh turned to face him, biting her tongue as her timidity and apprehension returned. She could feel her face flushing, and she was embarrassed to realize that she hoped it didn't clash with the color of her mask.

She knew she should have waited. This was a question for maybe a second or third date. Following up on her serious articulation a few moments ago about how little time they had, she was being partly facetious.

But only partly.

And she wasn't saying that she was in love with Tyler, by any means, or even confessing that she believed in love at first sight. She was only asking if he did. She told herself she was just making conversation.

Still, observing the inscrutable expression on the part of his face that she could see, RubyLeigh was mentally kicking herself. It looked as if he was struggling to know what to say. She was about to apologize and excuse herself when Tyler responded.

"I never did," he said.

RubyLeigh silently sighed with relief at the fact that he was honestly answering her question instead of telling her to hit the road.

"But after what you said earlier about the shortness of our lives now, I can see how that could come into play in developing relationships."

RubyLeigh looked at Tyler, considering his response. He looked up at her and continued haltingly.

"I don't know how much information you want."

RubyLeigh didn't either, and she shrugged and shook her head.

"Well, as I was walking here this morning," Tyler continued, "I was thinking about my past and how I need to grow up. To not base potential relationships on superficial things, but to explore her personality, her likes and dislikes, the way she expresses herself. And then, coincidentally, I meet you here at the grocery store."

"And?"

"And I like you. It's crazy, but in the short time that we've been talking, I feel close to you, comfortable. I've enjoyed sharing things I know with you, but I've also enjoyed hearing your thoughts and opinions."

"Maybe that shortened life expectancy we were talking about adds a sense of urgency to developing a relationship, if one is open to it."

"Maybe," Tyler said, pondering. "I wonder how we can determine if it's urgency or desperation."

RubyLeigh smiled.

"I guess we'll just have to keep getting to know each other."

"I think you're right. So, RubyLeigh, where do you come from?"

"I was born and raised in Kansas City, Missouri," she laughed.

"Are you serious? We were neighbors from the start!"

RubyLeigh began briefly telling her story. She liked the fact that Tyler was interested in her, in who she was, not just what she looked like. She was still a little apprehensive about him seeing her without her mask.

But that was a subject for another time.

HABITATION

We spent the next several days getting settled in our new home. Those logistical issues I had mentioned occupied my time, and I used my father's tools to dig a toilet hole for us.

I found another door that opened, one facing the east. It seemed as if it was a little less prominent, and it would have been somewhat hidden from view when all the skeletal trees on that side of the building were still alive. That's where I dug our toilet hole. And I wedged a piece of metal under the door to keep it closed.

I also spent a few days, probably more time than I should have, using the auger that my father had to drill a well. Actually, I drilled several until I finally was able to tap a viable water source. I had to go a few blocks west before I finally struck water, but at least it wasn't as far away as the river which, by the way, according to the atlas that I had smuggled, is called The Potomac.

I'm well aware that I made more work for myself than I should have, not only initially, but every day after that. The well was at least twice as far as the river was from our previous home, so each day started with a much farther hike there, through the tunnel, and back.

Also, our toilet hole required that we descend multiple flights of stairs to use it, then climb said stairs again when we were finished. Fortunately, in a short time, I found a large bucket in a storeroom, and we kept it covered in a nearby room to use as a portable toilet. I took it down once a day to empty it, so that eased our burden a bit.

Still, all of this admittedly made our lives harder than they had been at our old home. But we were so enamored with the Library that we both agreed it was worth it.

Besides, having made the move due to fear, the greater security was worth the extra trouble. We both felt that we could defend ourselves much more efficiently in this building, should the need arise.

We set up our home in that room that we had discussed our next move in. The sofa provided cushions for us to sleep on, once they were augmented by additional cushions we found in other rooms. We bundled all those cushions together on the floor to make a comfortable bed, which served us for several days. In time, though, we replaced it with a real bed that I found in a nearby house. This room was plainer, much less decorated than many of the other parts of the building, but we opted for taking the physical high ground.

We spent several days just cleaning. Having found brooms in that storeroom, we were able to sweep up the glass from the broken skylights. We swept up years of dust and grime.

We also gathered human remains, by now little more than dry skeletons draped with flimsy bits of fabric. There weren't many. I suppose when people were sick and dying, they wanted to stay at home. But there were a few.

We gathered the bones into a room that we decided to set aside solely for this purpose. We didn't just toss them into a pile. They were — or had been — people, so we tried to be respectful. We arranged the bones into what I thought of as individual grave sites. Having seen cemeteries, I knew a little about how people used to do it.

Since we didn't know who these individuals were, though, there were no grave markers. I thought it was sad that people who had lived lives, who were, presumably, loved by others, should now be gathered in anonymous graves, unremembered.

In time, our lives took on a rhythm, a pleasing routine, as we settled into our new home and took time to explore it. It was after I had found and read a book on solar energy and storage that we made it a point to locate a system. It took a few tries before I found one that was connected exclusively to its own battery storage unit, and not to what they used to call "the grid."

A number of appliances had been left in the house, so I was able to try a few items to make sure it worked. The first two didn't do anything but, besides the thick layer of dust, there was some rust visible on their exterior. Without taking them apart, I couldn't say what kind of condition they were in on the inside.

They were old, *really* old, and they hadn't been used in ages. Also, based on the rudimentary understanding I had from my reading, I thought that the warm, dry climate may have protected them. But not knowing for certain what some of them were or how they worked, I couldn't be sure if they were still in working order or not.

Determined not to be discouraged, though, I scoured the house and found several other electrical items, and I gathered them all up. I had little success with many of these other items.

The next item I tried, which I think was some kind of radio, had been stored in a closet. Having been protected—somewhat—from the hotter temperatures and the dust, it did turn on. Obviously, since there were no stations broadcasting anymore, nothing came out of the speaker except a little occasional static, but the fact that that much happened told me that the system was still gathering and storing energy.

I tried another after that, an item that, if I recall correctly, was called a toaster. I had seen references to such items in a couple of books that I had left at our old home. When I depressed the lever on the side, some metal coils inside began to turn orange and get hot. The blanket of dust inside the toaster ignited.

I was convinced!

I enlisted Frida's assistance over the next several days to help me dismantle the system and transport it, little by little, back to the Library. We worked during the early morning hours when it was, at least, a little cooler.

I hoped I was understanding the book correctly as I assembled all of the parts up on the green copper roof, but when it was done and I pressed the switch on the utility light I had found, it lit up!

The proud smile and the look of admiration on Frida's face at that moment is something that I will carry with me till I die.

It was a few weeks after we had moved into the Library that I had the idea of creating a garden on the roof. Yes, I had read a book about unconventional gardens, and I figured it was worth a try. Of course, that meant that I had to transport more water, up a longer distance. And, unfortunately, the sun was so oppressive that nothing grew for the longest time.

It was only after I used some of our hemp fabric to create a little shade that I achieved any results. It wasn't enough to nourish us on its own, but it helped to supplement my daily foraging ventures.

I had an idea, something that I wanted to do for Frida. I made a cautious trip back to our old home to dismantle the loom that my father had built for my mother. After they were gone, Frida had continued using it to make fabric for our clothing, as well as canvases to paint on, so I wanted to be able to present that to her.

There seemed to be no change, no disturbance anywhere around the old neighborhood. There was no evidence that anybody else had been there. I felt a little silly at the fear that had sent us scurrying away, but our happiness with our new home definitely eased the embarrassment.

And the happy tears in Frida's eyes when I presented the loom to her in the Library made it all worth it.

FOOD CHAIN

After so many other smaller seafood chains have shut down during the past year, Cod Smack is finally calling it quits. The board of directors voted unanimously today to dissolve the popular seafood corporation. In a press release, they cite financial hardship as a result of the SHePF virus, as well as the recent collapse of the worldwide fishing industry."

"Shit," said Joe as he and his friend Tom sat in the dark on the front porch. The VidScreen was playing just inside the open door. Joe's wife, Kathy, liked to have the news on whenever she was busy with chores around the house. She wanted to keep up on current events. Joe took another sip of his homemade okra whiskey, and he grimaced as it went down.

"I'm surprised it lasted this long," Tom replied knowingly. "But it was just a matter of time."

"I suppose you see this as proof of your fuckin' climate change," Joe said, adopting a skeptical tone of voice.

"You're telling me you still don't see it?" Tom asked incredulously, "after all this time, and all this evidence?"

"What evidence? You say it's getting warmer. So what? I'm fine with a little warmth."

"A little warmth? Do you realize that a hundred years ago, the average high temperature here in Nome was in the teens? Alaska was held up as a standard for cold places. Now look at us. We're sitting on your porch in January in jeans and sweaters, sipping your nasty whiskey."

"Sounds like an improvement to me," Joe replied, sneering at Tom's remark about his whiskey.

"The temperature may be pleasant here, but it's the winter time. It's supposed to be cold and snowy. And it gets more miserable, and even dangerous, the farther south you go."

"Well then, it's a good thing we don't go anywhere."

"God, why do I hang out with you?"

"Must be my pleasing demeanor and sparkling personality," Joe said, grinning at his friend, and trying to hide the scowl as he took another sip of whiskey. He looked out over the neighborhood. It was pretty sparse. Several of the neighbors had caught the SHePF virus and died. Joe had thought that they would have been more protected from it up here.

Others who had managed to avoid or survive the virus moved away, some to more isolated locales. Others moved to cities where family members lived, having learned the importance of that family connection. As it stood now, roughly eight out of ten houses in the neighborhood were empty.

"Okay," Joe said, "I'll agree things have changed. But it's not something we've never seen before. The climate is constantly changing. Temperatures rise and fall, and they have for as long as the earth has been around. It's just the natural cycle."

Tom shook his head.

"Alright, look at the ice age," Joe continued. "That didn't stop man. Humans adapted and continued. We'll adapt and continue again through the rising temperatures."

"Okay, but during and after the last ice age, the earth was still capable of supporting life. But now, after homo sapiens has fucked up the environment, the weather every single day in most places around the world consists of continued dry heat with zero chance of rain. Now, the atmosphere is getting thin enough that you have to be sure and dress properly when you go out so you don't get skin cancer."

"But, like I said," Joe replied, exasperated, "that's just the natural cycle. It's not our fault. The climate just naturally changes over time."

"But it's not natural," Tom insisted. "Not this time. Earth's natural reaction to trauma has always been to heal and regenerate. New plant life forms, animals move in and begin the cycle of life *again. The earth isn't able to do that anymore. The trauma is too deep, too permanent.*

"Extinction is forever, and more species than we can even count have disappeared over the last couple of centuries. Nobody's seen a bee in a long time. You know how many plants have to be manually pollinated now? And what food we can still grow is often unappetizing and contains little nutrition, because the nutrients in the soil have pretty much died out."

He held up his glass containing the noxious liquid.

"Hell, okra is a heat- and drought-resistant crop that never used to grow as far north as Alaska. Now, it's one of the few things that will grow here. Face it, Joe, the age of man is over."

He motioned toward the sound of the VidScreen, where Cod Smack stockholders were still telling their sob story and lamenting the disappearance of seafood.

"The oceans and rivers didn't overfish themselves." He looked out across the dark neighborhood. "When was the last time you saw any salmon running upstream? It's been years."

"Okay," Joe said, "but that's likely just because of the atmospheric issues you mentioned. That's not man's fault. You're always going on about car exhaust before we went electric. Shit, cows fart tons of methane. There's your greenhouse gas right there."

"It is partly because of how long gasoline-powered cars went on," Tom countered, "belching tons of carbon into the atmosphere over the last couple of hundred years. But the livestock issue, since you brought it up, is because of man's voracious appetite for meat. That in itself is a horrendous waste of resources. Think about this: counting what was required to grow the feed, it takes over 400,000 gallons of water to raise a single cow to slaughter, while poor countries, and even some poorer American communities don't have enough clean water to drink."

Joe took another discreet sip from his glass, but didn't respond.

As they sat there, the silence was disrupted by a deep snuffling sound to their left. Simultaneously, they turned their heads to see the cause. A big grizzly bear was lumbering across Joe's yard, his head up, sniffing the air.

As they sat there perfectly still, watching the bear, hoping the breeze was blowing in their favor, they heard what sounded like a raspy, throaty roar from another bear perhaps a block away. It was accompanied by a frantic, terrified scream, which abruptly stopped.

The beast in front of them stopped and lifted its head, looking around and sniffing the air again. It turned its head toward Joe and Tom, and they each held their breath, trying not to react to the sounds they just heard several houses away.

Searching the air currents, the bear began moving ahead again, slowly swinging its head back and forth, trying to find some easy prey. Joe and Tom relaxed once the bear was halfway across the next yard.

"What the fuck?" Joe hissed.

"Well," Tom replied thoughtfully, "there aren't any bees making honey anymore. And they're not pollenating flowers, so there aren't any berries out there. Seafood's not on the menu anymore. Looks like we're next on the food chain."

He held up his glass in a sardonic toast.

Joe harrumphed and took another slug.

RELATIVE HAPPINESS

That routine that we settled into became our life for several pleasant years. Although, admittedly, "pleasant" is a relative term. From numerous books that I read during our time in the Library, I realized how much more difficult our lives were than daily life had been in the past. It was during this time that I began referring to that past as man's *Golden Age*. They could do anything. The sky was the limit, to use a phrase from that time period.

Although, even that phrase was not accurate. They had gone to the moon and to Mars and had sent spacecraft into the farthest reaches of space. What couldn't they do?

Of course, given our current situation, appearances were, obviously, deceiving. There were any number of things they couldn't do, and many, based on my reading, that they could have done but didn't, which led to where we are today.

Still, my life with Frida was most agreeable. It was as if she was the most bright and pleasant version of what would fill whatever gaps existed in myself and my life. I could only hope that I was something comparable to her.

§

I watched from the doorway as Frida used a hammer to tap a tack into place, securing a portion of a canvas to the sticks she was using as a stretcher. It wasn't perfect, though it was better than her previous canvases.

She had found a tool called a plane in a workshop attached to the house we had gotten the solar power system from. After we found out what it was and how to use it, she had started using it to smooth the sticks we found for her stretchers, which made her canvas surfaces a little flatter and more uniform.

I've read from several sources about people being able to sense something as intangible as somebody watching them. I don't know if science backs that up in any way, but Frida seemed to sense me watching her. She looked up at me and smiled a curious smile.

"What?" she asked.

I just shook my head. How do you describe a feeling so intense that just watching the source of that feeling can affect your mood? Frida was the source of that feeling for me. Just watching her for a few moments could raise my spirits if I was feeling down.

"What?" she repeated, pushing her golden hair behind her ear and smiling. Her warm brown eyes bored gently but persistently into me.

I shook my head again, but I had gathered my words by then.

"I love you," I said, pushing myself away from the doorway.

Frida put the hammer down on the table and leaned back in her chair. Her eyes warmed as I approached.

Love was a concept that had, well, not quite disappeared from vocabularies, but at some time in our past, it had suffered a definite decline. I don't know for certain when it happened, but I'm sure it was after the fall of the *Golden Age*, when book writing and publishing had gone by the wayside. When daily survival became one's main focus, of what use were abstract emotions that didn't directly help one's individual survival?

But feeling what I felt for Frida, I couldn't imagine surviving in our current situation, much less thriving, without her.

"More than that," I continued, "I'm *in* love with you."

"You're what?" Her eyebrows scrunched together.

"I'm in love with you," I repeated. "People used to write about being in love a lot in the past."

"I know what love is," she replied, but with a slight hesitation. "But 'in love'?"

"Even though so many were absolutely certain that they were in love, many also wrote about how difficult it was to define what love actually was." I frowned. "And now that I'm trying to explain it to you, I'm finding myself in that same situation. Words are so inadequate sometimes."

I pulled another chair over near hers and sat down.

"Being 'in love,'" I continued, "referred to an intense feeling of attachment and affection for someone else. Romantic feelings of attraction and intimacy. It's like the attachment we felt for our parents, but deeper and stronger in a lot of ways."

Frida looked away as she thought about that for a moment. Then, she looked back at me. She smiled warmly and nodded, and we spent a few moments just gazing at each other's faces.

"I think I'm in love with you, too," she finally said.

I leaned forward and kissed her, and she responded, pressing her lips to mine. I reached up and placed a hand on her face, opening my mouth to hers. My other hand slipped under her top, caressing the smoothness of her skin.

People in various times in the past wore multiple layers of clothing. It seemed to me that this meant that getting undressed could be a complicated and time-consuming ordeal.

In our time and climate, multiple layers were not necessary, at least not inside. It didn't take any time at all for my fingers to come in contact with Frida's breast, and I felt the moment intensify.

While heat was a constant and unpleasant thing in our world, in the moments that followed, the temperature seemed to rise a little more. Except, not in an unpleasant way.

I felt *myself* rising, as well, making my trousers fit a little more snugly, and I glanced down at the bulge.

"I think this is part of being in love, too," I said.

Frida looked at what I was referring to, then she looked back at me and smiled. She stood up, pulling her top off, revealing the body that I loved so dearly, and she took my hand, leading me to our bed.

BOTTLENECK

Randy turned on his radio. It was practically his only link to the outside world, and even that was sporadic. A week ago, Will Kane at WDCO – "Western Denver Colorado: We Do Country the Old-Fashioned Way" – announced that due to the tragic loss of life that had been occurring because of the SHePF virus, the local power plant was operating with a skeleton crew, and two more workers had called in sick that day.

The CDC, bowing to pressure from President Armstrong who had vowed to continue all the work his late predecessor had begun, had postponed enacting Section 361 of the Public Health Service Act. They had urged prudence on the state level, but seeing how opposed many governors, businessmen and citizens were to isolating, and even simple precautions like wearing masks, many in the CDC had expressed deep dissatisfaction with the results, and discouragement at the growing number of deaths.

Many essential businesses were feeling the effects, including the power plants. Those who were left were frantically looking for skilled workers trained in the operation of a generating station. The company, with stations all along the Front Range, was consolidating its workers into fewer locations, and there still weren't enough.

Realizing their fears, the power station ground to a halt a couple of days ago. Ever since then, WDCO, making judicious use of a generator, would only go on the air at the top of the hour to broadcast news and pertinent local announcements, then would go silent again.

Randy was really missing his classic country music, Kenny Chesney and Toby Keith, Waylon Jennings and George Jones, Hank Williams and Willy Nelson. Even though WDCO didn't play music anymore, Randy still tuned in every hour on his battery-powered radio to hear what was going on in his neighborhood and around the world. He sat there listening expectantly as the radio came on.

At first, it was silent. It wasn't quite the top of the hour. Then, there was a burst of static, the sliding steel guitar tones of the WDCO jingle, and Buck Johnson, sounding like a Texas cowboy, began delivering the news. Randy still thought it was weird to hear the familiar voices of his favorite DJs not introducing music.

The SHePF virus was still galloping across the country, debilitating millions and killing, on average, over half of those it infected. Randy couldn't imagine that many people dead. He had been glad that his company had let him start working from home, so he could decrease the potential of exposure. As a customer service rep for a sporting goods company, he could work anywhere.

Of course, that was a moot point now that there was no power and he couldn't get online. And since his company had closed down, Randy was now living off of his savings.

Back to the news, the various hot spots were, to some extent, still hot, and the war in Algeria was still building, though there seemed to be little information about any of them. When day-to-day survival was at stake, people didn't want to know about battles on the other side of the world, several of which few people cared much about to begin with.

"Next up," Buck continued with a shuffle of papers, "as y'all know, the pumps at Colorado Water quit when the power went out, so ain't nobody getting water in their homes. Grocery stores all across Denver have reported being out of bottled water and other necessities for about a week now.

"Colorado Water has announced that they'll be delivering water to various locations. Trucks will be dispatched to every King Soopers and Safeway store still open in the Denver Metro area at 1:00 this afternoon. Individuals can purchase gallon jugs of water, limit two per person, after which any that's left over will be available on the store shelves."

Some forward-thinking individuals had recommended filling bathtubs, jugs, pans and any other suitable containers with water early on. Randy, realizing he likely wouldn't have thought of it himself, was grateful for the advance warning. But his apartment didn't have a bathtub, only a shower stall, so he didn't have as big a reserve of water as some likely did. He had been stretching it for the last couple of days with pans, pitchers and glasses.

He looked at his watch. It was just after 11:00. He had nearly two hours. He turned the radio off and pushed himself up from his chair. He had to get dressed. Since he stayed home pretty much all the time, he didn't see the point in changing out of his pajamas. But he decided that, for a trip to the store, getting dressed was called for. Especially since not dressing properly could result in serious bodily harm.

His particular apartment didn't come with a garage space, so his car was, as always, parked in the sun. Once he got the door open, he climbed in and began taking down all the shields he had placed in the windows. Even with them in place, the temperature inside the car was blistering.

Leaving his door open to allow the car to air out as long as possible, Randy pressed his thumb against the pad on the dashboard. Naturally, it was hot and he jerked his hand away, but it was long enough to start up his car. The flashing red light next to the charge gauge reminded him that the car had almost no power. He kicked himself for not getting charged the last time he was out. Parking spaces with charge stations were more expensive, and he had opted for a basic space and buying his charge when he was out.

But that's okay. He still had plenty of time.

The navigation system in his car had stopped working several months ago. He figured it probably melted in the heat, but he didn't know for sure if that could actually happen. Other things had stopped working, too, and he couldn't afford to fix them. At any rate, it was up to him to drive to the store.

Holding the steering wheel gingerly between his fingertips, he pulled out of the parking lot of his apartment complex and turned toward his local charge station. It was only April and it was already an inferno, and there wasn't a cloud in the sky. With his battery so low, he left the air conditioner off and his windows down. He was still miserable.

He was distracted from that thought, only slightly, when he approached a foul-smelling river of sludge pooled in the road. The car just ahead of him plowed through it, but a man in a mask and an orange reflective vest walked into the road and stopped Randy, as other masked workers started unloading orange cones from a truck.

He held his breath as he approached.

"Sorry," the young man said, directing him down a side street, "the pumps at the sewage treatment plant stopped working." Assaulted by the smell, Randy nodded, only too happy to comply. It would just take him a little out of his way. It was only 11:30. He still had time.

But the detour ended up taking him several blocks out of his way, onto Colorado Boulevard. In the best of times, Colorado was a busy thoroughfare that he usually tried to avoid. Now, it was exponentially worse, as none of the traffic lights were working. Drivers, already angry about the traffic delays or any number of other frustrations, were slowly trying to work their way through intersections, horns blaring and swear words flying.

Randy was a little surprised. As so many people had been infected and died, he was amazed that there was still so much traffic. But the mandatory lockdowns and curfews that the CDC had hinted at a few weeks ago hadn't yet materialized. He tried to stay calm. At the next intersection, he would be able to turn and get out of this traffic.

He cursed car manufacturers who, despite the science fiction writings of the past couple of centuries, had still not created flying cars. That would certainly solve his current problem, although he admitted that, knowing people as he did, it would likely create a whole slew of additional problems. As many bad drivers as there were, how could things be better if they were flying?

Nearly ten minutes later, he reached that intersection, and he heaved a heavy sigh as he was able to move again, back toward his charge station. There was still an hour before the water truck would be at the store. He still had time.

As he approached the charge station, though, he began to have his doubts. Cars were lined up waiting for one of the twelve charge ports, and Randy had to stop in the street, and wait for the line to proceed enough for him to pull out of traffic. Drivers accelerated around him, often leaning on their horns as they sped past.

As Randy got closer, he noticed the sign in front, and he shook his head. Randy never imagined he'd ever have to pay five dollars per minute. And a hand-written sign taped under the price on the sign stated "cash only," and that there was a three-minute limit.

After nervously watching the numbers decline on his gauge, he was glad the engine didn't use any juice whenever he stopped. He was also nervously watching the clock on his dash. By the time Randy pulled up to the next available port, it was 12:50. As long as the water truck didn't get to the store early, he still had time.

Randy put a mask on and got out of his car, rushing to the attendant's booth to pay his cash.

"Only three minutes?" he asked, exasperated, pushing fifteen dollars through the slot.

"Afraid so," the kid said behind the glass, through the scratchy speaker. "We don't have much power available. We have to ration it."

The attendant locked in three minutes on the charger and nodded to him.

Randy ran back to his car and pulled a paper towel out of the dispenser. He wrapped the paper towel around the handle and shoved the plug into the outlet on his car, watching the gauge tick down toward zero from three minutes. It seemed slow as he stood there watching it, but it was too quickly for what he paid.

As it approached one minute, he heard scattered cursing, just as his own charger clicked off. He heard a burst of static, then the attendant's voice came out over the speaker mounted above his booth.

"Sorry, folks," he said. "That's all. I'm afraid we're out of juice. If you didn't get the charge you paid for, come to the booth and I'll refund the remainder."

Randy sighed. As he saw the people already lining up at the attendant's window, he considered just leaving it and rushing to the store. In the "old days," he likely would have done that. But with no income, and no end in sight, he decided he needed those five dollars.

He put the plug back and got in line.

By the time Randy finally got up to the window and collected his change, his pulse was pounding. He knew he was going to be late and would have to go back home without any water. He started up his car and growled impatiently as he had to jockey for space to pull away from the station among other customers and those who didn't get a charge.

Maneuvering through traffic again, he inched through another intersection with dark traffic lights, where an accident had just occurred. Nobody was hurt, but there were angry words being ex-changed, and Randy was glad when he was finally able to get past them.

By the time he pulled into the parking lot at King Soopers, it was 1:40. He remembered hearing stories about supermarkets, and the wide selection of goods they used to carry. He hadn't seen that in his lifetime, though. They were just stories told by older folks about the "good old days." Grocery stores now were pretty small and utilitarian.

He scanned the lot looking for a big truck, or for a large crowd of people. There were a few people, most of them wearing masks, fortunately, and holding umbrellas against the blazing sun. They were all loitering around the front entrance, leaving plenty of space between them.

But there was no truck.

Randy got out of his car and approached them, making sure to stop at least six feet away.

"Has the water truck already left?" he asked.

A couple of them shook their heads. One man wearing a white shirt and tie, and a name tag that said, "Geoff Borden, General Manager," spoke up.

"I'm afraid he hasn't gotten here, yet."

"Oh," Randy replied. "I would have thought there would be a lot more people here."

"There were," Borden answered. "Most of them gave up and left. Some of them said they were going to try their luck at a different store."

Randy nodded, looking around at the few who had stuck it out.

"I figure he's probably just stuck in traffic," Borden continued. "Traffic in the city can be a bear nowadays."

Randy nodded knowingly, lifting his hat and wiping the sweat from his forehead with his sleeve. He looked around as a box truck drove up. There was a collective sigh from the people around him, and everyone seemed to be fighting back the urge to crowd closer around the truck.

The driver and a passenger, both wearing masks and latex gloves, got down out of the cab, the driver shaking his head as he approached Borden, while the other man opened up the back of the truck. The waiting customers had their cash in their hands, and Randy followed suit.

"Oh my god!" the driver exclaimed to Borden.

"Rough drive, huh?"

The driver shook his head in exasperation, exhaling heavily into his mask.

"It's practically impossible to get across this town anymore."

Randy was next in line at the back of the truck, and he handed the man his cash, taking two gallon jugs from him.

"And I needed to get a charge, too," the driver continued, rubbing his face with his hands, "and after waiting in line for a half hour, some asshole ahead of me got the last drop of juice."

Randy hurried to his car.

SETTLING IN

I was a reasonably good shot with my father's bow, especially considering that I didn't use it very often. So, when I came back from my daily foraging expedition with *two* rats, Frida was ecstatic.

We hadn't had that much meat in one day since my father had come upon a starving deer years before. She had collapsed by the time he found her, but was not dead yet. Killing her, he said, had been a mercy, both for the doe and for the rest of us.

Both of the rats were fairly plump, and I wondered where they had been getting their food.

From my reading, I knew that rats, in most countries, had been considered disgusting and disease-ridden, and were not used for food. Some cultures, though, even during man's *Golden Age*, considered them acceptable as food.

In our current situation, we just didn't have the luxury of being too picky.

After leaving the rats with Frida, I went up onto the roof to inspect and water my garden. The green copper roof was slanted a little, but I had grown accustomed enough to it to be able to walk comfortably. It had also required me to build slanted stands for my planters, so that they were level. And this garden necessitated more water for me to transport.

By this time, I had finally developed a satisfactory shading system, with just the right amount of hemp fabric, set at just the right angle, allowing just enough of the oppressive sun that my plants were actually growing. From photographs in books that I had found about food of the past, I knew that my crops bore little resemblance to those in the *Golden Age*, but it was better than what I usually found in my foraging trips.

One of the crops that was doing reasonably well was watermelon. At maturity, they were small enough to hold in one hand, but their sweetness was welcome, and their seeds, besides the ones I saved for replanting, provided a little much-needed protein.

A couple of them were nearly ripe, but I let them be. The rats would provide enough protein for us today.

I realized that I felt slightly cooler than usual, and I looked up. I was in the shade of a rather large cloud. That's not to say that the heat wasn't still intense, but the relief was tangible. It was so rare to see clouds, and when we did, they usually burned off quickly. I didn't get my hopes up.

I went back down into the Library, relieved as always to be in the relative coolness of inside. I began peeling off the garments that were necessary for being outside, hanging them on nails that I had driven into the wall for the purpose of drying our sweat-soaked clothing. While I was inside, at home, I usually only wore shorts.

I plopped down into a chair and I saw what Frida had been working on while I was out. The painting, done entirely from memory, was a portrait of her parents. The fact that I recognized them was a tribute to her amazing talent, and her memory.

She came back into the room and sat in her own chair in front of the canvas. She looked at me and I shook my head in awe.

"You have such a gift," I said softly.

Her face pinkened slightly and she smiled, as she turned modestly back toward the painting, looking at what she had done so far. This was her usual reaction to my compliments, but I know it was not just an affectation. Her modesty was sincere, and in proof of that, she turned back to me with tears resting on her lower lids. Reaching for my hand, she tilted her face a bit, which sent the tears cascading out the downhill side of her eyes.

"You know," I said, "people used to have cameras."

She knew about cameras, since we had discussed how the photographs of paintings were printed in the art books that were filling her burgeoning personal library.

"I don't mean just the authors of your art books, but virtually everyone. Cameras were even built into their communication devices. In fact, I suspect that's what most people used their personal communication devices for.

"My point is that people in the past took photographs all the time, of friends and family, pets, even their meals." Frida's eyebrows went down in disbelief at that. "I don't know why," I quickly added, getting to my point. "But they had pictures of their family members that they could carry with them and pull up to view whenever they wanted to."

We both looked back at her painting of her parents.

"They didn't know how good they had it," I concluded.

A clap of thunder sounded outside the open window, and we both uttered a sigh of relief as we heard a light pattering of rain outside.

"Come to bed with me," I said suddenly. Frida looked up at me, a curious look on her face. "I've read that people used to think of this as particularly romantic," I explained, "making love during a rain storm. I want to try it."

Frida smiled and leaned into me. Our lips found each other as we walked a little sideways toward our bed. Since I was only wearing shorts, Frida had already gotten me completely naked before I even had Frida's tunic up over her head.

Rubbing my hands over her already slippery back, I pressed my mouth harder against hers, loving, as always, the feeling of her bare breasts pressing against my chest. I was finally able to slip her shorts down, and we collapsed onto our bed.

We knew the rain wouldn't last very long or amount to much measurable moisture, but we had learned to appreciate even little things when they came along.

Nicki tossed her last bag in the trunk and pushed it closed. There was a little light in her garage this early morning, shining through the windows of the garage door from the streetlight across the street. So, the power was back on, for now. It had been spotty for a while. At least she wouldn't have to disconnect the garage door from the track to open and close it manually.

As she looked around for anything else she might need, her eyes were red, but they were dry. She had done enough crying for a while.

She got in her car and pressed her thumb against the pad on her dash. The car started and the garage door began rising. The sun wasn't even up yet, and it was already hot. As she fastened her seatbelt, her eyes were drawn, against her will, to the pickup next to her. But she forced her attention back to the navscreen in her own car as it started backing out of the garage.

She was amazed and horrified at the turn her life had taken in just a couple of weeks. She had been certain that they would be safe. They were young and healthy. They didn't bother much with the masks or gloves. And social distancing was fine for some, especially for those more susceptible. But she had always been gregarious. They had friends, friends who were also young and healthy.

The garage door began moving back down as the car backed out of the driveway. As she drove down her street, she glanced at certain houses, homes of friends. She knew that a few of them were fine. Several of them, though, were gone.

Lights flickered in a couple of the houses as she drove past, then went out, as did the streetlight in her rear-view mirror. "Just in time," she whispered to herself.

She turned on the radio, tuning it to the Public Radio station on her satellite radio service. The morning news program had just *started. The first story, the big one across the country, was about the CDC's announcement that they were finally initiating Section 361 of the Public Health Service Act. Starting at nine p.m., a nationwide mandatory lockdown was going into effect for everyone except a select few essential personnel, particularly in health and emergency services. Anybody caught outside their homes, whether on the roads or just on the sidewalk, would be subject to arrest unless they could supply irrefutable proof that they had necessary business "of an allowed nature."*

Nicki was fine with that. She finally recognized the wisdom of social distancing, of keeping isolated when an insidious threat like SHePF was going around.

She just didn't want to be isolated in her house.

Her first stop was Front Range Bank of Colorado Springs. She knew it wasn't open this early, but the ATM was all she needed. She had to have cash if she was going to be in extended lockdown away from home. It was just a few blocks away, so it didn't take long for her car to pull in to the drive-up ATM.

As she had feared when driving out of her neighborhood and seeing the lights go out again, there was no power. But she had hoped that they had backup power. Still, the "Out of Order" sign taped to the front of it told her that, power or not, she wouldn't be getting any cash from the machine. She had some, but she had planned to empty her account. She sighed, knowing that she'll have to delay her trip, and come in personally to close her account.

As her car pulled through the drive-up lane around the front of the bank, she noticed that some of the windows were darker than others. There were no reflections as she drove in front of them, and she could see the interior of the building. The windows had been broken out.

She sighed again. She hoped she had enough cash for today.

The Public Radio commentators were talking now about sporadic power outages happening across the country, some of them quite extended. They told about some companies, including banks, Nicki noted, which had gone out of business because of having no power and being cut off from the internet. If you can't connect to your customers, your markets or your service providers, you can't do business.

Kind of a moot point now, she thought, in light of the CDC mandate.

Nicki wondered if whoever broke into the bank actually got away with any money.

She shook her head and sighed. She hoped she would have better luck at the grocery store. If they had power.

As she drove toward the store, she remembered the barbecue they hosted on their back deck a couple of weeks ago. It had been their first of the season, and Nicki loved it as much as Tim did. Getting together with friends, enjoying the sweet barbecued pork ribs and potato salad, the grilled chicken and fresh roasted vegetables. It was hot, of course, but she didn't mind that. She had always liked the heat. It was the perfect beginning to the summer.

As the eastern horizon lightened, the next story on the radio caught her attention. A Federal Reserve spokesman was speaking about numerous factors, from the average cost of groceries and electricity, to foreign markets — when they could be reached. It was his determination that the value of the dollar had plummeted to nearly nothing.

Nicki had a bad feeling about the amount of cash she had in her purse.

That meant little, though, when she pulled into the parking lot of the grocery store. The store opened early, and she expected to have it pretty much to herself. She was surprised by the number of cars in the parking lot, some of them parked haphazardly around the front doors.

And not just the cars; the people! They were everywhere! Some were running in to the store at breakneck speed, fighting past those slower than them. Others were running out of the store, their arms loaded with necessities that they had gotten. The fact that the goods were not in bags, and that the people were running, implied to Nicki that they hadn't purchased the items, but looted them.

As she pondered whether she should try going in or not, police cars, their lights strobing, their sirens wailing, converged on the place. If the previous scene had suggested panic, the frantic activity in front of the store now screamed outright anarchy.

Police officers poured out of the cars, some with nightsticks in hand, others with guns drawn. Some of the looters dropped their spoils and ran, while some tried to run with their plunder still in hand. Physical conflicts erupted in one place after another, while a couple of the more courageous souls tried to snatch up things that others had dropped.

Nicki saw flames erupt near the front door, and if there was still any doubt in her mind, the gunshots that rang out convinced her that it wasn't worth it. In the trunk and the back seat, she had coolers and bags of virtually all the food she had. That, and whatever she could get at Ken's Corner Grocery, would have to do.

She spoke her next destination, and her car quickly pulled out of the parking lot and headed toward Highway 24.

The commentator was talking about how some businesses were considering instituting a barter system. Others, including some doomsday preppers and survivalists, were arguing in favor of using precious metals and gemstones as currency.

"Can't eat those, either," Nicki said under her breath.

Despite her plans being foiled on two counts, she felt better when she was finally on the highway heading toward her destination. She had inherited her father's cabin in the mountains, southwest of Colorado Springs, on the other side of Pikes Peak. With the increasing tension in the city, she decided that, if she had to endure isolation, the cabin would be a much more peaceful location for her to do it.

Manfred, Colorado was little more than a bulge in the sporadically-paved road off Highway 67. But it had a gas station, a coffee shop and a little grocery store. This will be the first time she had gone there alone, but she felt good about it. As good as she thought she could.

She was anticipating a dinner cooked on the stone barbecue pit, right next to the clear, cold stream that tumbled over the rocks behind the cabin. Nicki always thought that food cooked outside tasted better, and food cooked outside in the mountains was the best.

She didn't know for certain if there was any difference. Maybe it was just her imagination. But it was something to look forward to, anyway. It had been a while since she had anything to look forward to.

A week after the barbecue, when Nicki felt the cold coming on, of course the virus was in the back of her mind. But then, she got over it. She was fine. Whether it was SHePF or a cold, she had fought it off.

Then, Tim got sick. The cold symptoms hit him a little worse, but again, they ended. The nightmare had passed them by.

But it was just beginning.

She shook her head and redirected her attention back to the road. And the scenery! Driving in the mountains, the forest gliding past her, always made her feel better. The forest was mostly brown, now, but still, it was like returning to an old friend. She couldn't help smiling, even if the sadness was still there in her eyes.

Other than a few brief patches in the canyons, the satellite radio had performed admirably, keeping her company for the whole trip, although Nicki's attention tended to drift from time to time. But now that she was approaching the cabin, she was more focused. The gravel washboard road was hard to ignore. Her car slowed down to reduce the vibration.

Her car turned onto the long dirt driveway, lined with pines and aspens on either side. It took nearly a minute to drive the length of the driveway before she emerged into the clearing. The little cabin appeared in front of her, and she sighed. It had been months since she had been here. Now that she was back, she could feel the tension melting away, or at least diminishing.

The cabin rose golden from the forest floor, its varnished pine logs warmly aged. The forest wrapped around it and closed back in behind it. Nicki's car pulled up in front of it and stopped, powering down.

She felt the tears threatening to return again, but she wouldn't let them. Not yet. She wanted to get everything carried in and put away first. After she was settled, there would be plenty of time for crying.

§

After unloading her car and getting everything put away, especially the food, she took a leisurely walk around the grounds. First, she went out back and was glad to find that the fuel oil tank was nearly full. Almost 350 gallons of oil, which she would use only for refrigeration and occasional cooking, when she wasn't cooking outside, should last a while. It was old-fashioned, but effective.

There was already quite a stockpile of wood cut, thanks to Tim on their last couple of visits here. She would only use it in the fireplace if it got particularly cold at night, which was not likely. Mainly, it would be used for fires in the fire pit.

She found a few spots where deer had come and grazed, leaving deposits of their smooth round droppings. She found dark, coarse fur stuck in the bark of a pine beside the stream, and two sets of parallel gouges a few feet above it, where a bear had stopped to scratch its back, and possibly to mark its territory.

Though the forest was in better shape here, still several of the pines were a reddish brown. Whatever ones the pine beetles hadn't killed, the thinning atmosphere and blazing sun were tirelessly working on.

She heard the songs of a few birds in the forest, though, and she smiled at the proof of life around her. People may be screwing up the planet in more ways than she could count, but it wasn't too far gone. Not yet, anyway.

The happy sound of the stream lifted her spirits a bit, although it was little more than a trickle, now. And she couldn't help but be reminded of happier times spent here when she wasn't completely alone. She slowly wandered in random directions, just looking and thinking, remembering those times.

The sky was a pale blue, shining cloudless above her. She remembered her father reminiscing about when he was a boy, and the bright blue sky that Colorado had, years ago, become famous for. She didn't recall ever seeing what he described. Now, it was usually bright, pale and cloudless.

After a time, which could have been an hour or three, she found herself back at her starting point behind the cabin. She pulled one of the folding camp chairs out of the little shed beside the fuel tank and opened it up in the shade beside the stream. Plopping herself down in it, she sat there completely still, pondering the trickling water. That sound, more than anything else, along with the sights and smells of the forest, always helped her empty her mind of bad thoughts and memories, and she certainly had some that she was happy to be rid of.

A couple of hours later, feeling drained, and yet, curiously, energized, she pushed herself up from the chair. She went back inside and ate a granola bar since she realized she hadn't eaten anything since her meager and rushed breakfast hours before. Picking up her purse, she went out to her car. Time for a supply run.

She didn't want to wait too long. The nationwide curfew was set to begin at nine o'clock, and the sun was going down. She didn't know how strictly they would be enforcing out here in the middle of nowhere, but still, she expected to be back at the cabin well before then.

She remembered the last supply run she had made, back home. Tim had been so sick, wheezing and coughing until he doubled up in pain. Nicki felt bad for him and decided to run to the store for a cough suppressant and some NyQuil.

From where he lay on the sofa, he watched her leave. Nicki promised she would only be gone a few minutes. The look on his face tugged at her heart.

"Radio," she said, looking at the dashboard. The screen lit up and the Public Radio evening news program was on. She didn't necessarily want to listen to anything, but she liked the noise, the drone of voices in the background. She didn't feel so lonely then. She wanted to purge the memories.

As she approached Manfred, the little town captured her attention as it always did. There may have not been much to it, but she loved it. The buildings were quaint and well-kept, better than the run-down buildings in some other mountain towns.

She could feel her tension melting away again. She had always adored the Victorian-era trim on the houses, the picket fences, the colorful flowers in the flower beds – although she noticed that the flower beds seemed neglected now. If SHePF was a big concern up here, too, it was certainly understandable. They had more important things to worry about than tending flowers.

She didn't see anybody out and about, though. That seemed odd to her. It had always been such a friendly little town. People out for a stroll would make it a point to smile and wave, even at strangers. But the blazing sun and the soaring temperatures were likely keeping people inside.

She took a deep breath and sighed as Ken's Corner Grocery showed up ahead. It was a small store, but they always had a surprising selection of everything she had needed. But as she drove up in the deepening twilight, she could see that it was dark inside.

She must have waited too long. She'd have to come again in the morning when they opened.

As she prepared to turn around in the little parking lot, though, her headlights illuminated the sign on the door showing their hours of operation. They were supposed to be open until 9:00. She pressed her foot on the brake pedal, overriding the auto-drive. With her headlights shining through the glass, beyond the sign, she could see a few empty shelves inside.

She puzzled over her suddenly changed situation, as the words in the current story on the radio caught her attention. A correspondent was telling of a trend in small towns across the country. Larger cities had more and larger grocery stores and other suppliers of goods. People in some rural areas were perceiving this as a greater guarantee of security in these uncertain times, and were abandoning their homes where supplies might be scarce, and moving into dirt-cheap apartments in metropolitan areas.

Nicki lifted her foot from the brake pedal and spoke her next destination, the cabin. The car shifted into reverse and pulled out of the parking lot. Manfred suddenly looked a lot different. She headed back toward her cabin, looking at the dark windows in the houses of this new ghost town.

Her last run to the store had been more successful, though the memory was one she wished she could forget. She had a large bottle of NyQuil, a cough suppressant, and several cans of chicken noodle soup. She was going to heat a can of soup for Tim right away. That, along with the medicines, would make him feel better for sure.

The sight that greeted her eyes, though, was one that she had, thus far, been unable to purge from her memory. It revisited her whenever she closed her eyes, especially before she went to sleep. If she was able to sleep.

She had come in the door and found Tim lying on the sofa where she had left him. He looked at her, panting, exhaustion weighing heavily on his eyelids. But that wasn't the part that Nicki kept seeing.

Tim held a wad of tissues in his hand, and they were saturated with blood. He had tried to contain it when he started coughing, but in time, as the coughing continued, he no longer had the strength to hold his hands up to his mouth.

The blood was soaking the front of his pajamas, the back of the sofa, and had even sprayed on the wall behind it, and was dripping from the framed oil painting. Nicki froze when she saw him, her breath stuck in her chest, wavering between wanting to rush to him and comfort him, and horrified by the grisly scene.

Each inhalation gurgled in Tim's chest. Each exhalation caused blood to bubble at his lips. Until the last one. The wheezing and gurgling stopped. But even without that, she would have known. There was something about his eyes, the way they looked a little past her, or through her, not quite focused.

She wiped the tears away, watching the bumpy road, now deep in shadow from the encroaching forest and the fleeing sun. She almost missed the narrow driveway that cut through the trees, but fortunately, her car didn't, and when she finally stopped in front of the cabin, the headlights emphasized the darkness of the windows like those in the other houses in town.

The car powered down, plunging her in darkness. The sky overhead was a washed-out reddish color, and when her eyes adjusted, it illuminated her view a bit, but the dark forest rising up behind the cabin looked sinister and threatening.

She hurried from her car into the cabin, quickly closing the door behind her. As she lit an old-fashioned propane lantern, she marveled at how oppressive the empty, isolated cabin suddenly seemed to her. She picked up the lantern and carried it to the sofa, placing it on the table in front of her.

She sat down and shivered, despite the heat. She pulled her feet up on the sofa and wrapped her arms tightly around her legs. The

*tears returned, now, unbidden, as she put her head down on her
knees and cried.*

ALMOST PARADISE

I wish I could have seen this place in its heyday. I can imagine it, looking past the rubble and the dust and the rot. But to actually see it at its best! This place must have been constantly packed with people seeking the abundance of knowledge that it contained.

The shelves containing the books are my favorite part of the place, but I've become quite fond of what the Library's informational materials humbly call The Reading Room. This magnificent room, located in an enormous rotunda under the main dome of the building, directly to the west of our living quarters, contains tables and chairs arranged in a circle around what seemed to be a central altar, although it was likely the station of librarians, assigned to assist the learners.

I've spoken about how my days go, scrounging for food and other usable items. I've also mentioned how our time was so much harder than days in the past. And all of that is true.

But still, my life with Frida, despite those hardships, was a good one. Neither of us had an easy life. Since we didn't live back in man's *Golden Age,* only the few years in our own lifetimes were all we were able to compare to. And compared to those, despite the absence of both sets of parents, and the friends that we had lost, we agreed that the years we spent living in the Library of Congress together were the best of our lives.

I honestly didn't spend that much time outside. It was too deadly. Okay, potentially deadly, but definitely uncomfortable. Some of my time was spent exploring the Library itself. Not just the books and the art, but the doorways, the rooms and passages. That was how I discovered the tunnels.

Apparently, in the past, the subway, an underground train system, stopped near the Library. Those tunnels that the train traveled through had passages up to ground level. After I found that, I wedged some debris under the one door at the main entrance that opened, to discourage any others who might stumble across our home.

After that foraging time in the early morning was done, I spent my time perusing the shelves of books in the Library, and reading them in The Reading Room. Besides history tomes and biographies and the so-called "do-it-yourself" books, I had developed a fondness for adventure novels. Once I understood the concept of fiction, I began to marvel at how authors could weave stories that were not real, but that still were able to pull the reader into them, making them care about the characters in the novels, and about what happened to them.

Frida and I were both growing our own personal libraries up in our living quarters, and we spent some very happy times lounging together on our bed browsing the books that we had brought up to our room.

She would delight in sharing with me a beautiful, luminous landscape by an artist named Maxfield Parrish, and I would show her how houses in the past were equipped with refrigerators, large appliances that would actually generate and enclose a cold atmosphere in order to keep food fresh for days at a time. We had a refrigerator in our old house, but it didn't do that.

My library was growing, partly, with books that were little more than nostalgia, like books about historical figures or events in the past. But it also contained books that were useful to me, like books on xeriscape food gardening and maintaining a solar energy system, as well as my adventure novels.

Frida's library was now bulging with books on artists, some whose names I knew from my own reading, and some that were completely unfamiliar to me. Da Vinci and Mucha. Michelangelo and Van Gogh. Botticelli and O'Keeffe.

She also gathered books on textiles. We didn't have access to a wide variety of fibers as our forebears did, but some of what she learned she applied as she made new garments for us, incorporating little decorative details. In the grand scheme of things, since we were the only ones around, they didn't make any difference. But they were attractive little details that we appreciated.

Some of our favorite times were after we had exhausted the new books we had found and put them aside. Lying side by side on our bed, we would often turn to each other and begin a different exploration, our hands caressing the other's body, pushing aside the clothing that separated us from paradise.

My exploration of the library had led to some surprising discoveries. People in the past seemed to write books on absolutely everything imaginable. Sex was a main topic to which pages and pages were devoted.

I brought a few volumes up for us to investigate, and I must admit that our lovemaking took on a new dimension as we tried some suggestions. Others, honestly, did not interest us at all and were roundly dismissed.

But those times we spent together were the best of our lives.

Up until the darkness came.

POWERLESS

Marlis scratched a match to life and touched it to the wick of the lavender candle beside her favorite chair. Before the match burned out, she lit the honey-scented candle next to it. She loved the combination of those two scents more than any other, and burning next to her chair while she read made for a relaxing experience.

Marlis was a devout introvert. In her past life, she had spent a great deal of time online. Most of her friends were people that she had never actually met, online entities who shared her introversion, and with whom she could be completely herself.

When the CDC's lockdown order went into effect, a lot of people lamented not being able to go out and socialize with their friends. But Marlis was fine with that. Her life didn't really change at all. She already worked from home as a contributing blogger for a number of companies' web sites. As long as she got her blog entries done on time, she could make her own hours.

Those hours allowed her plenty of time for one of her favorite activities, reading. A lot of people spent their time watching TV. The SHePF virus had proven to be a windfall for the numerous streaming networks.

Marlis, though, preferred to let her mind create the images. She was a voracious reader. It was safe to say that she had spent half her life in the company of Austen and Wilde, Orwell and Tolstoy, Brontë and Brontë, and several modern authors, as well.

She was drawn into the stories she read, living them for the duration of the book. The images that the words conjured, the people that her mind materialized, became her life while she was in it. Real life just didn't compare.

When the first SHePF-related death occurred in her building, the threat became more real to Marlis. The elderly woman wasn't someone that Marlis knew personally, but she had greeted her a *few times. Marlis passed by her door to get to the mailbox. She seemed nice.*

Now, she was dead, and despite the limited contact that Marlis had ever had with her, she was shaken. The violent fleetness with which the virus struck and took its victims filled Marlis with a fear unlike any of the numerous fears she had ever experienced in her life.

Within a couple of weeks, seven other people in the building contracted the disease. Five of them died. SHePF anxiety now strengthened Marlis' already firm resolve to keep to herself.

But overall, despite that fear which was always there, the lockdown didn't really affect her life much, aside from having her groceries delivered, a luxury she had never indulged before. But that simply gave her more time for reading, her favorite therapy.

When the power started going out a few weeks before, though, that was a different matter. It was sporadic at first, with pockets of power in scattered places around the country. But the virus had been relentless, particularly when people resisted lockdown orders. Essential workers, like those at power companies, worked valiantly to keep it going, but people were still dying, and there weren't enough knowledgeable people to go around.

When the grid went down completely, so did the internet, and so did the phone networks. So that meant that she was also now unemployed. Virtually everyone else was, too, though, so she wasn't alone in that. The hardest part for her was going cold turkey from her online friends. She was an introvert, but she still felt the need for a certain amount of human interaction. The internet provided that for her. And now, it was gone.

While she missed the virtual friends that she had across the country and around the world, she sometimes made brief and cautious contact with others in her building. On those daily occasions in the past when she used to venture forth with mask and gloves, when the mail was still being delivered, she sometimes met a neighbor, uttering a concise greeting from a safe distance. Aware of the deaths that had occurred in her building, those face-to-face times were tense, but they did provide momentary proof that she wasn't the last one left.

Now, there was no mail. Marlis didn't leave her apartment unless it was absolutely unavoidable which, fortunately, wasn't that often. Groceries were still being delivered, though they were getting expensive and severely rationed. Marlis had lost weight, which she figured wasn't a bad thing.

And she had plenty of time to read.

Reading during the day was the easiest. Often, as long as she was shaded from the relentless sun, she would go out on her balcony with Mr. Knightley or Mr. Darcy, perhaps with Winston or Dorian. Going to bed when it got dark became her habit, and she never went to bed alone. She would always take one of her companions with her.

Although there were times when she just couldn't sleep. Like tonight.

Marlis had taken a couple of bags of trash down to the street that afternoon. The waste collection companies weren't officially in operation any longer, but a few hardy individuals from them had taken it upon themselves to occasionally gather the trash in their neighborhoods and carry it away. Marlis didn't know where they took it, but she was glad to be rid of it.

Today, though, one of them told her that he had heard through his grapevine that they had officially stopped keeping a tally of the death toll. Marlis remembered back when she heard that more than twenty million Americans had died from this insidious virus, and it broke her heart.

Now, the death toll had gone so high, they couldn't even keep track. She couldn't fathom that many dead people. More than twenty million Americans? How many around the world? Millions? Billions?

No wonder she couldn't sleep. She hoped a couple of chapters and the relaxing honey lavender scent would help her to relax enough to fall asleep.

But Mr. Rochester was particularly surly tonight, and his irascibility, on top of the bleak statistical news she had received that day, meant that Marlis just couldn't loosen up. With a sigh, she got up out of her chair, blew out the honey-scented candle and picked up the lavender candle. If only she could take a warm bath. But those days were over, as well.

Marlis felt tears rush to her eyes. She didn't know if they were prompted by the deaths of all those – to her – total strangers, or if it was the grim and terrifying monotony that her life had become.

No wonder she preferred the worlds her literary companions invoked.

She carried the candle into her bedroom and, her body shaking, she got undressed.

§

It took a while, but Marlis finally slept fitfully for a few hours. When she awoke in the half light of dawn, she turned, and her eyes came to rest on Edward Rochester. His brooding face was softened by a hint of a smile.

Marlis was certain it was a sympathetic smile. Her lovers always understood the trials of her life. And who understood trials better than Edward? What a sorry and unhappy life he had led, being stuck with that madwoman, Bertha! No wonder he spent so much time away from home.

Just the opposite of Marlis' troubles. She couldn't get away from home.

Not that she wanted to.

Especially now that Edward was with her, things were looking up. Marlis snuggled into his arms and sighed, smiling at this happy turn of events. Tomorrow night, she might be with Dorian, or Heathcliff, or perhaps Fitzwilliam.

But for now, her strength drained away, and she gave herself entirely to Edward.

DARKNESS AT DAWN

What's wrong with me?" Frida asked me. I helplessly shrugged my shoulders. I wanted to be more help than that. I really did. But we just didn't have doctors anymore. Not for quite a long time. I didn't know what was wrong.

For several days in a row, Frida had woken up vomiting. At first, we had thought that what she had eaten the night before was not agreeing with her, as the old saying went. But I had eaten the same things. Why wasn't I affected?

Once again, we felt the lack, the disadvantage—well, one of them—of not having any other people around. We had nobody to talk to about shared complaints or similar experiences.

I spent much of that day in the library doing research. What I found was a little surprising.

"I think," I said haltingly, "you might be pregnant."

Frida looked at me for quite a long time. After a while, I began to think that she hadn't heard me.

"Did you hear me?" I asked.

"I did," she replied, quite a bit more calmly than I felt. Her eyebrows were already formed into a frown. Then, she cocked her head to the side as she started to reply. "I thought I couldn't get pregnant," she said.

"That was purely an assumption, since nobody in our group ever did."

Tears pooled in her eyes, and I knew they weren't happy ones.

"Press, I know we only have, at best, a few more years here." I hated that she knew that. "How can we bring a baby into this?" She spread her hands, gesturing around her, and while I looked around me, I knew she meant more than just our wonderful Library home. I knew we both felt the same way about bringing a child into the world, especially if we were both, likely, going to end up abandoning it before it was even able to take care of itself.

We spent the rest of that day holding each other.

Then, the headaches started.

Frida had complained of a headache a few times recently. Initially, we hadn't thought much of it. But they were becoming more prevalent. One afternoon, she tried to ask me what the problem might be, but she couldn't think of the words.

Then, there was her fatigue, which was becoming common more days than not, along with the aforementioned nausea. But her headaches were getting to be more commonplace, as well, and of greater severity.

Again, I didn't go foraging. I went and got our water for the day and emptied our toilet bucket, but I stayed in after that. I spent the day in the Library, doing research.

I didn't like what I found.

§

"I think it might be something called a 'brain tumor.'" I spoke quietly, but Frida, unfortunately, heard me.

"That doesn't sound very good," she said a little shakily.

"No," I replied. I couldn't meet her gaze. I kept my eyes glued to my hands clasped in my lap. "If . . . if it's cancerous, you—" My throat closed up and I had to force myself to push ahead. I took a deep breath and let it out slowly while I closed my eyes. "You may have twelve to eighteen months at the most."

When I finally opened my eyes again, I couldn't see anything except for basic shapes and colors through the tears. I rubbed the tears away and looked at Frida. Her eyes were dry.

"Are you sure?" she asked. I shook my head.

"Of course not," I said, my eyes filling again. "I have no way of being sure." I reached out and took her hands in mine. She didn't fight it. She just sat there. "All I could do," I continued, "was research your symptoms."

"My headaches and nausea and fatigue," she said.

"And," I said hesitantly, quietly, "your inability to think of words." I looked down at our hands as if I was ashamed, as if the words I was saying were accusations. "And I remembered the last time we made love. I noticed your body was skinnier than usual. It looks like you've been losing weight."

She nodded, but didn't respond. As the silence stretched on, I closed my eyes, trying to blot out two images. First, the image of Frida that I was imagining based on photographs and descriptions of what cancer does to a person. The second was the image of the rest of my life without her.

Frida took a breath and sighed.

"Well," she said, "at least I won't be leaving a baby to this."

STILL EXPENDABLE

Cancer Alley was the colloquial name of a nearly 100-mile-long stretch of the Mississippi River in Louisiana that, during parts of the 20th and 21st centuries, was lined with countless chemical plants and other industries, built right among residential neighborhoods.

Up until just a few decades ago, oil refineries were also a part of that mix. But as petroleum sources dried up and new ones proved prohibitively expensive to tap, the automotive industry as a whole, with a certain general reluctance, finally made the total switch over to electric-powered vehicles. The refineries, depending on their fiscal preparedness, had either gone out of business or re-tooled for other industries.

But they remained where they were, dwarfing their surrounding neighborhoods with their ugly gargantuan structures. They either continued belching smoke and other exhausts, filtered just enough to accommodate the imposed bureaucratic standards, into the air and the Mississippi River, or rusted and disintegrated, all but forgotten.

§

Teddy Monroe was hot and miserable. And discouraged.

The HazMat suit she was wearing, combined with the merciless Louisiana sun beating down on her, made her hot and miserable. The result of their mission was the source of her discouragement.

She thought wishfully about the modern suits she had seen that were totally encapsulating, and circulated fresh, cool air throughout them. But The Spectrum Foundation, from its early days, was a non-profit organization. Charities, like even most for-profit organizations, were operating now with drastically reduced personnel and miniscule budgets. Money bought so little these days, and those who had any had to save it for the meager necessities it would purchase. Spectrum could not afford top-of-the-line HazMat suits. Teddy was thankful, at least, for the filtered respirator.

"Over there," she pointed. Ray Harmon, Teddy's partner on this mission, looked ahead to where she pointed. Two people were huddled in the entryway of a dirty apartment building.

Teddy got there first, though she already knew before she saw them up close. She saw the blood puddled around them, dried into crusty brown stains. She saw the swarms of flies scatter as she approached. Unable to escape as quickly as the flies, the maggots squirmed there, as well.

Teddy didn't need to disturb them in order to confirm the theory that she had been forming. Actually, not so much a theory as a fact. And it wasn't even hers, but she had adopted it as her own. And here, it was confirmed. She could see the dark brown skin, the tightly curled black hair.

She reached up to wipe away the tear that had broken free from her eye before she remembered the plastic face plate above the respirator.

She heard Ray sigh as he reached her side. He lifted the old, scuffed tablet with the scratched screen and the blurry image, and he made two marks with the stylus.

Teddy looked sadly at him as she shook her head and stepped past the latest corpses they had found and reached for the door. It opened with no resistance. Folks in this neighborhood, she had found, rarely had any kind of security entrance.

She stepped inside, but then she stopped and leaned against the wall.

"Teddy?" Ray said. "Are you okay?"

She echoed Ray's sigh and looked at him.

"I wanted to help people, Ray," she said. She looked down at the tablet in Ray's hands. "I didn't want to just tally the dead. I wanted to actually make a difference in the world. That's why I joined Spectrum in the first place. I thought that I might be able to get past the color barrier that has existed for over two hundred fucking years and actually help people, for a change, regardless of their skin color."

"I know, baby," Ray replied. The term of endearment escaped his lips before he had a chance to reel it in. But after it was out there, he was glad. He had been attracted to Teddy for a while now. Her compassion mirrored his — in fact, her compassion seemed to dwarf his own. She was truly empathetic and moved by the plight of others, and that made her that much more appealing to him than just her physical appearance.

To his chagrin, though, it seemed as if she had missed it.

"Do you remember that book we studied in our sociology class, Expendable – Exploring the Link Between Racism and the Death of Planet Earth, written by Dr. Jodi Alexander?" Ray nodded. "She really put herself out there, experiencing, for a short time at least, what the Sioux at Standing Rock experienced, and the Blacks in Georgia, and—"

"Yeah," Ray nodded again, "I remember. She was definitely a badass!"

Teddy looked at Ray, her eyes boring through the plastic face-plate.

"I wanted to be like her. I wanted to actually help these people," she motioned toward the corpses showing through the glass of the door, her eyes filling with tears, "not just count their dead bodies!"

"I know," Ray said, grasping her shoulder, wishing he could hold her without the HazMat suits between them.

"The whole point of Dr. Alexander's book," Teddy continued, "was that people of color were always exploited. Water treatment plants or oil pipelines or refineries were always built in or near their neighborhoods, because privileged white people didn't want that shit near them."

She motioned out toward the street they had just walked in from.

"In all these decades since she wrote her book, not a goddamn thing has changed!" She moved her hand up toward another tear, then, disgusted, just blinked her eyes to push it out and down her cheek. "We still put the refineries and the factories in the neighborhoods of people of color, because we don't want them near us. And they're still the ones who die."

"Honey, a lot of white people have died, too. SHePF hasn't paid any attention to skin color."

"No, but I'll bet you a million dollars that, when we get back to the office and start compiling the numbers with the other groups, black people and brown people will far outnumber white people in number of deaths."

"Why? What does their neighborhood have to do with whether they're taken out by a killer virus?"

"They're almost always poorer," Teddy replied. "Like Dr. Jodi Alexander said, they don't have the money to fight corporations who want to build a water treatment plant in their back yard, or run an oil pipeline through their sacred land. They don't have the sympathy and the backing of the general public to get behind them."

She saw Ray's eyebrows scrunch together behind his faceplate and realized that she lost him.

"They're the undesirables. They're expendable. They get what nobody else wants. If they do get anything beneficial, it's only after we've taken what we want from it.

"Remember early on when SHePF took us by surprise, and stores ran out of face masks and disinfectant and alcohol wipes?"

"Sure. People had gone out and emptied the shelves before the stores started placing a limit on purchases."

"People who could afford it emptied the shelves," she corrected. "Chances are people in neighborhoods like this didn't get to stock up. And when the things were available again, the first shipments went to those who clamored for them the loudest.

White, affluent, educated. People in neighborhoods like this are the poorest of the poor, one step up from homeless.

"They can't afford anything beyond the most basic education, if any, because if they do get any money, it has to go toward food and rent."

"What does their education level have to do with it?" Ray asked.

"People of lower socioeconomic status, including lower levels of education, are likely to die earlier and have a higher incidence of disease than others. And that's not even counting when a killer pandemic is wreaking havoc around the world.

"Without education, their reading skills and comprehension are likely poor, so they may not even understand the importance of the most basic precautions. Look around. I haven't seen a single mask on any of these bodies."

Ray looked back toward the corpses huddling on the other side of the dirty glass in the door and nodded sadly. Teddy took a deep breath and blew it out as a long sigh.

"Come on," she said, turning down the hallway, "let's get this over with."

Ray followed morosely behind her to start knocking on doors. The first apartment they came to, they were greeted by silence. After knocking a second time, Teddy tried the doorknob. It was locked. She turned and looked at Ray and nodded.

Ray stepped up. When they had started out on this venture, he had looked forward to a little display of manliness in front of Teddy. Now, he just felt gloomy.

He threw his weight forward as he lifted his foot, kicking the door right beside the doorknob. The door exploded inward with the splintering of the door jamb, wood that was at least forty years old, likely more.

The apartment was a mess. Dirty and cluttered, as Teddy had expected, but more than that. It was as if someone on the verge of death panicked and knocked over anything that wasn't nailed down.

A few steps into the apartment told Teddy that her assessment was probably pretty accurate.

A Black woman, perhaps twenty-five years old, lay on the floor, a baby grasped in her arms. Both had old blood caked around their mouths and noses. Flies swarmed away temporarily at the sudden movement near them, then resumed their places.

A sob caught in Teddy's throat at the sight. Ray sighed heavily and made two new tick marks on his tablet.

"Stay here," he said, and he made his way into the apartment to finish the inspection on his own.

"Just the two," he said quietly as he got back to the entryway. He put his hand on Teddy's shoulder, gently directing her out the door. Their instructions were to not disturb anything, just to make a quick inspection and count.

The remaining three apartments on the first floor were unlocked, and yielded seven more bodies, four of them children. Ray could see after the first apartment how it was affecting Teddy, so he entered the apartments himself and made the count while she waited in the hallway.

"Shall we go to the second floor?" he asked, but Teddy was already turned away from him. He frowned as he watched her, thinking she might be on the verge of running away crying. But she stood at the base of the stairs, her head tilted sideways, turning slightly to try to get the best angle.

Then, he heard it, a metallic banging upstairs.

Teddy was already racing up the stairs as quickly as the baggy HazMat suit would allow. Ray was right behind her.

She stood outside apartment 2C, listening to the noise.

"That's not a rhythmic sound," she said, her eyes wide. The sound stopped for a few moments, and she looked quickly at Ray. When it started again, she pounded on the door.

The noise stopped again, and she stood there waiting, an almost wild, anticipatory look on her face. Then, the banging started again. She looked at Ray, then she turned toward the door and tried to turn the knob. It was locked. Not waiting for Ray, she threw herself against the door. The door jamb splintered like the one downstairs.

Ray followed her into the apartment, which looked much like the first one as far as the squalor and the clutter. The first room off the entry was the living room. Aside from the filth, it was empty. Across the hall was the kitchen.

A woman, her head-full of cornrow braids pulled back into a thick ponytail, lay on the floor, completely still, her mouth and nose caked with old, dried blood. Two feet away from her sat a little girl, a toddler, her own hair pulled into two short unkempt pigtails, sat looking up, surprised, at Teddy. The wooden spoon and the saucepan in her hands were paused in mid-strike.

"Oh my god," Teddy said breathlessly.

She stepped forward toward the little girl and dropped to her knees in front of her. Ray dragged his eyes away from the scene only long enough to make a single tick mark on his tablet.

"Honey," Teddy said, "are you okay?"

The little girl, recovered from her surprise, smiled and started banging on the bottom of the saucepan again. Teddy reached out and took the spoon and the pan out of her hands and put them down on the floor. She picked up the little girl and stood up.

"Do you see this, Ray?" she asked. "The blood?"

Ray looked at the little girl. Her mahogany-colored skin had camouflaged it, at first, but now, up close, he could see it. She had blood caked around her nose and mouth, just like her mother.

"She had the SHePF virus herself, but she, obviously, recovered from that advanced stage."

Ray thought it could just as easily, maybe even more likely, be the mother's blood, when the child kissed her or something like

that. Still, she had been closely exposed to the virus and had survived, so that was something.

But he looked at Teddy, seeing the hopeful, almost happy expression through her faceplate. He felt alright leaving her for just
a moment while he made a quick inspection of the rest of the apartment. Aside from an almost overflowing potty chair, he found
nothing of note in the rest of the apartment.

He came back to the kitchen and Teddy looked up at him. Her
face expressed such sublime satisfaction at the result of their inspection that he decided to call it quits for the day, making a quick
note on his tablet.

"Come on, honey," he said, putting his arm around Teddy and
leading her toward the door, "let's get her back to civilization."

Teddy smiled at him, and she allowed him to guide her down
the stairs. As they got out on the street, she leaned her head against
his shoulder.

EASE HER PAIN

The room that we had made into our living space was a large one, and it served our purpose well, once we pushed tables and chairs aside. This allowed us to clear space against the wall that had windows facing east. That was where we put the bed that we had found in a nearby house, along with one of the tables on each side, where we each kept several favorite books that we liked to peruse in bed.

This room, the Rare Book and Special Collections Division, according to the Library's documentation, contains books originally owned by Thomas Jefferson, a historical figure of some import when civilization was still intact. I had examined some of the books early on and found many of them to be, while informative, somewhat dry.

So, many of these books began to be displaced by our own growing personal library as we brought new favorites up from the stacks. This became even more true as I continued my extensive research on Frida's symptoms, and on cancer, specifically, when it became certain that this diagnosis was the correct one.

A lot of the time, in the past, when I was doing research on certain subjects, I would do it down in the main part of the Library, in The Reading Room, returning the books to the shelves when I was finished, unless I found a book that I liked enough to keep. In this case, though, I decided to gather piles and piles of books and lug them up to our living quarters to do the research. I didn't want to spend any more time away from Frida than I had to.

I decided that I could ease Frida's burden a bit by doing more of the tasks that she had traditionally done. In this way, my routines changed somewhat as I would come back from my foraging expeditions and prepare our breakfast with whatever I had found, supplemented by whatever was available or usable from my rooftop garden.

By this time, Frida would be waking up and we would have our breakfast together in bed, although, admittedly, some days she did not feel like eating. Some days, she only felt like vomiting. We kept a small bucket beside the bed since she often couldn't make it quickly enough to the area that contained our large toilet bucket.

On days when she felt strong enough, Frida would paint. When she didn't, I would read to her. Sometimes, it might be a book on a particular artist or art style, and she would enjoy the pictures in the book that I shared with her. However, by this time, she had also developed a fondness for classical romantic literature, so I might, instead, read to her from a novel by Jane Austen or Emily Bronte or Catherine Cookson.

I don't mean to say that she deteriorated quickly. It seemed quick to me, but a lot of days, she continued her previously accepted role. However, when she didn't have the strength, I was ready to help her with tasks that I hadn't, before, taken on.

These included things of a more personal and unpleasant nature, about which I won't elaborate, but which we both, admittedly, were embarrassed about.

But she was my Frida.

The money man cometh," Ed Bodsworth said as the helicopter touched down, blowing snow in all directions against an impossibly blue sky.

"Nah, he's not the money man," Joe Parker said coldly. "He's nothing more than a figurehead." He looked askance at Bodsworth. "You don't really expect anything good to come of this, do you?"

Bodsworth shrugged, though it was barely noticeable through his heavy parka.

They had known for a while that a consultant from the National Science Foundation was coming. Most of them were pessimistic about his visit. As with numerous other government agencies in recent years, the National Science Foundation had less to do with science now, and more about business.

They saw the figure climb down out of the helicopter and reach back for a suitcase.

"I hope he snores," Parker said. Bodsworth looked at him with his eyebrows scrunched together. "If he snores like you do," Parker explained, "I'm gonna shoot him. Problem solved."

Bodsworth shook his head as he turned back toward the approaching visitor. The wind had whipped out a lock of long, auburn hair from under the hood. Bodsworth and Parker glanced at each other as the figure pushed the hood back, revealing a head-full of that same auburn hair.

"Hi, boys," she said, holding out a hand covered with a down-insulated mitten. "Alex Patton."

§

The wind had become fierce, so relaxing in the main shelter with a cup of warm something was welcome as the howling continued outside. Alex Patton sipped a cup of hot tea. She studied Bodsworth and Parker, as they returned her look.

"How many people work here at Polynya Station?" she asked.

"We're a small station," Bodsworth replied. "There are eight of us who work here permanently. Mainly geologists and climatologists." Alex nodded.

"What exactly is it you do here?"

"We've published three papers so far," Parker said, sniffing the Scotch in his glass. "You haven't read them?"

"To be honest," she replied a little sheepishly, "I was sent to observe and advise. I'm afraid I don't know your history."

"Do you know science?"

"What do you know about the polynyas?" Bodsworth quickly asked, hoping to defuse Parker's simmering tension. Alex shook her head. Parker sighed, but Bodsworth tried to contain his frustration. "They're holes that open up periodically in sea ice. You probably passed over the Witherington Polynya on your way here, just before you landed."

"You mean that big lake out there?"

"Yes, except it's not a lake. That's a two-hundred-mile-wide hole in the ice shelf, with the ocean coming up through it. They used to appear every few years here in Antarctica, and for decades, they went unexplained. Now, they're happening more and more frequently, and in different places. We're trying to determine why."

"Do you have any theories?" Alex asked.

"Some," Bodsworth started, but Parker took over.

"They're mainly related to climate change," he said, watching for her reaction, "which I know you guys still have a hard time accepting, despite the overwhelming evidence. But I don't suppose you care to hear that."

"I want to hear the facts," Alex said simply, taking another sip.

"I didn't think facts mattered to your administration."

"An all-too-common misconception. We just have a few disagreements as to what constitutes a fact and an opinion." She smiled, but it wasn't returned.

"I'll be honest," Parker said, "I wasn't a bit broken up when SHePF killed McCauley."

"That's true," Bodsworth added with a snicker. "In fact, he did a little jig." He stopped, immediately sorry that he had shared that tidbit. Parker smiled at the memory, though. But then, the smile faded.

"As it turned out, though, Vice President Armstrong has proven himself to be an even worse president than McCauley was. A fact that I would have found extremely difficult to believe a year ago."

"President Armstrong is going to be at least as tough as President McCauley was," Alex said, ignoring the negative remark. "He cares about the environment, but he also feels that a strong environment will be useless if our economy is in tatters and the American people can't prosper and enjoy it."

"Maybe McCauley should have initially been a little more responsive to the threat of the virus."

"I'm afraid that virus took everybody by surprise," Alex replied, her calm showing signs of strain.

"That would probably be news to the previous administrations which had put virus response mechanisms in place, only to have them dismantled by McCauley. He just didn't want to be bothered by a deadly pandemic. He was too fucking worried about casting a pall over his reelection, and didn't think about the fact that people need to be alive to vote."

"He was reelected fair and square."

"He was reelected. I wouldn't say it was fair and square. You guys have a hard time winning elections when everybody can vote. And without your Electoral College, which should have been eliminated a couple of centuries ago.

"And incidentally, it occurs to me that you could be a little more responsive, as well."

"What do you mean?"

"Despite the rosy reports your beloved **Führer** keeps spewing, the virus is still going on. People are still dying every day, and you come here to our isolated outpost and don't even bother to wear a fucking mask! You people are so convinced of the rightness of your opinions, despite any and all evidence, and to hell with anybody who disagrees with you!"

"Haven't you heard?" Alex replied. "They've come up with a vaccine. I've been inoculated, despite the feelings of many to the contrary."

"We haven't," Parker replied. "Your own super-progressive efforts notwithstanding, this vaccine is still very new. How do we know you're not a fucking carrier?"

"Uh, Parker," Bodsworth said quietly, "are you forgetting that our funding may be dependent on Ms. Patton's testimony? Maybe we should stick to science and leave politics out of it."

"They don't believe in science," Parker gestured toward Alex.

"On the contrary, Mr. Parker. We believe in science. I just told you I've been vaccinated. We just don't believe in the pseudoscience gibberish so many insist on supporting."

"Such as?"

"Such as global warming."

Parker smiled a mirthless smile.

"Okay, so the fact that measurable scientific facts show that the average temperature of the earth has increased a little over two degrees in the last century and a half is known to be fake by you non-scientists in Washington?"

"Two degrees is negligible."

"But measurable, and with far-reaching consequences."

A fierce gust of wind shook the shelter and Alex pulled the neck of her sweater up and took a sip of her tea, which was quickly cooling off. She gestured toward the wall that was still shuddering.

"It's way below freezing out there," she said. "How does that fit in to your theory of global warming?"

"You probably had breakfast today, too," Parker said, "which, of course, disproves the myth of people dying of starvation."

"Okay," Alex said as she lifted her head, a confident smile appearing on her face, "what about rising sea levels? That's such an easy one to disprove."

"Really? How?"

"Try to remember back when you were hot and you had a glass of ice water. What happens if you don't drink it and you just let it stand there?"

"I stay hot and thirsty?"

"The ice melts. And what happens to the water? Does the glass overflow? No," she answered, not waiting for another of Parker's smartass responses. "The level of the water actually goes down." She raised her eyebrows at him as if she had sufficiently proven her point.

"Fascinating!" Parker said. "But what if you have a plate with a big pile of ice cubes on it? What'll happen if you just let it sit there?" Alex looked at him apprehensively, frowning as she tried to follow his analogy. "You're going to end up needing a pretty big wad of paper towels to clean up all the water that flows off that plate."

"What does that have to do—"

"That's what we're sitting on, sister!" Parker snapped. "Five and a half million square miles of rock covered with ice. Where do you suppose the water's going to go when the ice melts? Into the oceans, making them rise. I know it's hard to wrap your super-scientific mind around that spooky voodoo magic, but that's the way it is."

Alex was still processing the information. She had always pictured icebergs. She never thought of an actual land mass under the ice of Antarctica.

"But," she said, looking again toward the buffeting wall of the structure, vibrating violently under the force of the wind, "we don't have to worry about that, do we? I mean, how can the ice melt, as cold as it is here?"

"It's already melting," Bodsworth spoke up softly, not wanting to contribute to the tension. "For one thing, there are the polynyas that we're here to study, although those are over the sea, not land. But also, there's water between the ice and the rock. In fact there are whole rivers and lakes of water below the ice."

"If all the ice in Antarctica melted and ran off the plate," Parker added, "along with all the other ice, that would be enough water to raise the sea level around the world as much as two hundred feet. Washington D.C. would be underwater. Which would be a definite improvement.

"And it's melting faster than previously expected. And not just melting, but calving, chunks breaking off into the sea more frequently than before."

Alex seemed shaken by that revelation, but Bodsworth tried to calm her fears.

"That two-hundred-foot rise is not going to happen, though," he said. "The consensus is three feet to possibly a maximum of six feet rise in sea level in the next century."

"Yeah," Parker said, "we'll completely fuck up the planet in some other way long before the rest of the polar ice melts."

A door opened, allowing a blast of freezing air into the shelter as six people noisily filed in from their day's work. They quieted down when they noticed the almost tangible agitation in the air.

§

"Mr. Parker certainly is a cheery soul," Alex said. She was bunking with Julie Allen and Debbie Hamilton, both climatologists, and the only women permanently posted here at Polynya Station.

Alex was wearing a mask, now, just in case.

Dinner had been a noisy, but generally pleasant affair, even though they made her sit at the end of one of their tables while the rest of them crowded at the other end of that table or around the second one.

Just in case.

Still, it felt good to relax now in the relative quiet. Relative, because the wind still raced outside.

"Yeah, he's kind of an asshole sometimes," Julie acceded.

"What's even more maddening, though," Debbie added, "is that he's seldom wrong about anything."

"Just ask him. He'll tell you," Julie laughed.

"Hmm," Alex responded, his comments about the melting ice and the rising sea level still on her mind.

"So, you were asking about all of us at dinner," Debbie said. "What about you? What's your field?"

"My field?" Alex asked nervously.

"Of science."

Alex took a deep breath, remembering how poorly matched she had been with Parker and Bodsworth in their discussion of natural science.

"I'm not a scientist," she admitted. "I guess you could say I'm a glorified accountant."

"I don't understand," Debbie said, confused.

Alex looked back and forth at the two of them and sighed.

"My husband and I made a large contribution to President McCauley's campaign. He . . . well, he showed his appreciation by appointing us to positions in his administration."

The cold, hard expressions that appeared on Debbie's and Julie's faces rivaled the bitter, howling wind outside.

"I don't know anything about science," Alex continued. She was glad she was wearing a mask. The combination of embarrassment and incompetence she was feeling in her present company probably didn't look very good on her. "I was sent here for no other reason than to determine the financial feasibility of continuing this station."

228

Julie silently shot her a withering look as she reached up to flip the light switch off. Not a moment too soon, Alex thought. She couldn't bear the looks they were giving her.

As the light went off, the room remained bathed in the dim glow from the window. Despite the window coverings pulled closed, the twenty-four hour November sunshine still found its way inside. Without looking, she was sure Julie and Debbie were still glaring at her.

She sighed and pulled the covers over her head.

§

They awoke to a deep, explosive rumble and their beds shaking. Julie and Debbie were immediately sitting up and pulling on boots. Alex looked around in a panic and decided she should follow their example.

The ground was still again as the women ran out into the common area where the men were gathering. The emotions seemed to range from flustered to frightened. Some of them were picking up books and equipment that had fallen or tipped over.

"Shit, that was a lot bigger than the others!" Debbie said.

"Wait," Alex exclaimed, "this has happened before?"

"Not this bad," Bodsworth answered. "Just the sound of distant cracks and echoes. It's never been this loud before. Or this kinetic."

Alex looked at the others, faces she met over dinner the night before. One was missing, though.

"Where's Mr. Parker?" she asked.

"He went outside to have a look around," explained Tex, a geologist. The fresh-faced kid from Corpus Christi was pulling on a heavy parka. "I'm going out, too."

"Maybe we all should," Debbie replied.

"Are you sure?" Alex asked. "I thought that, if you're caught in an earthquake, you were supposed to stand in a doorway, or something like that."

"Well, that wasn't an earthquake," Gotlieb said. Could have fooled Alex, but Gotlieb was a geologist, so he'd probably know better than she did. "And this isn't a typical structure. It was built to withstand the crazy wind out here, but I don't know anything about its ability to stand up to a violent shaking from the foundation."

"It's probably fine," said one of the others, whose name Alex had forgotten. Still, his voice sounded a little shaky and unsure. Besides that, he was pulling on his parka and heading out the door, as well.

The unspoken consensus seemed to be to go outside, as everyone bundled up and filed out the door into the sunlight. Alex glanced at her watch. It was 2:30 in the morning.

Once outside, everyone slowly scattered in different directions, looking around for any signs of what had happened. Aside from some of the weather and communications instruments being tipped askew, there seemed to be no evidence of whatever seismic violence had taken place minutes before.

Alex didn't see Parker anywhere around, but when she scanned the horizon, she saw a small, dark figure against the ice, near the shore of the big lake she had passed over the day before, which she now knew was the polynya. Another tiny shadow near him, shaped vaguely like a snowmobile, told her how he had gotten out there so quickly.

Suddenly, there was another loud cracking sound, and the ground dropped a few inches beneath them. A couple of them managed to stay on their feet, but most, Alex included, ended up on their hands and knees on the ice.

She winced at the pain from her knees hitting the ice as she pushed herself back up. She looked out toward Parker and saw violent waves of water churning around the edge of the polynya from the downward impact of the ice against the sea. Parker was scrambling to stay on his feet and get back to the snowmobile and start it up. Then, Alex noticed that there was no longer a solid, stable ice field out there. It had, apparently, broken up, and enormous chunks of it were bobbing up and down at different levels all around Parker.

"Ed," she said, grasping Bodsworth's arm. He looked in the direction she was looking.

"Oh my god," he muttered under his breath. "The ice is thinner and weaker out there where it's melted through. It must have broken apart from the shock."

"The ice shelf is disintegrating," Julie said. "It's turned into a bunch of growlers."

"Growlers?" Alex asked.

"Smaller chunks of ice that break off an iceberg or ice shelf," Bodsworth explained, watching breathlessly.

Parker was on the snowmobile now, accelerating as he did a sharp turn back toward Polynya Station. The growler he was on bobbed upwards a bit, and Parker rose off the seat as the snowmobile dropped down a couple of feet to the surface of the adjacent fragment.

The growlers were bobbing at different speeds and levels, depending, likely, on their size and weight, and they were beginning to drift apart now. Parker was zigging and zagging, trying to avoid the big, jagged chunks that rose in front of him, looking for the narrower gaps that his snowmobile would be able to jump across.

Without warning, Parker and his snowmobile dropped abruptly as the growler he was on broke apart. The skis had made it onto the edge of the next growler, but the weight of the snowmobile, and of Parker, hadn't made it there yet. Bodsworth and the others caught their breath, keeping their eyes focused on the last place they saw him, where the skis pointed straight up, then disappeared down into the ice. Where the growler had been, several small chunks of ice bobbed up and down, tilted at different angles as the space around them grew and they sought their center of balance.

Parker was not there.

There was no time to grieve him, though, as the whole plane they stood on shifted again, as if whatever was holding it in place finally gave out. Everybody reached out, grabbing on to each other for stability, as miles of ice suddenly began moving with a loud, nauseating grinding sound. It moved slowly at first, downward toward the polynya, where they last saw Parker.

Alex felt sick to her stomach as the motion continued, and she could see the water rushing toward them as the leading edge of the sheet of ice far ahead of them plunged under the sea. The polynya was now gone, its encircling ice having slipped under the surface of the water. She wanted to scream, but her throat felt locked, holding her breath tightly in her chest.

There was another sudden drop as the back edge of the unbroken sheet of ice cleared the land that Alex, before last night, hadn't known existed. As that edge, somewhere miles behind them, splashed down, the front edge rose up above the surface of the sea, hurling gallons of seawater toward them.

Everyone grabbed for something, some trying to race shakily toward the building. They didn't make it inside before they were drenched with ice cold water.

§

Like a giant ocean liner whose engines had died, the former ice shelf drifted on the sea, the little science station still firmly rooted to it. Seven of the eight people inside the common shelter sat huddled together in front of a space heater, having changed into dry clothing. Their faces were grim, looking at the heater, or the floor, rarely at each other.

Bodsworth sat before the radio, powered like everything else in the station by long hours of daylight, repeating the Mayday call. After a few minutes, he stopped.

"I'll try again later," he sighed.

"Has this ever happened before?" Alex finally asked, trying not to panic at their current situation.

"Never," Julie replied with a sharp edge to her voice. Alex looked at her. Julie held her gaze for a few moments, then looked back down at the heater.

"Calving occurs all the time," Bodsworth added. "That's where chunks of icebergs or glaciers break off and go adrift on their own. But I've never known an entire ice shelf miles wide to just slide off the supporting land mass under it. That's just unprecedented in my experience."

"What could cause something like this to happen?" Alex pressed.

"Well," Bodsworth said, looking up at Alex, "Joe and I were talking to you about it yesterday. The changes in the climate, particularly the increase in temperature, are having adverse effects on various ecosystems. That two degree rise that Joe mentioned is an average. I told you there were rivers and lakes of water between the ice and the land, fed by ice melt or by seawater. If that water circulating under the ice warms up and increases its area, it could conceivably undermine the ice's roots, its connection to the land-mass."

Bodsworth's calm tone, free of blame or accusation, as well as his logical explanation of science, affected Alex deeply.

"So," Debbie said, "what are you going to tell POSOTUS?"

"Who?" Alex asked, scrunching her eyebrows together.

"Piece of shit of the United States," Julie said. "Just one of the many affectionate nicknames we have for him."

"Sorry," Debbie said, "the President."

"Ah," Alex replied with a nod. She took a deep breath. "Well, I'm afraid he's not going to be very happy with me, but I'm going to report that our understanding of climate science has been greatly flawed and shaped by our political prejudices, and that the work you're doing here is important." She looked around. "Not that you can keep doing it here."

"Obviously we'll have to move now," Bodsworth said with a shaky smile.

"Since we broke our last place," Tex added, "I don't think we'll get our deposit back."

"Maybe our new place should be called Parker Station," Gotlieb suggested. Everybody responded with reflective nods.

"I hope you can have a new station," Alex said quietly. "My trip down here was pretty much just a formality connected to a foregone decision. With all the deaths from the virus, and the subsequent crash of the economy, the country is in a shambles, and the government is pretty strapped for cash."

She looked around, chagrined, at all the faces watching her, drawn, sad and exhausted.

"But I'm going to argue very strongly for keeping you in business," she insisted. "Assuming I can ever get back home to file my report."

"You will," Julie said.

Bodsworth tried the radio again, with no luck.

"I'll go out and check the connections to the antenna," he said.

"Meanwhile," Tex spoke up, "anybody else hungry?"

REFLECTIVE

On the spectrum of humanity's relatively short existence on this planet, they have accomplished some truly magnificent things. At the same time, they have also perpetrated horrendous things, and many things, in varying shades of good and bad, spread out across the scale in between.

Our current condition is a result of a confusing combination of those things. The invention of the automobile, for instance, was quite a leap forward in transportation. Not long after that, air travel was another great advancement.

However, since both required the burning of fossil fuel, and the fact that so many people seemed to gravitate toward the monstrous "gas guzzlers," that advancement began endangering our existence, as so-called greenhouse gases were belched into the atmosphere in such huge quantities.

We were warned about the consequences of this, but since we couldn't be dissuaded from whatever we felt was our God-given right, little was done.

Scientists in the *Golden Age* determined that, before the nineteenth century industrial age, carbon dioxide levels in the atmosphere were at about 280 parts per million. By the early twenty-first century, they were at 420 parts per million.

Many recognized the dangers that those numbers, that the trend we were on, represented, and efforts were made to curb CO_2 output. Treaties and agreements were signed, but changing administrations and agendas frequently invalidated whatever good might have been done before.

There continued to be those who "buried their heads in the sand." This was an analogy using a long-held but mistaken belief about the ostrich, a now likely extinct flightless bird that was thought to burrow its head into the earth thinking that this would prevent it from suffering whatever danger was facing it.

"Deniers" continued to push against the scientific data, thinking that, somehow, they knew more than the experts. "This is the way it's always been. The earth, and its atmosphere, moves in cycles."

Which, of course, is true. From the dawn of time, the earth's atmosphere had experienced numerous peaks and valleys of carbon content. But those alterations were naturally-occurring events. They were not, previously, brought on artificially by earth's most voracious user and abuser of resources.

We continued to use up available resources, until the resources were no longer available.

All of this was on my mind as I sat here watching my Frida waste away. I know that people back in the *Golden Age* got cancer, too. But they had the advantage of being able to receive medical assistance. Depending on the type and stage of cancer, it might or might not be successful. But they had hope.

That option was no longer available. Neither was hope.

The appellation *Golden Age* was not without a degree of irony. As I said earlier, the sky was the limit. They could have done anything!

They chose to fuck up the planet.

And my Frida was going to be their next victim.

§

My moods fluctuated between angry and sad and magnanimous. What lingered through all those moods was a certain philosophical attitude.

It was during this time that I started writing little profundities on the wall outside. Sometimes, they were scriptures picked from my father's *Holy Bible*, other times they were thoughts from *The Talmud* or from *The Code of Hammurabi* or Oscar Wilde. This day, I chose a quote from Confucius, a visionary from a distant ancient land.

> The gem cannot be polished without friction, nor man perfected without trials.

It seemed a strange mix of dark and uplifting, which was in keeping with the way I was feeling.

I can't say why I started doing that. I hadn't seen anybody in ages, and when I had seen signs of possible human "others," we ended up fleeing in fear. I guess I always had hopes that there might be others like us.

The prospect of losing *my* "other" was just a little too hard to contemplate.

REPO MAN

Bill Keaton *frowned. Sitting on the sofa in his home in Arlington, Virginia, he leafed through the papers in his hand. He had known that the report had been on its way, and he had delayed leaving for his office at the Department of Homeland Security since he had no way of contacting the investigator to tell him of a change in plans. Plans simply could not change at the last minute anymore, if they involved other people. He had to be here to receive it.*

The report in front of him was troubling, not only because of the information it contained, but also because of the time frame. During the last three years, since the beginning of the SHePF virus, he still had not gotten used to the marked transformation of their way of life.

He had read about the COVID pandemic that took place in the last century, and the many mistakes that had been made in dealing with it. A few years after it made its appearance, after over seven million worldwide deaths, they stopped collecting data on deaths by COVID. But by that time, they changed its designation from pandemic to endemic. COVID was now a regular part of their lives, with annual flareups just like the flu or the common cold.

The SHePF pandemic was so much worse, but they had not, apparently, learned from their mistakes. Many of the errors from the past were repeated, with PPE shortages, supply chain issues, and on and on.

The SHePF virus took out seven million Americans *within only a few months. By that time, the workforce had been reduced to the extent that power shortages, water treatment issues and grocery supplies had been affected to a major degree.*

After President McCauley succumbed to the virus and Vice President Armstrong assumed the office of President, Armstrong, after putting it off as long as he dared, finally declared martial law. Bill thought he should have done it a lot sooner than he did, possibly as one of his first acts as President.

But that was in the past. So many of the things that doomsday preppers had warned about had come to pass. The power grid was virtually non-existent. Solar panels had saved them to an extent, but even at that, the national grid could not be depended on. Individual homes, office buildings and stores had power, if they had their own battery storage.

Access to communications, though, was another story. Connecting to cell towers was hit or miss. If a person still had old-fashioned copper wiring in a landline, they might have access to phone service, but copper wiring was rare these days. A solar charger for a cell phone meant that the cell phone could power up, but being able to connect to a tower and put a call through was, more likely than not, not going to happen.

The White House was an exception. Due to the fact that fiber optic communication was susceptible to power grid failures, they had kept the copper wiring connected as a backup plan.

Bill didn't have copper wiring, though.

The report he was looking at was hand-written. Computers, printers, email, telephones, even fax machines were rarely available or effective, so they had been reduced to something more like nineteenth-century technology. The envelope had been delivered to him by hand at his door, and it was now several hours after the investigation had been completed and the report had been written.

President Armstrong was in danger, and it was now up to Bill Keaton to warn him of the danger.

§

With the collapse of communications came the collapse of many businesses, including banks and lenders. Some were able to adapt, sometimes depending on the type of business or the size. In some cases, the very small ones had more flexibility, while the very large ones had more money to throw at the problems. Those in between often failed.

But each of the problems came with their own new set of difficulties, further complicating this new life. In almost every case, one of these difficulties involved the availability and speed of information.

Lenders, for instance, needed to know that products they were financing were being paid for in a timely manner. In order to pay for merchandise, customers needed easy access to their money.

But with so many electronic systems failing, producers of goods and services, and their consumers, were gradually learning that things they had taken for granted for their entire lives could no longer be depended on.

As much as a century ago, autopay had become the standard whereby payment was made for goods and services received on a regular basis. The consumer set up their account online to access their bank account, and the appropriate amount was withdrawn for the payment. Once this was done, they didn't have to think about it again.

As communications systems became sporadic, though, payments would not go through. Merchants' online systems were programmed to follow through with a notice of non-payment, in hopes that the consumer would realize the error and rectify it.

But, since communications systems were sporadic, many of those messages were not getting through to the customer, nor were the customers able to connect with their bank to see account activity, or lack of it.

§

Just after homes, automobiles were the most-often financed merchandise. Self-driving cars had become the standard a few decades before. Solar chargers for cars had, fortunately, drastically reduced in size over the last several years and in many cases, including the model that Bill owned, were actually built in to the paint and other surfaces. So, powering the car was not a problem. There was always plenty of sunshine.

Since SHePF, though, connecting a self-driving car to the network was often an issue. Most people didn't even bother trying to use the self-driving feature anymore. If the network went out while they were en route to their destination, the car would simply stop in the middle of the road until it picked up the signal again, if it did. Many crashes had resulted from such an occurrence, since those manually driving their cars would not be affected by the cessation of the network, and did not react as quickly as the self-driving cars would.

Built into the programming of all cars nowadays was a fail-safe mechanism designed to protect the lender. Many lenders had actually begun demanding it when inflation was preventing many people from making their payments.

After a certain number of notices to the customer, if payment still was not made, the repossession programming would activate. The car would automatically drive itself to the lender, assuming a connection could be made to the network.

In Bill Keaton's case, the car connected to the network and pulled out of his driveway as he was looking at the report that had just been delivered to him. His car did not make it all the way to the lender's location before the network went down again, but by the time Bill opened his door to rush to the White House, his car was nowhere in sight.

He had feared that it was already too late.

Without a car, it definitely was.

want to paint you," Frida said. I looked at her curiously. She was sitting in front of a fresh, blank canvas. Though I couldn't bring myself to speak of when she would no longer be here with me, the thought occurred to me that, at that time, I would much rather have a portrait of her than of me.

"Why?" I asked simply.

She smiled tiredly at me.

"So I can still see you when you've gone out foraging."

I nodded. I thought that sounded like a perfectly reasonable request.

"Do you think you can do a self-portrait?" I asked. "I'd love to have a painting of you, too."

I saw a flicker of sadness in her smile. I'm sure she recognized the reasoning behind my statement.

"I'll do that next," she agreed.

"Alright," I said, putting my book aside. "How do you want me?"

"Standing, I think," she said as she regarded me thoughtfully. She squinted her eyes a bit as she tilted her head. "With your bow," she continued, "looking off into the distance."

Always eager to please her, I rushed to get my bow and the quiver of arrows. I also grabbed my articles of clothing that were hanging on their nails. Inside, I was only wearing shorts.

"No," Frida said when I came back with everything. "Just the bow and arrows."

She had recently discovered an enormous cache of romance novels, all of which had some version of shirtless men on the covers. While she often found the stories to be a little shallow, she found that she enjoyed some of the cover art.

I grinned at her.

"Ah," I said. "So, you're doing a romance novel cover painting?"

"No," she replied. "Classical. Lose the shorts."

§

That day was obviously a good day for Frida. She had been sitting up for hours working on the painting. I felt like a weak little baby when I asked to take a break twice. But then I was holding a somewhat unnatural pose, while she was seated in a comfortable chair. Still, as I stretched and walked around, Frida continued working, forbidding me to see the painting yet.

It was late afternoon when she had finished and invited me to see it. My hand resting on her shoulder, I stood beside her chair, still completely naked, or nude, as they used to say when it was not meant to be sexual. I looked in awe at what she had created.

"Frida!" I said a little breathlessly.

With all my reading of novels from the *Golden Age*, several exclamations came to mind. "Oh my God," or "Damn, girl!" or "Fuck!" But they weren't in the common vocabulary of our time, so "Frida!" seemed to suffice.

She had, true to her word, created something akin to a classical masterpiece, like a Rafael, or Botticelli, or Frazetta. I stood there, on her finished canvas, perched on a mountaintop, bow in hand, gazing off into the future like some mythical figure.

"My hero," Frida said.

At that complimentary and, I thought, completely undeserved, comment, I sighed. I didn't feel like a hero. I felt utterly helpless in the face of her illness. But looking at this

243

painting, seeing myself the way she saw me, brought tears to my eyes.

I turned to look down at her and, apparently, feeling my movement, she turned her head. But her eyes were not level with mine.

I twitched a little as her eyes focused on what was at eye level, and suddenly, I was no longer simply nude.

Jon watched nervously out the front window of Emily's apartment, down toward A Street NE. A cacophony of angry voices floated in with the hot air. His breath escaping from the top of his mask fogged his glasses, and he pressed the little metal strip tighter against his nose.

"Nothing good's going to come of this," he said, shaking his head. Emily had every window in her apartment open to try to vent some of the heat, and the noise was nearly overwhelming.

Emily warily came to his side and looked down toward the street. The crowd was no longer moving. They ebbed and flowed as if it was a single living, breathing organism, but the individuals could not progress ahead anymore, like blood in a vein, the heart relentlessly pumping it up against a clot.

"I'm surprised there are still this many people in D.C." Jon commented.

Hundreds of people filled the street, many of them armed, some heavily, but could no longer move forward due to the numbers in front of them. Those down below seemed angry that they could not move, could not partake in the activity that they had come for, their voices raised in shouts demanding justice.

"This is so surreal!" Emily said.

"I don't know what they hope to accomplish." Jon anxiously cracked his knuckles. "I guess they're probably just fed up."

"Well—" Emily hesitated and looked up at Jon. "I have a pretty good idea."

Jon turned to her expectantly, his eyebrows curved like horizontal question marks.

"A few weeks ago," she explained, "a friend gave me a slip of paper with some instructions on it. Apparently, this is a fairly well-planned event, with people from all over the country." She looked at Jon. "That's why there are so many."

"So?" Jon probed, his eyebrows rising. "What's their agenda?"

"To hold the government accountable." She raised her eyebrows and shrugged her shoulders, as if it was obvious. Jon leaned out and looked up the street toward where the United States Capitol Building stood just a few blocks away. Emily shook her head as she looked down toward the street.

"She knew I was disgusted with the government's handling of the virus," Emily continued, "and various other things, and she knew I could be trusted with the information. She just didn't think about the fact that I wasn't going to endanger my life for this. You know how the Jackboots have been facing down protesters, whisking them away, looking for excuses to shoot them. I mean if it was just me, I would be out there in a minute, but not when I have a little girl to care for."

She looked at her watch.

"Speaking of which, I don't want Livy trying to get through them alone." She went toward the door and picked up her purse.

"I still can't believe they're forcing kids to go to school during this pandemic," Jon said, shaking his head. "And this heat."

"I know. But there's no phone service anymore for online schooling. And it's reduced time and limited contact." Emily was suddenly laser-focused. "Anyway, will you be here when I get home with Livy?"

"No," Jon replied, glancing back down at the street. "I should get home. Robin didn't know any more about this than I did."

"Livy'll be sorry she missed seeing her Daddy."

"I know, Em." Emily opened the door and Jon slipped out. He looked back toward Emily. "Give her my love. I'll see her soon. But she has you. I need to get to Robin."

Emily nodded.

"Go out the back. Maybe it's clear behind the building." She put a hand on his shoulder. "And please be careful. You know the danger."

Jon nodded and adjusted his mask.

§

It was clear out back, but the noise was still overpowering, muffled into a less-recognizable din, reverberating off of every hard surface around him. Not just the buildings, but the cars. Several cars were parked there which Jon suspected hadn't moved in weeks or months. Electricity was so damned expensive, if you could even get it. Newer cars had solar chargers built in, but they were especially expensive, and driving, even without the air conditioner running, was only for the wealthy.

Jon looked around. North was Constitution Avenue and the crowd of protesters. He went south. In the white-hot heat of the sun, he didn't dare run, but he walked as quickly as he could manage, as the sweat ran in rivulets down his back and chest. His clothes were seldom dry anymore.

Jon could tolerate the heat better than some, certainly better than all those who had died from heat stroke during the last few decades. But even with the necessary precautions, the hat, the clothing that left virtually no skin exposed, the water bottle (which he had forgotten to bring with him), still, it was far from comfortable. Jon was often miserable.

Add to that the mask as protection against the SHePF virus, and the crowd, and he couldn't breathe deeply enough for him to exert himself with anything more than a brisk walk. Since he wasn't in close proximity to anybody now, he decided to take the mask off.

As he reached 2nd Avenue and the imposing edifice of the Supreme Court, he could see people running in different directions on the street, either to or from the surging crowd on Constitution Avenue, or to the east, in front of Emily's apartment building. Again, he went south.

Emily was always so strong. Back when they were married, she often amazed him with her courage and toughness. Even when he had told her that he needed a divorce, there were a few tears, but she was tough, thinking primarily about Livy.

What she had said about her being out there in the protest if not for Livy, he knew that was true. In fact, she probably would have been involved in organizing it.

In the next block, between the Jefferson and Adams buildings of the Library of Congress, Jon realized his mistake.

"Hey, where the fuck do you think you're going?"

He looked to his left where one of the gun-wielding zealots leveled his pistol at him.

Jon had vacillated over the last few months about growing a beard. He grew one early on, but Robin didn't think it looked good on him, so he had shaved it off. He wished now that he had given more attention to his own safety and less to Robin's personal preferences. He pulled his mask up over his face again.

"I'm not who you think I am," Jon said, holding his hands up toward his antagonist. "I just happen to look like him."

"Sure, you do," said the man, his eyes wide, as he approached Jon, his handgun quivering in his grip.

"Please," Jon said, "my name is Jon Wilson. My ex-wife lives right over there on A Street." He pointed back behind the man. "My little girl's coming home from school right about now."

"Shut up, asshole!" the man shouted. "Hey, everybody," he shouted even louder, "I got him over here!"

Some people turned and looked toward the commotion, and while Jon had hoped that they might continue on toward their original destination, several of them joined the zealot.

"It's Armstrong!" someone else shouted, and more people joined the group. Somebody behind Jon snatched the hat off of his head, and he squinted under the oppressive sunlight. Another hand pulled at his mask, snapping the elastic straps, and Jon winced at the gouging against his ears.

"You have to believe me," Jon pleaded, "I'm not Armstrong."

As people approached and crowded around him, he saw the recognition in their eyes. If only he had kept the beard.

He watched as rifles and handguns were leveled toward him.

§

"He left here three hours ago," Emily said, looking at her watch.

Robin frowned, standing in the doorway. Livy looked up at him from the table where she was doing her homework. Robin scratched his face, his stubble making a rasping sound against his nails.

"Okay," he sighed, "maybe he decided to pick up dinner or something."

"That wouldn't surprise me," Emily smiled. "He is definitely thoughtful like that."

"I guess I should get back home," Robin said.

His eyes didn't seem so sure.

Frida isn't eating much. She just isn't hungry anymore. I'm doing almost everything for the both of us. Aside from what makes it necessary, I don't mind. I would do absolutely anything for Frida.

My beautiful wife has changed over the last several months. Her body and her face no longer resemble the beautiful woman I fell in love with. She's still in there. I know she is. I still see it in her eyes, I hear it in her voice. I feel it in her touch.

But she looks like someone in one of the horrible photographs I saw of survivors of the concentration camps back in the first half of the twentieth century. Frida's face has become more taut and angular, the skin tightly hugging her skull. Her body is weak, just "skin and bones," as the old saying went.

Shortly after painting my portrait, true to her word, she painted a self-portrait. While it isn't as complimentary or true-to-life as the portrait she did of her parents, or even of the heroic painting she did of me, it is a good likeness.

I keep my portrait on display in front of the bed so she can see it when she's awake. I keep hers where I can see it. I've shed many tears while looking at what I'm in the process of losing.

§

Last night, it rained. It was the first time in months, and it lasted for quite a while. It never amounted to much, but this time, apparently, it did.

This morning, I found a pool of water near the Potomac River. The river had, evidently, swelled during the rain just enough for some of the water to spill over a rise. In that pool, I saw a couple of silvery flashes.

I had not seen any sign of fish in the river for years, so I assumed that these might have washed downstream with the rain. Maybe we should leave our beloved Library and move to a higher elevation.

Then, I remembered. Frida would not be going anywhere.

I stepped down to the pool. It was small and shallow, cut off once again from the river, and the two fish were trapped. I had never eaten fish before, but I remember from a nutritional book that I had consulted that they were supposed to be high in protein.

I know that Frida is too far gone, but still an irrational part of my brain couldn't help thinking that a good, nutritious meal would do her wonders.

§

I made a mess of the fish. I consulted a couple of books on cleaning and cooking fish, but never having done it before, and not having exactly the right equipment, it was kind of a haphazard endeavor.

A while back, I had created a grill up on the copper roof, with a space under it for a small wood fire. This is where I cooked the fish. I think they are small bass, based on pictures I found in that first book.

The fish started cooking fine, but when I attempted to turn it, some of the meat flaked apart and fell through the grill into the fire. I managed to save most of it, though it looked fairly pulverized, and a little overdone in places.

Still, it tastes delicious. I'm sitting now on the pallet beside Frida. She's awake and looking at me appreciatively as I slip small bites of fish into her mouth. Her dark eyes are dimmed a little, whether from pain or some other symptom, I'm not sure. She doesn't say much anymore. Her once beautiful golden hair looks more like stiff straw now.

I gaze at her face, peering into her eyes. It takes a few moments, but I find her, my Frida. Sometimes, depending on how bad she feels, it's harder to find her, but she's still there, the sweet, beautiful, creative woman I fell in love with.

Who fell in love with me.

Peter Brown frowned. Something weird was going on. He drank the last swallow and slipped his empty beer can down into the beverage holder built in to the arm of the mounted seat at the stern of his boat. He held the fishing rod with both hands, moving it around, testing how slack the line was.

It wasn't. But it wasn't exactly taut, either.

The boat seemed still. That was weird, too. It was rocking a little, but not as much as he would expect in open water.

Peter Brown, or PB as his friends called him, stood up and slipped his rod into the rod holder mounted at the front of the seat. He frowned again, scratching his head, as he stumbled toward the gunwale. Business was lagging, and he had spent a lot of time fishing alone, and drinking too much beer.

PB operated a small fishing tourism company, and his business had been doing well, even with the soaring temps and plunging economy. A few years ago, he upgraded his older boat to a twenty-five-foot inboard cabin cruiser, with three mounted fishing seats at the stern. Then, that damn SHePF virus struck. The virus had passed, and PB had, thankfully, survived.

But too many people hadn't. In fact, many businesses and service companies, those that hadn't gone completely out of business, were operating with skeleton crews since so many people had died. PB had read articles about delays and outright dangers, depending on the businesses, associated with the fact that there just weren't enough skilled people left alive in the country who were able to do the work.

Then, there were the riots, and the assassination of President Armstrong—and of that poor bastard who just happened to look like him. Besides businesses, the government was scraping by, well, he didn't even know how the government was still going at all.

Of those who had survived, though, apparently there weren't as many interested in fishing expeditions. Or, at least, it just wasn't much of a priority anymore. Recreation took a back seat to survival.

PB was only a few hundred yards off the coast of Maryland, near the mouth of the Chesapeake Bay, the twin stacks of the St. Elizabeth Nuclear Power Plant looming to the west. He was in a spot that had always yielded rockfish and croakers in abundance. Now, his fishing rod had been as still as the waters surrounding his boat.

He leaned against the gunwale and looked over the side. The water was moving, but it was different from the waves that typically lapped against the side of his boat. It moved sluggishly, as if it was syrup. He squinted and focused on the surface, and that's when he realized that it wasn't water. Not entirely.

His boat was surrounded by jellyfish. He rubbed his eyes and peered down, looking at details. The jellyfish were packed against each other so densely that it appeared there were more jellyfish than there was water. The translucent creatures were barely visible, but PB could see them jammed up against each other, many of them as large as twelve inches across.

He didn't know much about jellyfish in general, but he knew that sea nettles were common in the area. He knew that they had six-foot long tentacles dangling below them, and while their sting wasn't fatal, they could be extremely painful. Who knows what kind of damage they could do in this number and concentration?

It wasn't uncommon for blooms of jellyfish to form in this area. Swimmers got stung fairly often in the summer months, but PB had never seen anything like this.

He looked up at the water between his boat and the shore. It was all undulating densely, thick with jellyfish.

There had been some alarmists who had carried on about global warming, and the effect it would have on numerous ecosystems.

PB hadn't paid much attention to them, but he remembered now that some had warned that, with overfishing removing natural predators, combined with warming seas, jellyfish could take over. To PB, it sounded like disaster movie nonsense.

Looking around his boat now, he had to admit that maybe they had been right.

There was a sudden explosive sound to the west, and PB looked up toward the nuclear power plant. An enormous cumulus plume of steam was pouring from each stack, and a few yards above that, the wind was catching the plumes of smoke and pushing them out over the sea.

Toward PB.

Seeing the wall-to-wall jellyfish surrounding him, he remembered that seaside nuclear power plants had intake pipes several yards below the surface, to bring in seawater to cool their internal workings and the radioactive fuel. Even deeper now, with the higher ocean surface. It was becoming a fairly common occurrence for jellyfish to get sucked into those pipes and clog them.

Several nuclear plants had shut down. St. Elizabeth was one of the few remaining, but with not enough skilled workers available, he assumed that reaction times to emergencies such as that might naturally be delayed. PB's reaction time, despite the number of beers he had consumed, was not delayed. He didn't want to stick around and find out if that steam was radioactive.

He ran to the helm and started up the boat. He jammed the throttle forward and turned the wheel toward the south. He had expected his boat to surge into a tight turn.

What he got was a brief lurch and a strange sucking sound, followed by a gag as the inboard motor sucked jellyfish up its intake and stuffed them tightly around the impeller. The motor groaned, then stalled.

PB realized instantly what had happened. He could envision the gelatinous creatures packed in the intake. If he could even reach them, clearing it would require spending some time in the water. With the jellyfish, and their six-foot-long stinging tentacles.

He had a decision to make. And his options sucked.

He could get in the water with millions of jellyfish, clearing the water intake tube, enduring excruciating pain, and with that overwhelming number of jellyfish, possibly even death. Or he could sit and wait it out, hoping that the jellyfish eventually go away, while simultaneously hoping that the cloud from the nuclear reactor is not radioactive, or if it is radioactive, hoping that it doesn't rain its slow, rotting death down on him on its way over.

As his boat bobbed languidly on the ocean of jellyfish, PB watched the monstrous cloud as it approached his position. It was still spewing out of the stacks, filling the sky, casting a dark and ominous shadow over him. Maybe it wasn't dangerous. Maybe it was just a routine venting of steam. Or, maybe it would just float over him and away, into the distance.

Maybe he should have another beer.

He sighed and plopped himself down into one of the fishing seats at the stern of his boat. He reached into the cooler and popped open a can, making himself comfortable.

BACKTRACKING

After making sure that Frida is as comfortable as possible this morning, I make my way down the flights of stairs, carrying the water buckets, to my exit toward the tunnel. My heart is as dark as the last flight of stairs into the abyss. I've done this so many times over the past few years that I'm going down the steps by rote, not really thinking about what I'm doing.

So, it's a surprise when my feet splash into water.

Shaken out of my torpor, I reach into my bag and pull out my flashlight, thumbing the switch on. The light reflects off the surface of the water undulating a few inches up from the floor.

I knew the water was rising. Even yesterday, walking back from retrieving drinking water from the well, I realized that I was walking through water. There was still a dry path on the higher section of broken concrete in the tunnel, but I knew that it was steadily getting worse. I just hadn't expected that it would be so soon.

A few years ago, I had made a study of the Potomac River. I knew that there were a few small dams in various places upstream. Maybe one or more of them had given way, sending more water down here. Or maybe one of the last great chunks of polar ice had given way, causing the shoreline of the ocean to rise.

Or maybe the water table had already risen beyond this, and the structure of the tunnel that had been holding it off was simply giving way.

Not knowing the cause, I don't want to continue going this way and risk getting trapped if the water, for some reason, rises even more before I come back. So, I turn around and climb the stairs, back to the main floor of the Library. I look toward the main entrance, where we were first intro-duced to this place, and I take a deep breath. It was time to undo what I had done when we moved in.

I go to the main entrance, to the center door, and kneeling down, I work at the pieces of debris that I had lodged under it. I finally get it all out and work at opening the door. It's even harder than it had been the first time a few years ago.

The other door, on the east side of the building, the one I use to empty our toilet bucket, opens much easier than this one, since it gets opened every day. This one protests and creaks and groans, but I finally get it open. Once outside, I look in all directions to make sure nobody is around. After all this time, it's still my habit.

When I emptied our toilet bucket a few minutes earlier, I did the same thing, but being on the back side of the build-ing, and slightly shielded by the skeletal trees out there, it never seemed like a problem. I had simply dumped the bucket and covered the hole, then went back upstairs.

Frida hadn't moved by the time I returned then, and I hated the fact that I felt the need to come closer and make sure that she was still breathing. Satisfied that she was, I took the water buckets and headed back downstairs. Where I found my tunnel closed off to me.

§

Having to go out the front door makes it a longer trip to the well. This first time, it's even longer, since I have to go to the street-level exit of the tunnel a couple of blocks south to retrieve the rusty old wagon.

Walking to the well with the wagon in hand, I'm besieged by memories of when Frida and I first moved here, when we fled our previous home with our possessions loaded in this little wagon. It was years ago and, obviously, based on unfounded fears, but it turned out to be a good move for us.

Our years in the Library have been good ones, inspiring both of us in our own ways.

Our love for each other deepened so much during that time, and the thought of losing her and living the rest of my life without her brings tears to my eyes for only the eighth or tenth time this morning. I *can* imagine living the rest of my life without her, but only barely.

The Library will help, but its glory will be dimmed by not having my Frida to share it with. Our bed will be cold and empty and lonely with only me lying in it.

I'm surprised to see the buckets of water standing in the bed of the wagon. I don't even remember filling them. My mind is so filled with thoughts of Frida and the absolute dread of losing her that I seem to be going through my daily routines without thought of anything but her.

I realize that I may possibly end up being the last living person on earth. Obviously, it had to be one of us. Since I know that Frida loves me, there's some small consolation in knowing that she won't have to be the one spending her last few years without me.

Still, the idea of that beautiful woman wasting away in pain and starvation—it just makes me shudder. As does the realization that she's alone now. I don't even want her to have to spend her last *minutes* without me, so I start pulling the wagon along the uneven crumbling streets back toward the Library.

RISING WATER

Annie Coghill pushed her fingers through her glossy black hair, tying it back in a ponytail. She looked out the window toward the sea. She didn't have to look very far. The waves were licking against the foundation of the house. She sighed. It was time to go.

Again.

She picked up her bag and slung it over her shoulder and placed her wide-brimmed hat on her head. She took one last look around on her way through the family room. There wasn't much to look at anymore. Most of the things had already been taken.

She went out the front door, the side of the house away from the sea, but the ground was still soggy from high tide. It sucked noisily at her feet with each step until she reached a level of ground that the sea hadn't reached yet.

Annie continued up the hill, a few miles north of Palm Beach, following the road that roughly traced the edge of the shoreline. The next house she was ready for was several hundred yards from the last one, and it was situated higher up, a little more out of reach of the rising sea.

It was a nice house. All of them were and, as with the others, there were no cars, no movement, no sign of life. Still, she knocked on the door. She didn't want to surprise anybody again. That had been scary.

The man she had walked in on, a couple of weeks ago, seemed frightened when he saw her, not just startled. Annie suspected that he didn't belong there, either. Still, it could have been dangerous for her if he had been of a certain nature, and better prepared.

After knocking and ringing the bell, nobody answered, so she tried the door. Luckily, it was unlocked. A few of them had been locked, which hadn't really been a hindrance to her. But, still, it was easier if she could just walk in.

The conclusion that Annie had reached was that those who locked their doors retained some hope that the warnings had been a hoax, despite the proof of the rising sea, and expected that they might be able to return. Those who didn't bother locking up, she assumed, were ones who had accepted the certainty of their fate and knew they wouldn't be back.

Or, maybe they were taken by the SHePF virus, and there was nobody left to lock up after them.

Once inside, she looked around. Like the others, it had been pretty much cleared out. A couple of pieces of furniture that they hadn't wanted to bother with, two or three kitschy pictures left on the walls, but aside from that, empty.

She found the kitchen and started looking around. With no power, she didn't even bother with the refrigerator. But there was a fairly large pantry, in which she found a half-full box of crackers, a couple of tins of sardines, and a few other miscellaneous items that the previous residents hadn't seen fit to take with them.

Now, to see if they left a bed!

§

White-skinned, blue-eyed, blonde-haired Annie Coghill had suffered hard luck for most of her adult life. She had come from a privileged background in Miami, Florida, but had gotten in trouble when she ventured out on her own. A life of petty crime had been somewhat exciting, providing a few thrills that she hadn't experienced growing up.

She had managed to avoid getting caught for a few years, but the narrow escapes hadn't been enough to "scare her straight," a saying that her parents had recalled from their younger days.

It was after she got mixed up with Carlos, a bigger player in the world of crime that she realized that she was in over her head. Transporting illegal drugs promised a good payoff upon completion of the job. Unfortunately, she had been caught and arrested by a DEA agent before she was able to collect her pay.

Since it was her first offense, though, or at least the first offense for which she had gotten caught, and since she had dealt directly with Carlos and had information that could prove useful, she was offered immunity if she would provide testimony that would convict the kingpin.

Annie accepted the offer, telling them what she knew. Her testimony had been good, leading law enforcement directly to the big guy. Unfortunately, the charges had to be thrown out due to a technicality concerning the collection of evidence.

To protect Annie from Carlos, she was relocated to Memphis with a new identity under the Federal Witness Protection Program. A new life, a fresh start, was exactly what she needed.

§

The bed was a little harder than Annie liked, but she had certainly slept in much worse situations. Under the circumstances, she was able to put up with a firm mattress for a couple of nights.

She remembered one night in Miami a few years back. Her partner in crime at the time was also her boyfriend. It had been a toxic relationship, one that kept her firmly rooted in a life of crime. They had broken in to a house in South Beach and had gathered the things they wanted to take with them. During the course of looting the house, her boyfriend had found a number of papers, written plans that made him realize that the owners of the house were not just out for the day, but were away on vacation.

They spent the night there, sleeping in the master bedroom, when they weren't having sex. As she recalled, they had copulated at least three times there before they left the next morning with their loot.

The bed had been the hardest, most uncomfortable she had ever slept on. But it was a king size bed with some of the softest sheets she had ever felt. She managed to sleep well, despite the firmness.

Now, in this house north of Palm Beach, Annie had been frugal with the food, but still finished it off in those two days. That was okay, though. She had completed what she had wanted to accomplish by then. As the water kept creeping higher, she knew it was time to move on.

Using this house as her base of operation, she had checked out a few other houses nearby. One of them was still occupied by a retired couple who refused to be moved from their home, dammit! At least that's what Annie assumed. She hadn't actually made contact with them.

She began moving southward, passing the houses she had already eliminated. In the searing heat of early afternoon, she kicked herself for not starting out earlier. As she trudged south, she remembered the past year.

After numerous costly wars, a devastating pandemic, stock market crashes, billions of dollars paid out in several monster hurricane relief efforts, and other unexpected setbacks, what was left of the government had been struggling under a mountain of debt. They had been trying to help struggling corporations to stay in business, to keep supplying whatever goods or services they provided, while law-abiding citizens who needed assistance during those difficult times were left to flounder.

In the process, the government had sent themselves down a dark fiscal tunnel from which they had yet to emerge.

Annie was established in her new life, under her new identity, but due to financial difficulties of his own, her employer went out of business and Annie lost her job. She looked for another one, but others who were struggling as well weren't hiring. Her money had run out quickly, especially since the unemployment insurance program had been discontinued a few years earlier.

When she heard that law enforcement was suffering, and that organized crime was gobbling up large portions of cities unhindered, Annie made an assumption that her relatively little crime would not be on anybody's mind any longer. She had decided to venture out from Memphis.

There were still a few cars out that had power, and she found a couple of drivers who were willing to give her a ride. A few miles by car, several on foot. It was long and tiring.

A few weeks had passed since she began her search, but as the sea rose, she was beginning to lose hope. She wished she had kept that letter!

As she approached the house that she figured would be her next base, her eyes were constantly moving back and forth, carefully examining the area. There was no sign of life, no movement. That was a good sign.

She went up to the door and knocked, just in case. When nobody answered, she tried the door. It was locked. Shaking her head, she got out the little case that she had kept years ago, selecting the tools she needed for this lock. In less than a minute, the door was open and she was inside.

Annie looked around. The house wasn't completely cleared out. Most of the furniture was gone, but there were still a few boxes. Probably less important stuff that they had decided they didn't have room for. She lifted the flaps of the box nearest the front door, and she looked inside. It was mainly stuffed with articles of clothing.

Another box sat on the floor by the door into the kitchen. A few pans and miscellaneous utensils were tossed in it. She checked out the kitchen pantry and found a few items that might sustain her for a day or so. That made her happy.

She went out to the dining room and found another box. It was packed with wall decorations, knick-knacks, pictures. Useless personal treasures.

She heard a sound at the wall of the dining room. She looked out the window and saw the waves washing against the back of the house. It was closer to the water than she had realized. She was pushing the flaps back in place on the box when she stopped. Something caught her eye.

She opened the flap again and pulled out a frame, feeling her heart stop. It was a photo of a happy family in front of a different house. There in front was blonde-haired Annie, a big smile on her face, her mother's hand resting on her shoulder.

Annie felt a pang in her heart as she looked at the photo of happier times. She remembered the last letter she had received from her mother, before Annie entered Witness Protection. Her parents were moving out of Miami into a house looking out on the ocean north of Palm Beach. They hoped that she might join them and they could be a happy family again. Annie was too ashamed of her situation and didn't reply. That was the last she had heard from her family.

When the ocean started noticeably rising and she heard that people were moving away from the coast, she finally decided to venture out from her protective situation in Memphis. She hoped they hadn't been victims of that virus.

All she remembered was "north of Palm Beach." But she hadn't saved the letter and didn't have the address. She decided to work her way from house to house in an effort to find them.

Considering all the empty, abandoned houses, she had apparently waited too long.

As she looked at the photo through the tears filling her eyes, she heard another sound, this time from the front of the house. She looked up from the photo into the shocked faces of her parents.

SHATTERED

Many books were written by many different authors back in humanity's *Golden Age* about the various kinds of pollution that plagued them. Air pollution and water pollution seemed to be the two biggest ones.

Some of the books were written in an encouraging, motivational tone. *We can do this if we work together.*

Others took a more forceful, threatening tone. *Time is running out. If we don't do something now, it will soon be too late.*

Soil pollution, littering, radiation, and others, had plenty written about them, as well. In one way or another, Frida and I have been experiencing the aftereffects of most of these.

One form of pollution that was written about back then that doesn't seem to affect us at all is noise pollution.

Apparently, in the *Golden Age*, people were assaulted by noise from all sides. Traffic noise, construction, radios blasting, industry, lawn mowers. With billions of people taking up space on the planet, noise was an inevitable constant.

Now, it is as silent as can be. No traffic, no industry, no construction. There are no radios blasting because there are no radio stations.

Or people with radios.

And no lawn mowers because there are no lawns. There are no birds singing or dogs barking outside, and usually no wind or rain.

We don't even have any faint ambient noise in our building from things like electricity, plumbing, heating or air conditioning. The nearest thing to that I have is the electrical storage unit attached to the solar panels on the roof, which I use to recharge my flashlight batteries. I also have a utility light attached to it, but I seldom use that, so as to keep from attracting attention at night. Old habits die hard, as that old saying goes.

If Frida and I are not making any noise, it's as quiet as can be.

So, I instantly jerk awake when I hear the gentle rattling of metal bookends hanging on the wire outside our door. I get up out of bed and go quietly to the door, stilling the bookends. The wire was a precaution that I had installed years ago, connected to the doors as a primitive early warning system.

The first grey light of dawn is just creeping through the window. I return to the bed and look at Frida. She's still asleep, unaware of any disturbance.

As I always do nowadays, I gaze at her face, seeking the beautiful woman that I love. My heart aches for her, and for me, but I decide that I don't have the time to feel sorry for us.

I pick up my bow and arrows in one hand and my spear in the other, hoping not to wake her, but she's dead to the world.

I instantly hate that expression.

I creep out of our room and into the hallway, glancing in both directions. I turn to the left, walking through what used to be called the Hispanic Room, then I turn into the long South Gallery.

I hear a sound of a creaking protestation of the main door, and I realize that the bookends are probably rattling again. I'm on the second floor on the south side of the building, and the front door is on the first floor on the west, but in a completely silent world, sound travels when there are no other noises to interfere.

The sound doesn't last long. I still keep a chunk of metal wedged under the door from the inside. Suddenly, I hear the distant crash of glass shattering. Whoever had tried to open the door apparently wasn't deterred by my security measures.

I had thought a great deal about this moment, should it ever come, but it had been a long time ago. Now, my brain is fumbling for what to do.

Turning the corner into the Southwest Gallery, a slide to a stop in the south corridor overlooking the Great Hall, the main entry that had captured our hearts years before when we first discovered our new home.

I crouch behind the balustrade over the main entryway, trying to stay hidden behind the white marble columns, as I look down toward the front door. I count five figures stepping through the violently opened door. They spend some time looking around the Great Hall, though it doesn't seem to hold their attention as much as it did ours.

Still crouched behind the balustrade, just in case, I make my way toward my right, toward the East Corridor, as they disappear from my view under the balustrade in the direction of the Reading Room.

I had heard stories about Raiders, and they weren't pretty. The stories, or the Raiders.

A lot of the Raiders, the stories go, are mutated messes. Pollution, radiation, all of it had done something to their DNA, turning them into weird monsters.

I don't know if that's true or not.

The ones I saw coming through the door seemed normal enough. But I'm quite sure they were Raiders. They were dressed pretty much the same as I dress when I go out, though without the artistic embellishments that Frida had put on our clothing. Instead, they seemed to have gold and silver chains around their necks, some with jewels hanging from them.

And I didn't see any weird monster-like attributes.

But they definitely looked aggressive.

I take a deep breath, casting a glance back the way I came, and try to decide how to deal with this.

Above all else, I need to protect Frida.

SEPARATE WAYS

Steve stood nervously in the waiting room at Lake View Medical Center. Looking out the large windows of the ancient building, he thought it was amusing, in a dark and twisted way, that the view actually included the northwest corner of Graceland Cemetery. Lake Michigan, the one referenced in the hospital's name, was actually several blocks east and couldn't be seen from here, at least not from his perspective on the ground floor.

His face was tense, and glistening with sweat. The hospital had been running on old generators for weeks now and, he assumed, to save fuel, was running its air conditioning at a minimum. And it was so hot. It was always hot!

"Mr. Lieberman?" The voice was feminine, but with a hardness born of dealing with horrors on a daily basis. He turned around and saw a nurse, a woman whose face looked familiar, but he couldn't place her.

"Yes," he replied anxiously.

"Your mother's still unconscious, but we've got her on an IV. We're administering fluids and insulin, and we think she's out of danger for the moment."

"Oh, thank you!" he said, truly exhaling for the first time in at least an hour. "Does the doctor know when she might regain consciousness?"

"Actually, I'm afraid Doctor Melcher hasn't seen her yet. Hopefully in the morning."

"Really?" Steve asked, surprised. "Why so long?"

"Well, before the vaccine, the SHePF virus took a lot of our staff. We didn't have enough personal protective equipment and we tried to make do with what we had while the patients just kept coming."

"Oh, I'm so sorry." The nurse nodded an acknowledgment.

"Thank you. I'm afraid the entire hospital is down to only two doctors, three nurses and a couple of physician's assistants. Needless to say, we're stretched pretty thin. Although, admittedly, after the virus, this is a much smaller town than it once was. We don't have as many patients as we could have."

Steve sighed. He and his mother had been pretty lucky through the SHePF ordeal. But now, she was a peripheral victim, not directly infected with the virus, but affected by the aftermath.

"You don't remember me, do you?" the nurse asked. Steve looked at her face again, and again, he knew she looked familiar. He squinted his eyes at her, as if he were straining.

"Your face is right on the tip of my brain," he said.

"Tracy," she said, smiling at his expression. "We went out to dinner once. About ten years ago, I think."

"Of course!" Steve replied, smiling at her. "Tracy, I'm so sorry."

Steve had dabbled in online dating years ago, hoping to find the love of his life. Or at least someone who could tolerate him enough that he wouldn't spend the rest of his life lonely. He remembered Tracy now, though her face looked more drawn than he recalled. She seemed more than ten years older. Given her occupation, and the ordeal she had been through, it was understandable.

"No, it's okay," she replied. "You've got a lot on your mind."

"That's true," he agreed. "And it has been a while."

"Yes, it has." Tracy looked at him for a moment, then blinked and shook her head as if awakening from a daydream. "Well, Steve, I'm afraid I don't have time to visit with you."

"Oh, of course not," Steve said. "Your hospital staff is down to seven people."

"Come with me. I'll take you to your mother's room. Like I said, she's still in a coma, but you can sit with her."

"Thank you, Tracy," he said as he followed her into the eerily empty hallway.

"And I'll try to check in on her in an hour or two." Tracy stopped at the door to an examining room and pushed it open. Steve glanced at her appreciatively and nodded as he entered the room, looking at his mother, so small and vulnerable in the hospital bed.

§

"I'd been trying for months to get more insulin," Steve said, "but I just couldn't get my hands on any. We tried some of the insulin replacements that have been developed, but she didn't tolerate them well. At the same time, I'd have a friend stay with Mom while I checked with different hospitals, knowing that she was going to need one soon."

"And they were turning you away?" Tracy asked. Steve nodded, and she continued. "Yeah, several hospitals have closed down permanently since they just didn't have enough staff to keep them going. They divvied up their personnel and supplies among the rest of us, and even at that, we were barely able to handle the load."

Steve noticed her exhausted tone of voice, and the brief appearance of tears in her eyes, but he didn't say anything as she blinked them away. They passed a couple of moments in silence as they looked at his mother, still comatose.

"So," Tracy said, then paused. "Well, I was going to ask what you've been up to for the last ten years, but I remember seeing Alzheimer's on your mother's chart."

"Right." Steve looked at Tracy's face for a few moments, frowning in thought. "In fact, I think you may have been my last date. Mom started getting worse about then, and I knew I didn't have time for a romantic life."

Tracy smiled at him, sadly but admiringly.

"So, you've been her caretaker ever since?"

"Yeah. Only child. My dad died when I was a kid, so it fell pretty squarely on my shoulders." Another glance at his mother, then back to Tracy. "What about you?"

"Working, mainly," Tracy shrugged. "I went on a few more dates, but none of them went anywhere. I'm amazed at how many men mistook online dating for hookup sites."

"We're pigs," Steve said, smiling sardonically. "Haven't you heard?"

"I remember you being a gentleman, though. I was sorry I didn't hear back from you."

Steve was about to apologize for not calling her when the lights went out. A moment later, a battery-powered emergency light came on, dimly illuminating the room.

"Looks like my break's over," Tracy said as she stood up. "I'll see what's going on and get back to you when I can."

§

The exam room that Steve's mother was in became hot and stuffy very quickly. He had propped the door open to allow a little air in. He didn't see Tracy again until morning. When he did, her expression was bleak.

"Our solar panels were installed years before I was born," she said, looking at Steve from between eyelids stained from a lack of sleep. "As I understand it, they degrade over time. Well, they stopped working several weeks ago, and we don't have anybody who knows how to fix them. Somebody did find an old-fashioned gas generator, though, and managed to hook it up, but it's way too small to power the entire hospital. We've been using it only for essential systems.

"It's also practically impossible to find fuel for it anymore. So, we've been running it at an absolute minimum.

"Well," she sighed, "I've been told that there is no more fuel to be found, and the generator won't be coming back on."

"Oh my god," Steve said. "What does that mean for the hospital?"

"It means we're even more limited on what we can do for people now than we were with just our reduced staff. We've already lost

273

three patients overnight who needed life support. And, of course, our refrigeration won't work anymore."

She looked up at Steve, and her face was grim.

"There's something else." She took a deep breath. "I've been informed that, besides fuel for the generator, we're also out of insulin."

Steve looked over at his mother, only partly illuminated by the open door. He didn't know what to say.

"To be brutally honest, though," Tracy said, and she hesitated. She nervously looked down at the floor, then back up at Steve.

He finished her thought.

"It would just be delaying the inevitable."

"I'm afraid so," Tracy replied with an apologetic tone, but apparently relieved that Steve had followed her line of thought.

"It'll probably be a blessing," he said quietly. "The last few months have been pretty bad. I mean, she hasn't even remembered the situation, and what we've been living through which, I guess, is a lucky break. And, at the same time, she was scared quite often when she didn't recognize her surroundings, or even me, on occasion."

In an impulsive move, Tracy put her hand on his upper arm and squeezed. "I'm so sorry, Steve."

§

"Obviously," Tracy said, "billing and payment are not an issue anymore. We're moving all our patients who are in exam rooms into rooms with windows, so they can get a little fresh air. I know it's hot, but still, it'll be fresh."

Steve nodded. His eyes were red enough that Tracy could see it in the dim light of the room.

"She's gone," he said quietly. Tracy looked at Steve's mother, her body seeming even smaller and more emaciated than before. Against her will, the tears sprang to Tracy's eyes again.

"Oh, Steve," she said, wiping the tears away.

"I know," he said. "But it's better this way. Wherever she is now, it's got to be better than here. And, as the cliché goes, at least she's not suffering anymore."

Tracy looked at Steve and saw the conflicting emotions on his face and she couldn't help it. She stepped toward him and embraced him. He put his arms around her and held her tightly as the tears came.

"I'm so sorry, Tracy" he said in a torrent into her hair. "I wanted to call you. I liked you. I wanted to take you out again, but Mom was a mess. I didn't know what to tell you."

"I would have understood," she replied. "In fact, I could have helped."

"I know." The tears kept coming as he held on to her tightly. His tone carried sorrow and regret and so many other painful emotions.

Tracy held him until the tears stopped.

Finally, she let him go as he stepped back. He seemed embarrassed at his outburst as he clumsily wiped the tears away.

"I'm sorry," he said awkwardly.

Tracy shook her head.

"You have absolutely nothing to apologize for."

Steve looked at Tracy for a few moments, fondly remembering that last date he had. He remembered, now, her face across the table from him, ten years ago, but looking twenty years younger than she did now. He remembered wanting to kiss her as he walked her out to her car afterwards.

"What can I do?" he asked.

"What do you mean?" Tracy asked.

"You said you're moving patients into rooms with windows. I'm a caretaker. I want to help out. I want to help you."

Tracy stood there looking at Steve, seeing the warm, caring man that she had seen ten years ago. Knowing, now, his history, she knew it was real. She knew he wasn't just putting on airs to *impress her, to get her into bed like so many other men she had met online. She could see his soul, and she cringed inwardly at the cliché while, at the same time, recognizing its truth.*

Putting him to work wouldn't be a problem. There was plenty to do. But she felt more than just gratitude for his offer to help. She tentatively reached out and took his hand.

He squeezed her hand in return and, with a final glance at his mother, followed Tracy out of the room, drawing strength from her touch.

This time is going to be different, *he thought.*

BLOODBATH

Adrenaline is an amazing hormone. It's been found in numerous animals, including humans, and even in some plants. Produced by the adrenal glands, it's the main element that fuels the "fight-or-flight" response.

In this case, since Frida is sleeping in our bedroom on the other side of the building, flight is not an option. But I definitely feel ready to fight.

Since I can't see them now, I strain my ears, listening to the sounds. I can hear shuffling sounds, as if they're down on the first floor looking through our stuff.

I know, it's not really ours. Or, it wasn't ours when we came here. But I feel protective of it now, and yes, a little possessive. Frida and I cherish this place and its contents. I can't say the same for anybody else.

I think about the figures I saw stepping through the door. They're all armed, but that in itself is not an indictment of their character. I'm always armed when I go out, as well.

Their aggression seemed obvious to me when they came in. I can't say for sure how I knew that. It was just an impression.

But I don't want to hurt anybody based on just an impression.

"What do you want?" I call out loudly, adopting a more threatening tone than I usually use. I hope they can't hear the bluff.

It suddenly goes silent downstairs. I'm barefoot, and I make my way silently to the stairs leading up to the Visitors' Gallery, which wraps around the Main Reading Room, making use of all the white marble columns to hide behind.

"We don't want to hurt you," I say, figuring that pluralizing their opponents might make them leave us alone.

I know that's unlikely, but still . . .

Nobody has responded yet, and I don't like not being able to see them. I have the advantage of being on my home turf. I'm intimately familiar with the building while they are not, but I'm painfully aware that this doesn't help when I don't know where my enemy is.

Gripping my weapons tightly, I quietly walk back and forth, continually peeking over the balustrade for any movement on the first floor. I think about how many other stairways there are. They could, conceivably, come up different stairs at the same time and have me surrounded. I just don't know where they are.

I turn my head in all directions, not to see them but to try to hear the slightest sound they might make. Hearing a light shuffling sound, I slowly peek over the balustrade, and I see one of them. He's motioning in two directions, apparently instructing others to do exactly what I had feared.

I need to buy some time.

I move to my left, to the staircase that the man downstairs was closest to. I'm hoping that I can make it from here to the staircase on my right before the man he was directing on that side gets there.

Just as I get to the winch, I see a man approaching the base of the stairs. I flip the switch, admittedly feeling a little smug about my ingenuity.

Did you really think I set up that solar power system just to charge my flashlight?

Years ago, and particularly after I acquired the system, I spent a great deal of time setting up some protections in the event of this very circumstance. These sorts of things, I believe, used to be called booby traps.

This particular one, and a similar one for the stairway on the north, involves a very large, very heavy section of book shelving. It had taken several weeks, and a great deal of help from Frida, but we managed to get the bookshelf hung from the ceiling high above the staircases.

Once I had determined to do it, it was still something that I was hesitant about. Not only because of how high it was. Fortunately, I had not inherited my father's fear of heights, but I did find some really tall ladders.

Rather, it was the fact that it required my damaging the beautiful artwork on the ceiling. In the end, I figured our safety was more important.

The top of the shelf unit was hung by cables from two heavy duty mounts I had placed in the ceiling. The bottom of the unit had a very long piece of cable which was threaded through a pulley, also hung from the ceiling, and which was ultimately attached to the winch, and had been pulled up into a horizontal position.

Each marble staircase used to have a brass rail going down the center of it, so I had to remove that so that the heavy shelf could swing down and completely block the stairs when the winch was turned on. I knew that it wouldn't entirely seal it off, since the stairway is still open on the side of the main entrance below. Whoever I was trying to block could still climb out and over the balustrade, and then back over it onto the stairs once they were past the shelf.

But it would buy us a little time.

Except that nothing happens. I'm afraid my smugness vaporizes in a panic-filled instant. I flip the switch up and down several times, the clicking loud in my ears, and am rewarded with—nothing.

I admit that this is something that I had been afraid of. I had read that solar panels degrade over time. There was probably enough residual energy in the storage battery to recharge my flashlight periodically, but not enough to do what I need it to do now.

The man at the bottom of the stairs sees me, and he smiles as if he sees an easy mark. He's carrying something like a large sword, with a fat, rusty blade. I think it used to be called a machete.

He starts up the steps towards me, his face displaying confidence in an easy kill. I'm sure he sees the panic on my face as I flip the switch a couple more times.

There's only one more thing I can do. I press on the manual switch that releases the ratchet, and I instinctively step back as the winch begins spinning.

The cable at the bottom of the shelf immediately loosens, pulling rapidly through the pulley. The shelf drops down in an arc, swinging wildly over the stairway, almost faster than I can follow. Except that I do follow it, and what I see imprints itself in my brain.

The man reaches the landing halfway up the stairs just as the shelf swings down. He puts his hands up in a panicked futile attempt to protect himself, but the shelf smashes into him, throwing his body against the top of the marble arch a few feet behind him.

My brain registers a splatter of blood left on the arch as his broken body falls to the floor just below.

The shelf swings back, and the weight of the thing, combined with the unexpectedly rapid motion, overtaxes the mounts I had placed in the ceiling, pulling them loose. As the bolts pull free from the ceiling, sending a cloud of plaster and dust into the air, the shelf crashes down onto the stairs, bouncing and sliding down the last few steps, until it crushes the body below.

I've just killed a man, and I'm not sure how I feel about that.

I don't have time to devote any thought to the man that I just killed, though, because knowing their intentions now, I know that I have another one to kill, the one that was directed to the staircase on my right.

I take off running in that direction, where I have another winch and bookshelf apparatus set up. Twin stairways, twin defenses.

Knowing that the winch won't have power, I slide up to it, the rough old mosaic floor scraping my bare feet, as the man on that side is running up the stairs, his gold chains bouncing and rattling on his chest. He sees me running toward the top of the stairs in a panic, and he gives an eager smile, anxious to engage. He likely saw what happened to his colleague on the other side, and he hopes to "beat the clock."

Knowing that nothing would happen, I don't even bother with the electrical switch. I pound my fist down on the manual lever and roll away as the ratchet lets go, and the shelf begins its ominous downward swing.

This Raider is armed with what looks like a Samurai sword. Where he got that, I'll never know. I won't even be able to ask him, because this shelf doesn't even survive the downward swing. Like the one on the other side, the bolts pull loose and before it can even swing across the landing, the shelf simply tumbles down flat against the stairs, crushing the Raider underneath it.

It occurs to me that I've now killed two humans in a matter of just a couple of minutes, and I have a fleeting moment of wondering what Frida would think of me now. The thought of Frida sleeping on the other side of the building spurs me on.

I look over the balustrade, and I see the first man, the one who had been directing the others, starting toward the steps on the left. I start running back toward that side, realizing that I had left my weapons where I dropped them on the floor by that winch.

I keep an eye over the balustrade as I'm running. This man has a spear clenched tightly in his right hand and a knife in his left. The sun has apparently risen enough, now, that the large ruby dangling from the gold chain around his neck catches the light.

He lifts his spear as if in an attempt to throw it at me, but I drop to the floor a few feet away from the winch, sliding the rest of the way, scraping my knees, this time, on the rough mosaic floor. The Raider, apparently, realizes that any attempt to throw his spear would likely be hindered by the balustrade.

Not so my arrow.

Lying partly on my side, I notch an arrow to the bowstring and aim between the balusters, but I'm afraid my actions are too rushed, and my position a little awkward. The arrow goes wide and splinters against the archway just behind him.

He instinctively ducks at the sound, and he looks up at me as he reaches the first landing, where the bookshelf is lying.

I quickly pull another arrow from the quiver and notch it. I move a little to my right to get a better angle between the balusters, and I sit up a little higher. This shot has better success. The arrow embeds itself in his left shoulder and he drops the knife.

A solid hit, but the man is still a threat.

I watch between the balusters as he transfers the spear into his left hand. With the arrow still protruding from his shoulder, blood soaking the sleeve of his garment, his left arm is useless for much more than that. Using his right hand, he grits his teeth as he climbs up over the heavy book-shelf, evidently giving little thought to his companion lying crushed underneath it.

I get another arrow ready, but he is now hidden from my view, crouching down below the ornate balustrade. I know he must be climbing slower than he would be able to in an upright position, but I don't want to wait for him to reach my floor.

I stand up, making sure I stay shielded by the column and my winch assembly. I take a deep breath and I step out from behind the column, directly in front of the stairs. He's only a few steps down, crouched low. I don't think he expected me to come out into the open. I note a look of surprise on his face as I send an arrow thudding into his chest.

I watch, shocked, as his body topples down the stairs, landing on top of the shelf.

Having removed these three threats, I'm very aware that there are still two more Raiders somewhere in the building, but I have no idea where. It's possible that they're exploring farther back in the Library and don't know what happened with their compatriots.

I'm already farther away from Frida than I would like, but I decide to slip quietly down the stairs, down to the first floor. I need to know where they are.

Zane pulled himself up through the brown crunchy grass and weeds, feeling scrapes and scratches on his belly and his elbows through his shirt. He slowly poked his head up above the top of the hillock and looked out ahead of him.

And there they were.

The great beasts were grazing very near where his father, Louis, had predicted a few days ago that they might be. Now, he just had to get himself in position.

From what he had heard, it might be difficult to kill one of them with an arrow. They had thick hide and muscular frames, but he hoped that he could get close enough to make it count.

He wished he could use a gun. He had a couple of them, a pistol and a rifle, but his father had used the last of the bullets in an effort to keep from being eaten by a bear. Having emptied the gun into the bear, he had succeeded in not being eaten, but not for a lack of effort on the bear's part. The bear mauled him badly, then fell dead on top of him. By the time Zane found him, Louis was more dead than alive. He completed the task sometime overnight.

That was two days ago. Zane buried him behind the house, after scraping a shallow grave next to his mother and his sister. He went back for the bear, but after a day of festering under the hot sun, and being gnawed on by scavengers who were not quite as particular as Zane, he decided that the carcass was best left to be disposed of naturally.

Both guns were now useless, collecting dust on the mantel in Zane's house. Ammunition had become scarce a long time ago. Several years back, Louis had talked about making their own ammunition, but he didn't know how. So, Zane was armed, now, with a bow and arrows.

His house was surrounded by farmland, but its sparce crops were now dead and chewed to bits by locusts. The only things that seemed to thrive now were weeds and short, ground-hugging shrubs. And some of them were being eaten by the locusts, as well. Zane had never seen so many of the damn things, and a while back, Louis had suggested a unique defense. They had devised a number of fine nets with nylon netting that Zane's mother had in abundance.

"If they were good enough for John the Baptist," Louis had said, "they're good enough for us."

Zane had a difficult time, at first, eating them, but once he tasted them, he decided, after a little experimentation, that they were tolerable. After roasting them and twisting off the heads, they actually weren't bad. If only they had a little honey, like John the Baptist ate them. Zane had never had it, but Louis had tasted it as a boy, and waxed poetic about how delicious it was.

Anyway, after a year, the bugs got really old.

Zane was amazed at how prolific the little bastards were. Especially now, when he was the only one of his family left, while so many other bugs had disappeared, there were still plenty of locusts to fill him.

But he was sick to death of the damn bugs!

A change of pace would definitely do him some good. As long as he didn't get killed trying to get it.

While he was out here exposed, he kept an eye out for bears, too, though he had little faith that his bow and arrow would be much protection. Historically, bears generally didn't come down here on the plains, but with food sources becoming scarce up in the hills, he knew that some had decided to venture down into the lower country.

Louis, if he were still around, could attest to that.

As he looked over the crest of the hillock, toward those fearsome beasts, Zane sucked a deep, quivering breath into his lungs. He wondered about the veracity of the stories that his father had related to him about the food of the past.

Their bodies were big and sturdy, their calls deep and ominous. Zane sucked in a deep breath and shook his head.

§

Scorpions were becoming prolific around here. After eating the locusts for a while, Zane and Louis had decided to branch out a little. Scorpions, it turned out, weren't bad, either. They had to cut off the stinger and the bulbous venom gland, but after that, the bug was fairly palatable.

But it was still a bug.

Ants and termites turned out to be doable, as well. To adapt his father's reasoning about locusts, if they were good enough for bears, the bastards, they were good enough for him.

But, again, they were still bugs.

He could really use a change in diet!

He looked ahead, at his current prey, and he took a shuddering breath. He had never hunted anything so huge.

During his lifetime, many animals had, apparently, disappeared, according to his father. The weather had changed. There were never any clouds, so there was never rain. Zane remembered rain falling on occasion in his younger days, but the closest thing to that that he got now was, and only occasionally, dew in the early morning.

The lack of rain affected the vegetation. Louis had drilled wells years ago, and they had used them to water the crops that they attempted to grow, but most of the crops had dried up. They were gone now, thanks to lack of water, and the locusts.

A few hardy grasses and weeds had proliferated in their area, and were, apparently, appetizing to these ponderous beasts before Zane now.

His fingers ached, and he realized that he was gripping his bow too tightly. He relaxed his hand and took a deep, slow breath, blowing it out, feeling a calm settle over him. He just hoped he could hold on to the calm long enough to make the kill.

§

It was like heaven, if heaven dwelled in smoke rising off a grill. Louis had told him that, years ago, they had used a tank of gas to fuel the grill. When that became too expensive, they used what he called charcoal briquettes, but those had not been available for a very long time. Zane used leaves, twigs, and bits of wood, which was not terribly plentiful, but the smoke did add a pleasant aroma to the grilling meat.

The heat was dying down, since he had to be frugal with the fuel. He used the well-worn tongs to lift the steak off the grill and placed it on a plate. Since the grill was in the shade of the back of the house, he usually ate his dinners there, outside.

He sliced off a bite of the steak and placed it in his mouth. As he chewed, he marveled at the delightful burst of flavor in his mouth. His father had taught him that grilling meat was a matter of timing. Meat should not be cooked so long that it becomes tough and chewy, or that the juices dry up. The juices and the fat were necessary to deliver the best flavor.

Zane congratulated himself on his preparation of this unfamiliar food. Bos taurus, which in the past used to be referred to under the catch-all word 'beef,' had been raised for centuries by man for food. Zane's father had spoken in hushed and sublime tones about the steaks and roasts and ribs that he had eaten on a few occasions in his early youth.

That was before civilization went to hell. Before SHePF killed so many people that almost every industry on the planet became undermanned. Before the climate change that people had been spouting off about seemed to be true after all.

It had been said for some time, according to his father, that beef production contributed a great deal to the climate issues that many had warned against, besides the car exhaust.

Zane hadn't seen a car that actually worked in his entire life, not even the later electric ones. They seemed like nothing more

than silly stories, mythologies dreamed up by a superstitious peo-
ple, like the gods worshiped by those even further in the past.

When SHePF and its various mutations came along and killed
over 75% of the working force, the feedlots and smaller ranches
were left untended. In time, the cattle that didn't die managed to
escape and adapted to life on the range. Having become wild, and
acclimated to the difficult life in the current world, Zane wasn't
so sure about how docile they might be.

Louis, had spoken of a romanticized period in human history, a
very long time ago, when men, "cowboys," would lead the cattle
to various areas for feeding and watering, fattening them up for
slaughter. They were docile then, as the cowboys could walk
among the cattle unafraid, or ride among them on their horses, an
animal that Zane had never actually seen in real life.

When he had chosen his target and let loose his first arrow, the
others scattered. It took three arrows to take down his prey, but it
had been worth it.

This cattle, this beef, was something that Zane resolved to enjoy
for a long time to come, if they stuck around.

SHOWDOWN

don't see them. I make my way silently through the Reading Room, but it's empty. I see a stack of books on a desk that I pass, from some research that I did a few days ago about how to make a cancer patient's last days more pleasant.

I don't remember reading anything about defending her from creepy killers.

I feel a very brief moment of shame that I had not put the books back. The feeling doesn't last long, though. I have more important things to worry about now.

I have my father's bow in my left hand, with an arrow already notched, held in place by my index finger, and my mother's spear in my right hand. I want to be ready for any eventuality.

The Reading Room is empty, though, and I come out the back side. I look both directions, up and down that hallway. It's also empty. I cock my head and turn slowly, listening.

Aided by the otherwise total silence of my world, I hear what sounds like footsteps upstairs.

What I had originally feared had actually happened. The other two Raiders had used a back stairway. They may not even be aware of what happened to their companions at the front of the building. If they heard the crashes, they may think it was just the sound of their searching and destroying, what I think used to be called smash-and-grab.

I rush up the nearest stairs, the ones I use every morning to empty our toilet bucket. They're more utilitarian and less ornate than those up front in the Great Hall.

I arrive on the second floor and I don't care where the Raiders are. I rush into our room to check on Frida.

And the men are there.

They glance briefly back at me, but only briefly. They turn back toward Frida, although I note that their bodies are more tense, as if prepared for a fight.

Or for something else, which I don't even want to think about.

Frida is still asleep, her flaxen hair splayed across her shoulders, one breast slightly exposed.

"You have a woman," one of them says, and I realize that I do have to think about it.

"I do," I reply, holding my spear in a death grip.

"What's wrong with her?" the other one asks. He's likely noticed that she hasn't stirred from their presence. I have to look a little longer at her to see that she's even still breathing, though weakly.

"She's dying," I reply, the words catching in my throat. I decide not to say what was killing her, in case they might be afraid of infection. Unfortunately, that doesn't seem to be a consideration.

"I haven't had a woman in, . . ." the first man says, lapsing into a long, reflective pause. It ends in a sigh. "I don't know how long."

"You'll not be having one now, either," I say.

Both men turn to look at me, apparently considering me more of a threat now than before. We regard each other for several moments.

"Are you the one who wrote the messages on the wall?" the first man asks.

"I am," I reply, stepping forward a little, not so much to engage the men, but to protect Frida.

"Where's the treasure?" he inquires.

"What treasure?" I ask, stopping in my tracks and wrinkling my brow at him. I'm suddenly aware, again, of the chains and jewels that they're wearing.

"You wrote about having gems and jewels," the second one says.

"What good is that?" I ask.

"Gold and precious stones are valuable," he says, turning a little more toward me. His free hand, the one not holding the Civil War era saber, fondles the chains around his neck. "When we climb back out of this depression, we'll be ready."

I don't know how to respond, and I narrow my eyelids at him, having a hard time believing that he thinks we're going to come back from this.

"Are you serious?" I ask.

"Fuck yeah, we're serious," the other man says, gripping the knife in his hand.

"This is the end, bonehead," I reply. I have a brief realization that it probably wasn't quite as forceful as calling him a shit-for-brains or fuckwit or asshole. I'm still new at dealing with idiots.

"Where's the treasure?" the first man asks, the sword gaining a little elevation.

"It was a metaphor, you fucking moron," I reply. I raise both hands around me in an all-encompassing gesture. I don't know if the weapons in my hands cancel out my meaning or not. "We're standing in what was, apparently, the largest library in the world. All the knowledge of the ages is located here. This is the treasure. Knowledge is the precious gem."

I step to the bed, concerned more about Frida than about myself, and the first man, the one with the knife in his hand, raises his weapon. My anger, my disbelief at their naivete, and at their total disregard for Frida's condition, makes me a little impetuous, and I make a wild slash with my mother's spear. The spearhead slices across the man's throat.

The other man raises his saber and plunges it into my chest. I feel a pain unlike any I have ever felt before. Feeling a sudden weakness spreading throughout my body, I fall on the bed next to Frida.

I realize that the bow is still in my left hand, the arrow still ready on the string and, somehow, I find the strength to lift it and pull the string back, and I let it go. The arrow strikes him—I don't know, somewhere.

He falls, I assume, at the foot of the bed. I don't even look to see what happens to either of them. I turn to my side, looking at Frida. Her eyes are locked onto mine for a moment.

As I hold her in my gaze, I notice that she stops breathing.

Images fire through my brain, memories of our lives together, a panoply of our sweetest moments. I smile, remembering her hands on me, her lips against mine, our bodies united in love.

I reach up and touch her face, engulfed in her affection, and I see her return my smile, as I close my eyes.

THE BEGINNING

Two figures clambered over enormous flat rocks across the wide, equally flat plateau. From a distance, they looked nearly identical. They both wore clothing made of thin, light-colored fabric and wide-brimmed hats, they each carried small packs on their backs, and one carried a bow, the other a spear. The blazing sun beat down mercilessly on them, and radiated its heat back up on them from the rocks.

Stepping to the edge, they looked down about a hundred feet to the top of a gargantuan haphazard litter of stones. Over the course of eons, the rock had peeled away and fallen, eventually forming a jagged talus slope filling the right angle between the cliff and the ground to a depth of perhaps an additional hundred and fifty feet.

One of the figures stepped warily back, taking the other's arm, coaxing her away from the edge.

Valencia looked at Bookman and smiled at his timidity, but she moved away from the edge.

"I'm sorry," she said, "I forgot about your fear of heights."

"It's not so much a fear of," he stammered, "as a healthy respect for." Still, he looked at his new and statuesque wife, the adventurer, with growing admiration. She was formidable.

§

Her name, Valencia, meant "Strong," and she had been given the name after proving herself as such when she had defended their settlement against a small band of Raiders.

The settlement consisted of six crude huts, arranged in a circle. Five of the huts were occupied by the people, while the sixth was used to store what supplies they had. There were only three men in their settlement, including Bookman, and they had been gone investigating a report of a herd of elk. It had been ages since any of them had brought in anything larger than a squirrel or rabbit, so this was important.

The herd, it turned out, was made up of only five weak and thin specimens, and while Bookman felt sorry for them, he decided it was an act of mercy to kill one of them, an act that would also be beneficial for the humans, as well. Its meat and organs would fill the bellies of their clan, its bones and skin would mend and supplement weapons, vessels and utensils.

They wished that they could have taken more, but with so little cover masking their approach across the barren landscape, the animals were alerted to their presence and bolted, leaving the hunters to take the weakest, slowest animal. Transporting more than one back to their settlement would have been too arduous for three men, anyway.

They had approached their camp, fully laden with every scrap they had gleaned from the elk, and stepping carefully as they followed the rocky trail down the incline into what had once been a vast inland sea. The sea was little more than a few scattered ponds and lakes now, fed by trickles from higher elevations. The water in the largest lake, the one they had settled beside, was perpetually warm and somewhat brackish, but drinkable.

As the hunters descended toward their home, they encountered something that had not been there when they left four days before. The body of a man, stripped of clothing, a gaping wound in his chest, lay draped across a large rock a hundred feet from the boundary of the settlement. His arms splayed out across the boulder, he seemed to issue a warning to any who would attempt to come near.

The story was related to them when they returned to the little village, how three Raiders had shown up with the intent to take their food and supplies. And the lustful grins that appeared on their faces when they saw only women.

Valencia, known then as Tree, a name she didn't understand beyond its historical significance, was standing behind the other three women and two children in the camp. The Raiders didn't see the spear she held in her right hand. As the apparent leader made his way toward the group, a knife in his hand, Tree gently slipped her left arm forward between the women in front of her.

When the man was just a couple of feet in front of them, Tree pressed her arm to the left, pushing those individuals aside and opening a space between them. In one fluid motion, she stepped forward and rotated, bringing the spear forward, plunging it into the man's chest, as the other women and children fell back in shock and surprise.

The dead man's two companions, one carrying a knife, the other a machete, moved forward to his aid. Machete was the first to reach her, and he had his weapon raised high, ready to swing it downward. Using the momentum of pulling the spear from the first attacker, Tree pivoted and slashed the point of her spear across the man's throat. He dropped to the ground instantly, leaving the third man hesitating, looking at his two dead companions and the wild woman with the spear dripping blood.

Without another look back, he turned and ran back the way they had come.

She really was formidable.

§

The hunters' return with meat and supplies was celebrated, as was Tree's victory over the attackers. Bookman had felt drawn to her for quite some time, and he had gotten the impression that she returned his feelings. As the other women told the story of how she had fearlessly defended them against their attackers, he felt his heart immersed in its growing need for her.

The others felt that it was time for Tree to shed her childhood name, that she deserved one that was more pertinent to her adult life. It was then that Bookman suggested the name Valencia. When he explained its meaning to her, Strong, she decided she liked it.

The renaming ceremony was simple but solemn. Tree knelt before Arch, the leader of the little clan. Arch scraped a shallow hole *in the dirt in front of Tree. Tree looked down at it and said the name that she had carried all her previous years, and Arch pushed the dirt back into the hole. As her old name was respectfully laid to rest, he spoke her new name, Valencia. He took her hands and pulled her to her feet, and she was known as Valencia from that moment on.*

It was that same evening that Bookman asked her to be his wife. To his delight, she agreed.

They had both been alone, Valencia's father having died a couple of years before. Bookman's parents had died when he was young, and he had been cared for by his brother, Montana, who now lived with his wife and son in the hut next to Bookman's.

By this time, marriage had become quite a simple affair, simpler even than the renaming ceremony, consisting mainly of Bookman publicly announcing to the clan that he wished to take Valencia as his wife, and Valencia then confirming her agreement to the arrangement.

"With my brains and your brawn," he joked to her, "we'll be a force to be reckoned with."

That night, she joined him in his hut which he had previously occupied alone.

Alone, that is, except for his rather prodigious collection of books. Bookman's love of reading is what had inspired him to take his name, and he had amassed quite a library from his own foraging, and from others who knew of his affinity for them. He had to push stacks aside so that Valencia could get to her side of his pallet.

After which they commenced kissing and fumbling with each other's clothing, and she simply fell onto the pallet on Bookman's side. Their lovemaking was awkward but tender.

Afterward, they lay quietly in each other's arms, their skin slick with sweat. In the dimming light, Valencia looked somewhat skeptically at all the books, a couple of stacks of which seemed quite unsteady. She had never been a reader herself.

"Have you actually read all of these?" she asked in a tone some-where on the scale between wonderment and incredulity.

"Most of them," Bookman smiled.

"What's so great about them?"

"Oh," he enthused, "there's so much to learn from them!" With his free hand, he reached toward the little table beside his bed and picked up the book on top of the stack. The cover was faded and worn, wrinkled and ripped in places. Most of the title, though, could still be seen, In a Sunburned Country, by Bill Bryson.

Bookman realized he needed both hands, and he slipped his arm out from under Valencia's neck, pushing himself up to lean his head against the wall. He opened a few pages in and began reading to her.

> But then that's the thing about the outback—it's so fast and forbidding that much of it is still scarcely charted. Even Uluru, as we must learn to call Ayers Rock, was unseen by anyone but its Ab-original caretakers until only a little over a century ago. It's not even possible to say quite where the outback is. To Australians anything vaguely rural is "the bush." At some indeterminate point "the bush" becomes "the outback." Push on for another two thousand miles or so and eventually you come to bush again. And then a city, and then the sea. And that's Australia.

"This book was written by a man who just set out traveling across Australia. And he wrote about his experiences." Bookman looked at Valencia expectantly.

"What's Australia?" she asked.

"It's a huge island. Once upon a time, it was a country, like this one."

"'Once upon a time'?"

Bookman looked around for a moment, gathering his thoughts.

"It's an expression from storybooks. Anyway, as near as I can tell from the Atlas I have around here somewhere, if you were to drill straight down through the earth from here, you might come out somewhere near Australia."

"Why did he travel across Australia?"

"Just to see it. To experience it." He saw the confused look on Valencia's face. "People used to travel for fun. Every day wasn't a struggle for survival. People went on what they called 'vacations.' They'd go away for a week or two just to see another part of the world."

From her expression, Bookman could see that it was a completely foreign idea, yet at the same time, she seemed intrigued. He could see the kindling of a fire in her eyes.

"I've only ever seen this basin," she said, "and a little way around it."

"I know," Bookman replied. "This is all I've ever seen, too. The farthest I've ever been is to the ruins of the big village, up where the western shore used to be, the place called Hamilton. But I've always wondered what it would be like to go farther and see other places."

"Why don't we?" Valencia asked frankly. Bookman looked at her, surprised. "Why not?" she persisted, feeling a little more enthusiastic about the idea. "There's not very much food left around here. We have to go farther and farther to find it. If we weren't here, there would be more for the rest of them. I don't have any family here," she added, "well, except for you, now." She smiled.

"My brother is here," Bookman pondered, "but you're right, this area can't really support this many people anymore." He looked at Valencia, feeling a nervous little something in his chest, and he smiled. "We could be the parents of a new world, like Adam and Eve."

"Who?"

§

They had broached the topic of the whole clan moving, to look for a home that could more easily support all of them. But they resisted the idea, for good reason. So little was known about the world around them. How could they know they wouldn't end up in someplace worse?

So, Bookman and Valencia took off on their own, to start a new life. They took only the necessities, which for Bookman meant he limited himself to only two books. It had been an agonizing choice, one that took him hours of skimming through his collection, but he finally got it trimmed down to The Holy Bible *and* Harry Potter and the Philosopher's Stone.

It was early on their fourth day that they came upon the massive cliff. They tried to follow rivers or streams where they existed, but for the most part, they were little more than trickles. Such was the one that led them to the place of the flat rocks.

Kneeling beside the trickle that once had been a mighty river, Bookman filled three metal canisters with the warm water.

"You know," he said, "according to one of my books, which I left behind," he pointedly added, "this used to be a popular destination for honeymooners."

"Honeymooners?"

"A long time ago, when people got married, they would go on a trip together, a vacation, to be alone in some romantic place."

"Romantic?" Valencia looked around at the barren, sunbaked landscape. Her nose wrinkled at the sight.

"Yeah, well, there was more water back then. And trees. Ny-a-gah-rah was supposed to be a beautiful place. Ny-a-gah-rah Falls, they called it. There was a wide river that filled this bed, and a great waterfall that poured over this cliff."

"Huh," Valencia grunted noncommittally. She had heard Bookman speak of great rivers in the past, but she had a difficult

time believing such stories. The ruins of the buildings they had passed a few minutes ago intrigued her more than this. Still, . . .

"I'm glad we can continue the honeymoon tradition," she said, smiling warmly at Bookman. "I don't want to see Ny-a-gah-rah with anybody else but you."

Bookman pulled Valencia into his arms and, unconcerned about the deadly drop-off a little way to their side, kissed her long and deep. Nothing else mattered now. She was the most important thing, the prime focus of his life.

Valencia looked deeply into his eyes, burning his face into her consciousness. As he held her, she allowed herself to be engulfed in his arms. She could push him away—she had proven that she could do that—but she didn't want to.

There was that other thing she had been feeling for the last few days, too. A strange feeling growing deep inside. Something she had never felt before, but that, somehow, made her feel profoundly happy.

But it could wait.

About this book

Parts of this book began taking shape in my mind in early 2020. When real life and travel bans prohibited exploration of actual settings and locations, though, it got pushed aside.

But even when writing new stories in my SpiritSense series, this story was always in the back of my mind. Science articles about the effects of climate change, news stories about how greed and corruption often trumped commonsense, the outrage expressed in social media about the handling of various issues, all of it sparked ideas for short stories that could be used to fill out this narrative.

This book wasn't meant to be light reading. I had in mind a cautionary tale, a warning about where I see us heading. Still, I tried to make the journey enjoyable.

Writing speculative fiction can be a tricky thing if you're hoping for accuracy. There were many varied sources I used in constructing this collection, and not surprisingly, some dealing with similar topics drew contradictory conclusions.

But through it all, my wife, Linda, was my adviser, critic, editor, and my greatest encouragement. So, for that, and so much more, thank you, Linda.

And thank you to my readers. The fact that people who don't *have* to like what I do, aka family, actually do like it is particularly heart-warming.

And if you *have* enjoyed reading *Worst Enemies*, please head over to Amazon and leave a review. It doesn't need to be long or detailed. In fact, the more concise, the better.

Reviews are crucial to writers, as they are crucial to other potential buyers. If your review encourages someone else to purchase my book, that encourages me to keep writing them.

Thank you!

www.ingramcontent.com/pod-product-compliance
Lightning Source LLC
Chambersburg PA
CBHW020915200626
46814CB00001BA/345